The Governess Tales

Sweeping romances with fairy-tale endings!

Meet Joanna Radcliff, Rachel Talbot,
Isabel Morton and Grace Bertram.

These four friends grew up together in
Madame Dubois's school for young ladies, where
they indulged in midnight feasts, broke the rules
and shared their innermost secrets!

But now they are thrust into the real world and
each must adapt to their new life as a governess.

One will rise, one will travel, one will run
and one will find her real home...

And each will meet their soul mate,
who'll give them the happy-ever-after
they've always dreamed of!

Read Joanna's story in
The Cinderella Governess

Read Rachel's story in
Governess to the Sheikh

Both available now!

And look for

Isabel's story in
The Runaway Governess

And Grace's story in
The Governess's Secret Baby

Coming soon!

Author Note

I have always loved writing about exotic and far-flung countries—there is something supremely exciting about conjuring up the sights, sounds and smells of a distant land and immersing yourself in a country's history until it becomes your characters' natural environment. In writing *Governess to the Sheikh* I had the opportunity to do something I had never done before: use a fictional setting—in this case the Middle Eastern country of Huria. I drew inspiration for the desert kingdom from the country of Jordan. Anyone who has ever had the pleasure of visiting Jordan might recognize the vast orange and red landscapes, the verdant pockets of lush vegetation and the hardy people who make the desert their home. Malik and Rachel even climb a rocky cliff face to a high place of sacrifice, something my husband and I did on a recent trip to Petra.

Some books are easy to write and some much more difficult. With its beautiful setting and the instant chemistry between Rachel and Malik, as soon as I'd written the first couple of chapters I knew *Governess to the Sheikh* was going to be my favorite book to date. I hope you enjoy reading it as much as I enjoyed writing it.

Laura Martin

Governess to the Sheikh

HARLEQUIN®HISTORICAL

Special thanks and acknowledgment are given to Laura Martin for her contribution to The Governess Tales series.

Recycling programs
for this product may
not exist in your area.

ISBN-13: 978-0-373-29901-0

Governess to the Sheikh

HARLEQUIN®
™ www.Harlequin.com

Printed in U.S.A.

Laura Martin writes historical romances with an adventurous undercurrent. When not writing she spends her time working as a doctor in Cambridgeshire, England, where she lives with her husband. In her spare moments, Laura loves to lose herself in a book and has been known to read cover to cover in a single day when the story is particularly gripping. She also loves to travel, especially visiting historical sites and far-flung shores.

Books by Laura Martin

Harlequin Historical

The Governess Tales
Governess to the Sheikh

Stand-Alone Novels
The Pirate Hunter
Secrets Behind Locked Doors
Under a Desert Moon
An Earl in Want of a Wife

Visit the Author Profile page at Harlequin.com.

For Sophie and Meic and your happily-ever-after.
And for my boys; you are my everything.

Chapter One

Rachel flicked open her fan and wafted it close to her face. She wasn't sure if moving the warm air around helped to keep her cool, but at this point anything was worth a try. She was hot, hotter than she had ever been before, and she was loving it. For the last four days, ever since she had first entered the desert Kingdom of Huria, Rachel had been overwhelmed by all the sights and sounds, but most of all by the heat.

'Not far to the palace now.' Wahid's voice came from outside the carrying chair.

Pushing back the thin cotton curtain that surrounded her, she gazed over the landscape. They were currently following a well-worn route, winding through the dunes, every minute taking them closer to Rachel's new life.

'Please be careful of the sun, *sayeda*,' Wahid said in perfect English, using *sayeda* to address her formally.

Wahid and his small band of guards had been there to meet her four days ago when she had crossed the border into Huria. He had helped her off her weary horse and ushered her into the luxurious carrying chair.

Ever since then Rachel had been treated like royalty and every care had been taken for her comfort. When she had accepted the job in a foreign country Rachel had mainly felt excitement, but there had been some anxiety, too. Naturally there had been worries that she might be moving to a country that was less civilised than England, but so far she had experienced a culture and environment that was worlds apart, but certainly not inferior to her homeland.

Rachel took a moment to turn her face up to the sun and enjoy the warmth on her skin. She hadn't been blessed with a porcelain complexion, her skin was naturally just a shade darker than was considered perfection, but it did mean she could enjoy odd moments in the sunshine without having to worry about turning a horrible red colour or developing freckles.

'You'll be able to see the palace once we reach the top of this dune,' Wahid said.

Rachel fixed her eyes on the horizon and waited. She had been travelling for weeks to reach Huria and during that time she had imagined a thousand different things—sumptuous palaces and whitewashed buildings, arid deserts and dusty plains—but none of her imaginings had prepared her for the sight that confronted her.

Rachel let out a gasp of pleasure. 'It's so beautiful.'

For four days Rachel had travelled through the desert and had seen no evidence of any water. When they stopped Wahid had passed her a water bladder filled with lovely, cool liquid, but never had she seen a single spring or stream or lake. There hadn't been one drop of rain, or even a cloud in the sky. Rachel had begun to think the whole kingdom must exist without water. The sight before her proved her wrong.

There was a wide, flat valley stretching out for a few miles in front of them, and the entire area was a lush paradise. Trees and plants covered the valley floor and the greens of the vegetation contrasted beautifully with the orange sands. Right through the centre of the valley was a vivid slash of blue, a narrow river that supplied this little oasis.

'The Great Oasis of Huria,' Wahid said, gesturing to the area before them.

'There's so much life, so much vegetation.'

Wahid gave a little chuckle. 'It's as though all the plants in Huria are squeezed into this little area.'

The palace itself was built amongst the trees. From the outside it was nowhere near as magnificent as some of the English stately homes Rachel had visited with school, but even from this distance there were clues that the real luxury was reserved for inside the palace. From their vantage point above the oasis Rachel could see magnificent courtyards with bubbling fountains and cool colonnaded passages, all surrounded by vibrant exotic flowers.

As they descended the hill Rachel pulled her head back inside the cotton curtain of the carrying chair and tried to compose herself. For as long as she could remember she had wished for this day. Ever since she was a little girl and her parents had been sending her letters detailing their adventures in far-flung lands Rachel had wanted an adventure of her own. She wanted to experience a different culture, a different way of living, and now was her time.

Rachel badly wanted to make a good impression;

she wanted the Sheikh to be impressed with the English governess he had sent for and she wanted to make a difference to his children's lives. Unlike many of the girls graduating from Madame Dubois's School for Young Ladies, Rachel had been excited to take up her position as governess, to start her life after school. Whereas other young women dreamed of marriage and a domestic life, Rachel had always wanted to see the world and experience the exotic. As the daughter of a baron, Rachel's natural position in life would be as wife to a titled gentleman, but she'd always dreamed of more. She wanted freedom and adventure, and to bring some love and affection into the lives of the children in her care.

She loved children. Her one regret about her determination never to marry was that she would never have a brood of her own, but her position as governess at least meant she would be surrounded by little ones her entire life.

As they entered the oasis Rachel took one last deep breath and smiled. This was what all the years of hard work had been leading to; she would not let nerves ruin this experience for her.

As soon as the carrying chair was set down the curtain was pulled back and a hand reached in to take Rachel's. Effortlessly Rachel was pulled out of the chair and she found herself being ushered up a wide set of stone steps and into a cool chamber.

'This way, *sayeda*. Watch your step.'

Rachel's eyes took a moment to recover from the bright sunlight, but when she had regained her vision she had to stifle a gasp. The room, although not large in size, was beautiful. Beneath her feet was an intricate mosaic that covered the entire floor. The coloured stones made a vibrant picture of what Rachel had to assume was the entire Kingdom of Huria. Deep oranges showed the vast desert and bright splashes of colour the scattered oases.

The beauty of the room did not end with the mosaic. Although the walls were plain they were more than made up for by the numerous plants and flowers that were arranged lovingly around the chamber. Rachel's eyes were drawn to a plant that had been coaxed to climb up one wall with stunning flowers of vivid pink.

Rachel felt her whole body suffuse with pleasure. Although she had hoped Huria would be the exotic paradise of her dreams, she had never imagined anything as magnificent as this. In all the letters her parents had sent her from their travels they had never described seeing anywhere like this small desert kingdom. A smile spread across Rachel's lips; she knew she was going to be happy here.

Slowly Rachel stepped further into the room, taking her time to soak up every little detail, not caring that people were probably staring and wondering why she was quite so enamoured with a sight they saw every day. She started to turn towards one of the archways, wanting to catch a glimpse of the courtyard beyond, when a man stepped through the opening and into the chamber. Their eyes met and Rachel felt her heart begin pounding in her chest.

It was the Sheikh, there was no doubt in her mind. He wasn't dressed richly and he didn't wear a crown or any jewellery that Rachel could see—in fact, there were other men in the room far more expensively adorned than he was—but Rachel knew he was royalty purely because of his bearing.

As he entered the room he didn't look from side to side to see who was there—he strode with purpose and vitality. It was the walk of a man who always got what he wanted. His back was straight, his eyes focused, and Rachel knew immediately he would be a hard man to deny anything.

He started to move towards her and Rachel found herself momentarily frozen. His eyes were still locked on hers and for a second she was mesmerised. It was only when he came to a halt before her that Rachel remembered herself and dropped hastily into a low curtsy, lowering her eyes to the floor.

As she rose from the curtsy she couldn't help but look up at the Sheikh, but as she did so she felt her mouth go dry and her lips quiver slightly. Up close he didn't just have a regal bearing, he was also disconcertingly handsome. Rachel thought it was probably his eyes that made most ladies swoon—they were a deep, dark brown, inviting and forbidding at the same time. Rachel felt herself swallowing nervously as she took in his perfectly shaped lips, caramel-coloured skin tone and short black hair. The Sheikh was a handsome man and a powerful one—it was a potent combination.

'Miss Talbot, it is a pleasure to make your acquaintance.' The Sheikh's voice was smooth and confident and Rachel was surprised to find he spoke English with only the mildest hint of an accent. 'I hope your journey was not too arduous.'

'You have such a beautiful country,' Rachel said with a smile. 'It was a wonderful opportunity to see so much of it.'

The Sheikh studied her as she spoke, and Rachel had to suppress a shiver that ran over her skin. Confidence and power emanated out of him and Rachel felt her pulse begin to quicken as he moved in closer towards her. She had an inexplicable urge to reach out and place a hand on his chest, to feel the hard muscles under her fingers and the heat of his body on her fingertips.

'We do not have many visitors to our small kingdom, but most who do come cannot see past the barrenness of the desert and stifling heat. They do not see the beauty in the rolling sand dunes and the fortitude of the people who can live under such a burning sun.'

Even though Rachel had only just met the Sheikh, there was enough passion in the few sentences he had spoken to her to show her he truly loved his country. She could tell he was proud of Huria and wanted everyone to view his kingdom with the same love and respect as he did.

'But enough of that for now,' the Sheikh said with a small smile that lit up his face. 'Wahid is always telling me I am far too serious when I speak about the merits of our country.'

'You cannot browbeat people into loving Huria as you do, Your Majesty,' Wahid said.

Rachel looked at the two men with interest. Everyone else in the chamber stood back from the Sheikh out of respect, but Wahid was at his side, more like an old friend than a subordinate.

'Please, come through to the courtyard. I will have someone fetch you some refreshments and once you are rested you can meet the children.'

Rachel followed the Sheikh through the archway

and into the courtyard she had glimpsed beyond. If she had thought the first chamber was beautiful, then the courtyard was even more so. The whole area was bathed in brilliant sunlight, although there were a few strategically placed trees in case shade was required. There was a bubbling fountain in the centre, surrounded by a small pool of water, and the rest of the courtyard was filled with plants and trees of so many varieties Rachel wondered if they could all be native to Huria.

As they walked Rachel took the opportunity to compose herself. Inside she was a jumble of nerves, her normal confident demeanour shattered by the Sheikh. She wasn't sure if it was his royal status or the intensity of his dark eyes that was making her feel a little shaky, but there was something about the Sheikh that made you notice him.

'Please sit,' the Sheikh said politely, indicating a small table under a tree.

Rachel sat and to her surprise the Sheikh took the chair opposite her. His manner was a little imperious, but there were flashes of normality beneath. Rachel had imagined him to be much more stern and haughty, but she supposed he was in truth just a man, born into a noble family.

Immediately a servant was by his side, setting two glasses down on the table. He served the Sheikh first, but Rachel noticed the ruler of Huria waited for her to take a sip before he picked up his own glass.

Rachel closed her eyes and sighed. She couldn't help herself. The drink was delicious; it looked like lemonade, but when you took a mouthful there were so many more flavours.

'This is divine,' Rachel said.

As she opened her eyes she realised the Sheikh was staring at her and she felt a blush start to creep to her cheeks as he did not drop his gaze. He looked as though he were seeing every bit of her laid bare before him. The air between them hummed with a peculiar tension and Rachel found she was holding her breath, wondering if he might reach across the gap and touch her. She wanted him to, she realised. She wanted him to trail his fingers over her skin or run his hands through her hair.

Hastily Rachel forced herself to return to reality. She wondered if it was the heat, or exhaustion after such a long journey—there must be some explanation for these strange thoughts. The Sheikh was a handsome and charismatic man, but that was no reason to start behaving like one of the airheaded heroines in the novels her friend Isabel liked to read. Luckily the Sheikh didn't seem to notice the inappropriate way her body was responding to him.

'You will find it all over Huria, every household, rich or poor, serves lemon and mint to their guests.'

He was still looking at her and Rachel had to stop herself from fidgeting. His eyes were so dark they were almost black, and Rachel thought she glimpsed a hint of wistfulness behind his expression.

Suddenly his manner changed and instantaneously he became the solemn leader Rachel knew most of his subjects would see.

'I am sure you are eager to meet the children,' he said, motioning to a servant who was hovering nearby. 'Then I suggest you rest this afternoon before commencing your duties tomorrow.'

Rachel nodded, glad to focus her thoughts away

from the attractive Sheikh and on to an area she felt a lot more comfortable with: her work.

There was a clatter of shoes upon stone and Rachel turned to see three young children filing out of one of the numerous archways that led into the courtyard. Even at first glance there was no mistaking that these three grave-faced children were related to the Sheikh. All had his dark, probing eyes and caramel skin tone, and the eldest had even perfected the slightly haughty look Rachel had glimpsed on the Sheikh's face.

Rachel had received a few sparse details about the Sheikh and his family before taking the job in Huria. Miss Fanworth, a teacher at Madame Dubois's School for Young Ladies, had known of Rachel's desire to travel and see the world, and when she had heard Sheikh Malik bin Jalal al-Mahrouky was looking for a new governess for his children she had acquired all of the information necessary for Rachel to apply for the position and had then encouraged her to do so. Rachel's correspondence with the palace had been brief and her application accepted almost immediately. The details about the children a palace secretary had sent in a letter had been functional and succinct. She knew the children were aged eight, six and four, and that their mother had died about a year ago. As to their likes and dislikes, strengths and weaknesses, she was in the dark.

Aahil, the eldest of the three children, stepped forward. Rachel could already see he was a Sheikh in the making. His back was straight as he gave a little bow to greet her, and his face unsmiling. From what she remembered he was only eight years old and already he was acting like a man. Her heart squeezed a little, surely there was still time for him to be a child for a few more years.

'Welcome to Huria, Miss Talbot,' he said, his English almost as perfect as his father's. 'We look forward to starting our lessons with you.'

Rachel's eyes roamed over the other two children, wondering if they, too, would be so formal at such a young age. Ameera, the young Princess, stared mutinously at her and Rachel got the impression she was trying hard not to stick out her tongue. Hakim, the four-year-old Prince, looked shyly at the ground.

'I can't wait to get to know you all,' Rachel said warmly. 'I'm sure we will have plenty of fun together.'

Aahil frowned, as if protesting at the idea of fun, but Rachel pressed on.

'You must tell me all about yourselves.'

Quickly Rachel gathered the children up and hustled them towards the shade of the tree. She noticed that the Sheikh hung back, watching his children closely, proudly, but not really interacting with them. She knew she shouldn't be too quick to judge, but she did wonder whether he encouraged the formal behaviour she had seen from Aahil.

'Right,' she said, perching on a little wall and gathering the children to her. 'Aahil, tell me what your favourite subject is.'

Aahil looked a little lost at being asked about his likes. He shot a quick glance at his father.

'I am privileged to learn about the history of our country,' he said almost mechanically.

Rachel smiled warmly. 'You must be very proud of your country,' she agreed. 'I think that is a wonderful favourite subject.'

The young Prince squirmed a little at her compliment and Rachel glanced once again at their father. She could tell immediately he was interested in his children, but she couldn't quite understand why he was not getting involved. Maybe he thought it best to let her get to know them first.

'Ameera,' Rachel said, turning to the pretty little six-year-old, 'what is your favourite game to play?'

Ameera gave her a haughty look that would have felled lesser women. 'We do not play games.'

Rachel felt her eyes widen slightly, but she tried not to show any outward reaction to the girl's words.

'That's a shame,' she said casually. 'I do so love playing games.'

'But you're an adult,' Ameera blurted out.

'Adults are allowed to have fun, too.'

Ameera pressed her lips together firmly as if she disapproved and Rachel could see she was going to get nothing more out of the young girl for now.

Rachel turned to Hakim, knowing she would likely have to simplify her language for the young boy and wondering what she could ask him to bring him out of his shell.

'Hakim,' she said gently, holding out her hand and taking his in hers, 'I do hope you'll show me round your beautiful home later. I bet you know all the best places to hide and all the best places to play.'

'Yes, miss,' Hakim said softly.

Rachel was pleased he didn't pull his hand out of hers, but she could see it would take a lot of work to make the three children trust her and open up.

'The children will take lessons every day in the morning and afternoon,' the Sheikh said.

Rachel could see that as their father spoke all three children stood to attention.

'I can't wait to get started,' Rachel said serenely, wondering if the Sheikh expected them to spend all day cooped up in a classroom. Rachel knew children needed formal lessons, but she also knew they learnt a lot more if they were given time to develop outside the classroom. She had a feeling the Sheikh might not approve of her teaching methods and wondered how she could make him see that fun was as important as French to such young minds.

Chapter Two

Malik reclined back on to the cushions and looked across the parapet and out over his kingdom. He'd invited the new governess to dine with him and was waiting for her to ascend the stairs to the rooftop so their meal could begin. He wasn't sure what to make of Miss Talbot and he knew he shouldn't judge her on first impressions, but he was eager they set some boundaries and rules before she began teaching his children.

She was young, younger than he had expected. He had *known* she would be barely out of the schoolroom herself, but when he pictured an English governess, Rachel Talbot, with her deep, soulful eyes and infectious smile, wasn't what he imagined. Surely a governess should be old, grey-haired and stern, maybe with a wart or two for good measure. His school teachers and tutors had never laughed and he'd certainly never seen such pleasure in their faces as he'd witnessed on Miss Talbot's.

He was pleased she saw the beauty of his country—too many visitors couldn't see past the arid desert and the nomadic lifestyle of many of his people—but he needed to ensure she would be suitably strict with his children. They were of royal blood after all, they had to learn to be serious and solemn as the occasion called for it. He doubted Miss Talbot had ever been solemn in her entire life.

Malik rose as he heard footsteps on the stairs. He had ordered for dinner to be laid out in the traditional style on one of the smaller flat rooftops of the palace, accessible from the courtyard via an outdoor staircase. Cushions were scattered around a low table, which would be filled with Hurian dishes when they were ready.

'Miss Talbot,' he greeted her as she emerged on to the rooftop.

She took a moment to take in her surroundings before a heartfelt smile blossomed on her face.

'Your Highness,' she said, bobbing into a little curtsy.

Malik watched as her eyes swept over the silk-covered cushions, the dark wood table and out to the palace beyond. He couldn't help but feel proud that it was his kingdom that was inspiring so much pleasure. More disconcertingly he found that as Miss Talbot was surveying her surroundings he was watching her, or more specifically her mouth. He found her lips just a little mesmerising, and he didn't think he'd ever met anyone who smiled quite as much as his children's new governess.

He reached out, took her hand and placed it in the crook of his arm, leading her over to the parapet. Although he had asked her here to discuss his children's education, Malik didn't see any harm in showing her a little more of the kingdom she would be living in for the foreseeable future. As they stood looking out over the palace and to the oasis beyond in the fading light of the evening sun, Malik heard Miss Talbot sigh contentedly beside him. The sound made something tighten inside him and he found himself quickly stepping away, trying to cover his confusion with a return to his formal behaviour.

'Please take a seat,' Malik said, motioning to the cushions on one side of the low table.

Miss Talbot sat, absentmindedly stroking the soft silk of the cushion beneath her, tracing a pattern over the smooth surface with her delicate fingers. Malik looked away and sat down himself.

'I asked you here so that we could discuss the children's education.'

Miss Talbot looked at him directly, nodded and smiled. Malik felt his train of thought slipping away. Hardly anyone held his eye now that he was Sheikh. Most of his advisors and chieftains averted their eyes out of respect when he spoke to them. Only Wahid, who had been with him since he was a young man, dared to look him in the eye and tell him what he really thought. And Wahid was certainly not as distracting as Miss Talbot.

'Wonderful,' the governess said. 'They seem such lovely children. I have so many ideas to help them blossom and have fun at the same time.'

Malik found himself nodding along with her as she spoke, even though he didn't quite agree with her words. He waited whilst a servant brought a tray of the first course and set the various bowls with hummus, dipping sauces and flatbread on the table.

'I think it is important that we discuss the objectives

and methods you plan to use before you get started with the children,' Malik said, surprised when Miss Talbot nodded eagerly.

'I completely agree,' she said. 'I think it is very important for parents to play an active part in their children's education.'

Not quite what Malik meant, but he pushed on anyway.

'Aahil is Prince of Huria, and one day he will succeed me as Sheikh. He will be the ruler of this small but proud kingdom and he needs to know how to conduct himself at all times.'

He paused. Although he had more to say, he could see the governess's lips had pursed and already he knew this meant she had an opinion she was eager to give.

'He is also just a child,' Miss Talbot said softly.

Malik considered his next words, wondering how to continue. Of course Aahil was still a boy, he knew that, but Malik also knew the weight of the responsibility of running a kingdom. His father had been strict with him, insisting he conduct himself with dignity and gravitas from a young age, and as a result, when his father passed away and Malik became Sheikh, he had already known what behaviour was expected of him.

'First and foremost he is Prince of Huria.' Malik expected the governess to drop her gaze and mumble acquiescence, it was what most people did when he talked. Instead she pursed her lips again and held his eye.

'First and foremost Aahil is a child. One day he will be Sheikh, but right now he is a boy like any other. He might have heavy responsibilities in the future, but that is all the more reason for him to enjoy his childhood.'

'Games will not teach him to run a country. Laughter will not show him how to deal with mutinous subjects.' Malik shook his head in frustration. He knew how difficult it was to rule a country, even a small one like Huria. When his father had died Malik had been just twenty-two, but he'd had to step up and do his duty. The first few months had been trying, but he knew he had been well prepared, and that was what he wanted for his son.

'You're wrong,' Miss Talbot said animatedly. 'Games can teach you strategy and forward planning. They teach you to read your opponents and come up with a way to out-think them.'

Malik didn't think anyone had come out and told him he was wrong since he'd become Sheikh. It was refreshing, but he found that since he was in fact right, it was also a little frustrating.

'And laughter?' he asked coolly.

Miss Talbot smiled. 'Have you never been in a negotiation with two people who want completely different things? The tension builds and no one can agree on anything. Knowing how to diffuse that situation with laughter is a skill every future Sheikh needs to learn.'

Malik couldn't help but smile with her. She was clever, this young governess. She might not be right, but she was certainly clever.

While he regrouped Malik motioned for Miss Talbot to begin eating. The food set before them was simple and traditional, food Malik had been served his entire life. The flatbread was baked in every oven in Huria and the accompanying dips found at every dinner table when entertaining guests. Malik loved the food of his country and he felt a glow of satisfaction as he watched his children's governess place a piece of bread covered in hummus in her mouth and begin to chew. As she ate she closed her eyes momentarily, as if not wanting to distract her tastebuds from the new flavour they were experiencing. He watched her lips as she chewed and noticed the slight curve to the corners of her mouth as she enjoyed what she was tasting. Hastily Malik looked away. Watching Miss Talbot eat was disconcertingly sensual, especially when she popped a finger between her lips and sucked off a stray bit of the sweet dip.

Malik rallied. He was ruler of Huria, a grown man, and he would not be distracted from his true purpose by this young woman's lips. He might have a body of flesh and blood, but his mind needed to be above such distractions as desire.

'You may find Ameera difficult,' he said.

In truth, difficult was an understatement. He knew it must be hard for all his children growing up without a mother, but it seemed to affect his daughter even more than he had ever imagined. Since their mother had died a year ago all of his children had changed. Aahil had become more serious, throwing himself into the role of Prince of Huria, eager to learn everything about the kingdom he would one day rule. Little Hakim had become quieter. Gone was the boy who used to run around the courtyards of the palace pretending to be an assassin or a genie. Those changes Malik could deal with and he knew were to be expected in boys who had lost their mother, but Ameera was different.

Since their mother had died Ameera had become sullen and withdrawn. She refused to utter more than words of one syllable to Malik and he didn't think he'd seen her smile in months. She was only six years old, but when he looked at her he saw a much older girl, someone who had experienced too much sorrow already in her young life.

He glanced at Miss Talbot. She smiled. She smiled more than anyone he had ever met before. Maybe she might be able to coax a smile out of his little girl.

'All the more reason to allow her to enjoy herself.'

Malik sighed. He wanted the best for his children, of course he did. He just didn't always know what that was. His own father had been viewed by many as a liberal. He had sent Malik to be educated in Europe, insisted it was good for his son to be exposed to different cultures and people, but he had also been strict. Malik had never once received a hug from his father, or even anything more affectionate than a warm handshake, and he'd turned out just fine.

'Ameera will one day be expected to marry into a good family,' he said. His daughter might only be six, but he had learnt from his own father it was never too early to look to the future.

'One day,' Miss Talbot said, waving a hand in the air, 'is a very long time away.'

'Not all that long.'

He had married Aliyyah when she was twenty. He had a horrible feeling time would speed by and suddenly his little Ameera would soon be the same age.

Malik waited until their plates had been cleared away and the main course brought up to the rooftop. He couldn't help but watch as his children's governess bent over the dish, inhaling the exotic scent and look-

ing on with anticipation a servant uncovered the side
dishes that accompanied it.

Most visitors to Huria from Europe were overwhelmed or outright disgusted that nearly all meals
were eaten with the hands. Miss Talbot just watched
him closely as he scooped up some of the spicy stew
with a piece of flatbread and then did the same.

'You will need to teach them arithmetic, geography,
languages and world history. I will employ a local tutor
to teach them the history of Huria.' Malik glanced at
Miss Talbot and wondered whether she would argue.
She had seemed to protest against everything else he
had said that evening.

'That sounds like a wonderful plan,' she said. 'Of
course I couldn't hope to know all the intricacies of the
history of a country like Huria.' She paused and then
continued mildly, 'I will also be teaching the children
music, a little natural science and engaging them in
physical activity.'

Malik put the piece of bread he had just broken off
back down on his plate and exhaled slowly. She was
infuriating. He'd forgotten what it was like to have
someone argue back, someone calmly pat you on the
hand and then tell you they would disobey.

'You will teach them arithmetic, geography, languages and world history,' he repeated, struggling to
keep his voice calm and level.

'Oh, yes,' she agreed. 'Those subjects are very important. Especially languages.'

Malik waited. He just knew she would have something more to say.

'But children need a rounded education. They can't
be cooped up in a classroom all day.'

He frowned. That was exactly what was supposed to happen. She was a governess, hired to teach his children. If she wasn't going to do it in the classroom, then where was she planning on taking his children?

'Miss Talbot,' he said sternly—it was a voice many of his advisors cowered from, but she just sat there and smiled sunnily. 'I have employed you to teach my children the subjects I see fit.'

'And of course I will do that,' she said. 'But when we're finished with arithmetic, languages, world history and geography we might branch out a little.'

How could you ever be finished with world history? Or languages?

She leaned forward and Malik found himself momentarily distracted by the swell of her breasts above her neckline. Hastily he looked away. Here he was preaching about how he wanted his children to behave and he couldn't keep his eyes from roaming.

'Why don't you let me do it my way for a few weeks? If you really don't like how your children are coming along, you can send me home.'

Malik opened his mouth to reply, then shut it again. She'd outmanoeuvred him. He was a skilled negotiator, always able to smooth things over with neighbouring countries or warring tribes, but he'd just been outmanoeuvred by a governess. He couldn't argue with her logic—if he didn't like how she did things he *could* always just send her home in a few weeks and employ someone more suitable.

He glanced at her again—maybe someone a little less distracting, with that grey hair, stern visage and the scattered warts he had been expecting. Maybe someone who didn't smile quite so much.

Chapter Three

'Enough,' Rachel proclaimed.

Three sets of dark eyes looked at her with surprise. It was eleven in the morning and they still had another hour of lessons to go until they broke for lunch.

'I think we need a change of scenery,' she declared.

None of the children moved. Insistently Rachel stood up and gathered one or two things from her desk. She needed fresh air and she needed to see some proper daylight. The palace was magnificent, there was no denying it; cool whitewashed rooms were never far away from bubbling fountains or beautiful mosaics, but the schoolroom had something to be desired. It was plain and boring, there was no way of getting round it. Rachel supposed the Sheikh or one of his aides had thought it best to keep the room as dull as possible so as not to distract the children from their studies. The result was a room Rachel was dying to get out of after just two hours.

'Come, children, we will finish our lessons outside.'

She had reached the door before anyone moved, but as she stepped outside into the bright sunlight she heard the scraping of the wooden chairs against the floor.

Rachel made a beeline for a shaded area, arranged her skirts around her, and sat down. The children followed awkwardly and stood looking down at her.

'Now to finish off the morning we are going to work on developing your imaginations.'

One of the toughest things Rachel was finding was tailoring her lessons to three children of different ages and abilities. Aahil was intelligent and probably the most confident of the three when it came to answering her questions. Little Hakim was still so very young, but Rachel could see that under his shy exterior he had a quick mind. Ameera had refused to answer any of Rachel's questions, instead preferring to scuff her feet along the floor and sigh loudly whenever Rachel spoke.

'Between us we are going to tell a story,' Rachel explained. 'I will go first, set the scene and introduce a character or two. Then we will all take it in turns to add to the story.'

It was a game Rachel had played many times with her school friends on cold, wet, winter afternoons. For a moment Rachel pictured herself back at Madame Dubois's School for Young Ladies and felt a pang of homesickness. She wondered how Joanna was faring in Hertfordshire. Of all her friends Rachel was most concerned for quiet, kind Joanna. Found abandoned on the steps of the school when just a baby, Joanna had never had a family, never known who her parents were. Rachel's friend wanted so much to belong somewhere and had been excited about the prospect of becoming part of the family she was being employed by, but Rachel just hoped they treated her kindly and not like a servant. Joanna had so much love and warmth to give, she deserved happiness.

Pulling herself back to the present before Aahil could protest this wasn't educational enough or Ameera could vocalise whatever criticism was making its way from her brain to her lips, Rachel began the story.

'Once upon a time there was an old woman who lived in a small cottage in the woods.' She turned to Hakim and smiled gently at him. 'Why don't you add something next, Hakim?'

The young Prince frowned and started to chew on his thumb.

'You can add anything you like,' Rachel said encouragingly.

'She had a pet,' Hakim said after a minute or two.

'What kind of pet?' Rachel asked.

'A pet dragon.'

Ameera snorted. Rachel ignored her for a second and focused on Hakim.

'That's very good, Hakim. Once upon a time there was an old woman who lived in a small cottage in the woods. She had a pet dragon.'

Rachel was delighted when Hakim gave her a small, shy smile. She'd have to remember he liked dragons, work it into one of their lessons soon.

'Ameera, it's your turn next.'

Rachel watched as the young girl's lips moved, but no sound came out. After a few seconds she spoke, a sly smile crossing her face.

'The old woman liked to eat children for breakfast,' she said. 'And her name was Miss Talbot.'

Ameera sat back triumphantly, crossed her arms across her chest and levelled a challenging stare at

Rachel. Rachel held her gaze. She had heard titbits of conversation from some of the servants about Ameera's behaviour with her previous tutors. The young girl had been rude, naughty and sometimes downright mean, but despite her previous shenanigans, Rachel knew she was still just a child. A child acting up most likely because of the loss of her mother.

Rachel hadn't spent years at a boarding school with lots of other girls not to learn how to deal with difficult characters. Ameera might be a little terror, but she was no match for Rachel.

Without changing the tone of her voice Rachel repeated the story so far. 'Once upon a time there was an old woman who lived in a small cottage in the woods. She had a pet dragon. The old woman liked to eat children for breakfast and her name was Miss Talbot.'

Serenely Rachel turned to Aahil and motioned for him to continue the story. Out of the corner of her eye she saw Ameera's face fall.

Aahil was quiet for a moment whilst he observed the interaction between his sister and his governess, then he realised what Rachel was doing and started to speak.

'One day a brave prince was riding through the forest and he stopped outside the old woman's cottage.'

Rachel turned to Hakim.

'And he saw the pet dragon.'

She smiled encouragingly, then motioned for Ameera to carry on.

'He killed Miss Talbot with his sharp pointy sword. The end,' Ameera said firmly.

Rachel clapped her hands together.

'What a wonderful story. We had an evil villain, a

brave prince, a happy ending, and of course a dragon—everything a good story needs.'

'Did you hear what I said?' Ameera asked, no longer able to contain herself.

'Yes, Ameera, I did.'

The young girl looked as if she were about to say something else when a shadow fell over them. Rachel looked behind her to see the Sheikh standing over them. She shivered slightly, telling herself it was because he was blocking out the sunlight and not because his dark eyes held hers for just a moment longer than was necessary.

'How are your lessons going, children?' he asked.

'We've been making up a story,' Hakim said, his face shining with pleasure.

Rachel saw the Sheikh's surprised look as his youngest son spoke without prompting and felt a stab of pride. Just a few more days and most of Hakim's shyness would be a thing of the past.

'It had a dragon in it.'

The Sheikh frowned. In the two weeks since Rachel had arrived at the palace she had barely seen him. Apart from the rather surreal meal on the rooftop he had been busy with state business. Sometimes she would glimpse him talking quietly with some advisor or discussing something animatedly with Wahid, but he had not approached her since their dinner together.

Not that she expected him to want to talk to *her*, of course, but seeing as she spent most of her day with his children, she was pretty sure he hadn't spoken to them either.

Rachel didn't profess to be an expert on how royalty normally interacted with their children, but she had experienced first-hand the heartbreak indifference from a parent to a child could bring. Her parents had always been kind towards her, they'd never beaten her, or even told her off. She had been well clothed, decently fed and well educated. All in all she'd had more than many children could expect. What she hadn't received was their attention. They'd always been more interested in each other than in her. Sometimes they hadn't even noticed when she had entered the room. As a child she'd craved their attention, their approval, and when they didn't do anything more than glance at the picture she'd painted or smile distantly when a governess paraded her in front of them on a Sunday, it had hurt more than if they'd slapped her face.

She wouldn't let the same happen to these children. She could tell the Sheikh loved them, she could see it in his eyes, but he just didn't know how to act around them. No doubt he had been brought up to focus fully on running his kingdom and didn't know how to engage properly with the three young children who loved him so much.

'A dragon,' the Sheikh said.

Hakim nodded. 'A pet dragon.'

'I'm not sure…' the Sheikh started to say.

'Doesn't Hakim have a wonderful imagination?' Rachel said lightly.

The Sheikh stopped speaking and nodded, smiling down at his son.

'Really wonderful.'

Rachel watched as father ruffled his son's hair and Hakim smiled shyly.

'Miss Talbot was in it,' Ameera said, stepping forward between Rachel and the Sheikh. 'She was the villain. I made sure she was stabbed with a really sharp sword.'

Rachel knew she was just doing it for attention so she smiled serenely and inspected her nails. She hoped the Sheikh would similarly ignore his daughter's provocation and Ameera would soon realise nothing was to be gained from this sort of behaviour.

'Ameera,' he said sharply, 'apologise at once.'

Ameera crossed her arms mutinously.

'No.'

'Apologise to Miss Talbot.'

'No.'

Rachel closed her eyes briefly and steeled herself for the disaster this was about to become.

'Ameera, you will apologise.'

'I won't.'

'I am your father. You will do as I say. Apologise to Miss Talbot immediately.'

Ameera stared at him silently, fury flashing in her eyes.

'Apologise.'

'Never.'

'Go to your room. You won't be allowed out until you apologise.'

'Good. Then I won't have to see her annoying face ever again.'

Ameera stalked off towards her room, not sparing a glance for her father or Rachel, making sure the door slammed loudly behind her once she was inside.

The Sheikh ran a hand through his hair and for a moment he looked beaten, but Rachel couldn't bring herself to feel sorry for him. He'd brought the whole episode on himself.

'Could we have a word, Your Highness?' Rachel asked excessively politely.

'I need to be getting back.'

'This can't wait. Boys, why don't you go and get cleaned up for lunch.'

As Aahil and Hakim scurried away Rachel saw the Sheikh turn as if he was about to leave, too. She caught him by the arm and proceeded to pull him into a little alcove that was sunk into the courtyard wall.

He was so surprised to be touched in this way that for a moment he followed her without any protest. Rachel saw the instant he rallied, but did not care if he was angry at being manhandled. She was angry at how he'd handled the situation.

'That was poorly done,' she hissed.

The Sheikh recoiled from her slightly and she wondered for a second when the last time he had been criticised to his face was.

'Ameera needs discipline.'

'She needs to see acting out will not get a reaction from us.'

'She needs to learn she cannot be so rude.'

'She's testing the boundaries, seeing what she can get away with.'

'And you would let her get away with that sort of behaviour?'

They were both talking in muted voices, but the anger was apparent in both sides. The Sheikh drew himself up to his full height and Rachel suddenly wished she hadn't brought him into such a small, enclosed space. His body was only inches from hers, his face so close she could reach out and touch his cheek without stretching.

Rachel felt a tingle of anticipation run through her body. She was angry with him, there was no denying it, but there was something else lurking inside her, too. She saw the passion flashing in his eyes as he spoke about his children, passion that matched her own, and she felt drawn to him. Even though they were arguing she wanted to reach out and pull him closer, to feel his body up against hers.

She rallied, trying to push all inappropriate thoughts from her mind and focus on the real issue.

'Ameera is craving attention,' Rachel said, forcing herself to speak calmly. 'She needs to realise that acting out will not get her attention, but behaving well will.'

The Sheikh looked as though he was going to say something more, but as he digested Rachel's words he fell silent.

'So you were just going to ignore her rude comments?'

Rachel nodded. 'And praise her when she did something well.'

'And eventually she will stop being rude.'

The Sheikh sank back against the wall. For a moment he looked just like a man, just like an ordinary father struggling with a difficult child.

Rachel watched as different emotions flitted over his face: sadness, helplessness and finally acceptance. She had another overwhelming urge to reach out to him, this time to comfort him, but just as she was raising her hand she stopped. He might look like an ordinary man right now, but she had to remember he was royalty. He was the ruler of a kingdom and so far above her in social status she probably shouldn't even think about speaking to him directly.

As she let her hand fall back to her side the Sheikh surprised her by catching her fingers in his own. For a moment Rachel thought there was a slight longing in his expression, but after a second it was gone and the façade he presented to the world was back. Quickly he released her hand and stepped out of the alcove.

'I'm sorry for interfering,' he said. 'In the future I'll leave such decisions on discipline up to you.'

Rachel felt him slipping further away and knew if she were not careful he might feel like it were best if he disengage from his children completely. Thinking quickly she spoke.

'This afternoon I was planning on taking over the kitchen for a few hours with the children. I know they would love for you to join us for a little while if you have the chance.'

Rachel saw him hesitate and then to her surprise he nodded without any further persuasion.

'I'll see if I can manage to join you for a short while in between the land disputes this afternoon.'

As he walked away Rachel sagged back against the wall. She had invited him to join them for the sake of his children, but she could not deny the flutter of excitement she'd felt when he'd agreed.

Chapter Four

Malik held up a hand for silence and immediately the raised voices fell quiet. He was developing a headache and he felt like they'd been cooped up in the mediation room all afternoon. As Sheikh it was his job to rule on all land disputes and intertribal quarrels in Huria. The kingdom was not huge, but the people were largely nomadic and had differing views of possession and ownership, which made disputes such as these very difficult.

The head of the Banjeree people opened his mouth to speak again, but Malik silenced him with a stern look. He'd heard enough. It was the age-old argument that the land belonged to nature and therefore the tribe should be allowed to wander anywhere to pitch their sturdy tents and take what they needed from the roaming livestock.

'Talid,' Malik said, addressing the head of the Banjeree people, 'you are right that this land of ours is a gift from nature. We need to nurture it and give back exactly what we take, otherwise we will be left with nothing.'

He turned to the other supplicant, a successful farmer who didn't like having his goats eaten by the Banjeree people, quite understandably.

'I also agree with your opinion, Yusuf,' Malik said in a conciliatory tone. 'You work hard to build a successful business and feel it is unfair when your land is used and your livestock taken.'

'They are not *his* livestock,' Talid said.

Malik frowned at him and the nomad fell silent.

'This is what will happen. Yusuf, you will allow the Banjeree to pitch their tents on your land, but only in places you are not currently using to grow crops or rear livestock. Talid, you will not allow your people to take anything from Yusuf's land. There is plenty of countryside and wildlife that belongs only to the population of Huria as a whole, there is no need to destroy this man's hard-built business.'

Both men looked as if they were about to argue, but Malik dismissed them before anything further could be said. It had been a long afternoon.

When the two men had left Malik stretched out on his adorned chair and glanced out of the window. He could hear giggles of pleasure coming from the kitchen where Miss Talbot had taken his children for an afternoon out of the classroom. He remembered her invitation and for a second he was tempted to go and join them, but something made him hesitate.

She was a little minx, his children's new governess. She was clever and quick with her words and far too attractive to make Malik feel comfortable. When she had pulled him into the alcove earlier to discuss Ameera and how they would deal with her she had been spitting fire. He liked how protective of his children she had become in two weeks and, although he had been annoyed, too, he had been able to admire the self-confident way she had dealt with him. Many people could not even look him in the eye when they spoke, but Miss Talbot always fixed him with a look that told him he would listen or there would be hell to pay.

She'd been right about Ameera, too—he *had* blundered in and made things worse, given her bad behaviour attention when it just needed to be ignored. Malik wasn't used to admitting he was wrong, he hardly ever had to do it, but he could see Miss Talbot's methods would work with Ameera, at least better than any of the previous tutors' had.

He almost stood, almost strode from the room and went to join his children in the kitchen for whatever lesson their governess had in store, but something made him hesitate. Of course he didn't approve of her taking them out of the classroom all the time, but he did have to admit Hakim was becoming a little more confident and Aahil a little less serious under her care. The problem wasn't with the location of the lesson, or the content, but with Miss Talbot herself.

When they'd stood in the alcove, so close he could have reached out and pulled her towards him, he'd wanted to do exactly that. He'd wanted to wrap his arms around her, pull her close and see what those lips that were always smiling tasted like. It had been a momentary urge, but momentary was long enough for Malik to know it was unwise on so many levels.

Malik hadn't felt desire like that for years. All the time he had been married to Aliyyah he had, of course, visited her bedroom, but for them both it had been a matter of duty, the need to produce children and heirs.

There had been no desire involved. Before Aliyyah, whilst Malik had been studying in Europe, there had been a couple of women he'd been intimate with, but he struggled to remember such fire and passion even with them. And since Aliyyah's death Malik knew he had been a little numb, not from grief—his wife had been so distant throughout their entire marriage her death was like losing a stranger—but from guilt. He could have saved her; if he'd just been more perceptive he could have saved her. Standing in that alcove with Miss Talbot, Malik had felt as though he'd woken up from a year-long slumber.

Telling himself it had just been a one-off, an anomaly, Malik stood. He would not be kept from doing what he wanted by a trifling emotion like desire. He would admire Miss Talbot's talents as a governess and her knack for making his children come alive again, but he would not desire her. It was all a matter of self-control.

Quickly Malik walked across the courtyard and stepped into the kitchen. It was chaos. For a moment he thought about quietly backing out and leaving them to it, but then Hakim spotted him and Malik was rewarded with a shy smile. He steeled himself and stepped into the disorder.

'Your Majesty,' Miss Talbot said as she spotted him, 'I'm so glad you could join us.'

Both of his sons spared him a quick glance and then plunged back into the mess on the counter.

'What are you doing?'

'We're making biscuits,' Aahil said, kneading caramel-coloured dough on the surface.

Malik just stared for a second. He'd become so used

to his eldest son acting like a man he'd nearly forgotten he was still a child. Standing in front of him, covered in flour with a stray bit of dough on his chin, Aahil looked like the boy he was.

'Biscuits?'

'Today I'm teaching the children to make English biscuits, and next week, if Cook kindly lets us take over his kitchen again, we will make something Hurian.'

Malik leant against one of the counters as he watched Miss Talbot instruct his two sons on how to roll out the dough and then cut the biscuits into the shapes they wanted.

'When I was at school in England I often used to beg our cook to let me take over a small corner of the kitchen so I could make a cake or a tray of biscuits,' Miss Talbot chatted easily to the children as they worked. It was a surprisingly comforting domestic scene, his two sons covered in flour and busy rolling out dough whilst Miss Talbot oversaw them.

'Where is Ameera?' Malik asked.

'In her room. You told her she could not come out until she apologised and, as of yet, she hasn't apologised.'

Malik felt a sudden warmth towards the young woman in front of him. Earlier that morning he had undermined her and tried to discipline his daughter himself. Now he realised he had gone about it all the wrong way, but Miss Talbot had not acted against him and allowed Ameera to get away with not apologising. She had let his method go ahead, even if she did not agree with it in principle.

Whilst the two boys were busy cutting out different shapes the governess moved over to where he was standing. In the kitchen full of the smells of baking Malik thought he could still detect Miss Talbot's own scent, a mixture of rose and lavender, a very feminine and English smell.

'Once the biscuits are in the oven and the smell of baking is wafting out into the courtyard I thought I might go and see Ameera,' she said softly. 'Let her know she only needs to apologise and she can come and sample the biscuits with us.'

Malik nodded his approval. He wished he knew how to deal with his children the way Miss Talbot did. It seemed to come naturally to her, like running the kingdom did to him. He thought back to his father and how he would have responded in this situation, but realised the old man hadn't ever really seen him outside of their once-weekly meetings where Malik would show what he had learnt that week.

Miss Talbot was standing next to him, leaning against one of the counters. She was close, but she didn't seem to be affected by their proximity the way he was. After a few seconds of watching the two boys concentrate on the shapes they were cutting, she turned back to him and raised her eyes to meet his own.

'Thank you for coming this afternoon, it means the world to Aahil and Hakim.'

There was such sincerity in her gaze that for a moment Malik could do nothing but stare at her. She was beautiful, he realised, not in the way Aliyyah had been beautiful, but beautiful all the same. Aliyyah had always been perfectly presented, a nobleman's daughter brought up to be the wife of a Sheikh, always dressed in the finest clothes and adorned with jewels. Miss

Talbot sparkled without any adornment. Even with her hair ruffled from spending the day with three children and her dress covered in flour, she was radiant. It was the smile, he thought, the happiness within her shone through that smile.

'They should really be in the classroom,' Malik said, knowing he was spoiling the moment between them, but needing to say something to stop that damn seductive smile.

Miss Talbot's face dropped and immediately Malik felt like a cur. He couldn't deny she was working wonders with his children, even if her methods were a little unorthodox. Aahil and Hakim seemed to blossom under her care and it would probably only be a matter of time before Ameera did the same.

'I plan to send Aahil to Europe when he is a little older to complete his education, I want him to be ready for that.' Malik tried to say the words softly, but even to his ears they had an edge to them.

'He will be,' Miss Talbot ground out.

Malik could see she was fighting to keep her composure in front of the children. Quickly she spun on her heel and whisked the trays of biscuits into the big oven.

'They will take about twenty minutes to cook, boys,' she said with a smile. 'I will keep an eye on them whilst you go and choose a book each for story time.'

Malik watched as his children dashed passed him. Hakim stopped on the way to give his governess a floury hug, his little hands leaving white handprints on her skirt. Far from being annoyed at the mess, Miss Talbot just laughed and ushered the boy out of the kitchen. Malik felt a little stab of disappointment that

Hakim didn't stop to hug him, but he supposed he'd never encouraged such behaviour.

There was a long silence in the kitchen as Miss Talbot seemed to consider her next words. Malik had the feeling he was going to see a side to her he had never before witnessed.

'Your Highness,' she said coolly, 'I think we need to acknowledge our very different priorities in the education of your children.'

It was the first time Malik had seen her without a smile on her face and he realised he might have pushed her too far.

'I would like to assure you that, although I may seem to indulge the children in fun behaviour, Aahil will be ready to study in Europe when he is older, Ameera will be suitably educated to marry well and whatever plan you have for little Hakim will be realised as well.'

There was a steeliness behind her eyes as she spoke and Malik couldn't help but admire her courage and determination.

'But I would like to make one thing clear...' She paused and stepped closer, so close that Malik could smell that enticing scent of rose and lavender again. 'If I am to remain as the children's governess, I will do things my own way. The children will learn everything that you wish them to, but I will not trap them in a classroom to wither in the dark. I will nurture not only their minds, but their bodies and their souls, too. There will be laughter and there will be fun.'

She stopped speaking and they held each other's eye for well over a minute. Malik knew they were at a vital point in their employer–employee relationship.

He didn't doubt—as much as Miss Talbot loved his children already and was enjoying her time here in Huria—that she would return home rather than teach in a way that went against her principles.

Suddenly Malik realised he didn't want her to leave. Ever since she had walked into the palace, her face glowing with pleasure, she had injected a happiness into a place that had been consumed with grief and guilt for too long. He hadn't heard his children laugh for months, but in the past two weeks every time he stepped outside there was a giggle or a shout of joy. Her methods weren't what he had expected, not what he had wanted when he had sent for an English governess, but he couldn't deny the children were responding to her. As long as they came out of it with an education, maybe it didn't matter too much how they got it. Even if his father really wouldn't have approved.

Malik took a step back. The proximity to the delicious-smelling Miss Talbot made something stir deep inside him that he didn't want to admit to.

'You will remain as the children's governess,' he said gruffly.

He wanted to say more, wanted to explain how in the past year he had felt adrift, with a chasm opening up between him and his children that he didn't know how to bridge. Malik knew he blamed himself for Aliyyah's death and knew the children probably did, too. He'd retreated into himself a little, giving everything to the kingdom as his own father had taught him, and not knowing how to help his sons and daughter grieve and move on.

Miss Talbot nodded once and turned back to clearing up the mess the children had made on the counter.

Malik rallied. He was Sheikh, ruler of the proud Kingdom of Huria, and he was good at it. No one had prepared him for the role of widowed parent, but he did know how to run his kingdom. He would just have to do his job and let Miss Talbot do hers.

Rachel took some deep breaths and started to count to a hundred in her head. Even though she was facing away from him, she could still feel the Sheikh's presence in the kitchen. His power and determination seemed to radiate from him wherever he went.

She couldn't quite believe how she had just confronted him, he was, after all, not only her employer, but also royalty, but Rachel had always felt her first responsibility was to the children in her care. When she was a child she had wished for a champion, someone who would stand up and tell her parents what she really needed, but instead she'd had governesses with weak personalities who just agreed with whatever their employers said.

Rachel reached a hundred and was surprised to find the Sheikh still standing in the same position in the kitchen. She knew others sometimes mistook her passion for rudeness or disrespect and hoped the Sheikh wasn't about to tell her to pack her bags and leave because of insubordination. Miss Fanworth, her favourite teacher at Madame Dubois's School for Young Ladies, had always cautioned her over her trait for speaking out, never trying to stifle Rachel's personality, but advising her to balance her forthrightness with a way to move forward after she'd said her bit.

The Sheikh was frowning, an expression that did nothing to mar his near-perfect features, and Rachel wondered not for the first time what was going on inside his head. She could see something was holding him back from his children, even from life itself, and although being brought up knowing your first duty was to your country would certainly change your perspective on life, Rachel didn't think it was enough to account for the distance he seemed to keep from everyone.

She supposed he could still be in mourning for his late wife, although in the two weeks Rachel had been at the palace she had heard quite a lot of gossip about their relationship. Rachel had always had a talent for making friends easily and people seemed to like opening up to her, so she had heard how the couple had remained distant despite being married for almost a decade.

Aahil, Ameera and Hakim were cared for, their father was ensuring they got a good education and were always safe, but Rachel knew something else integral was missing and she was determined to help this little family find it.

'If you do not have to rush back, I think it might be a good idea for us to go and see Ameera together.'

She saw the Sheikh glance towards the door as if wondering if he could make a speedy escape. Rachel found herself holding her breath, wondering if this father would step up and make an extra effort with his children, even though he was struggling.

'Of course,' he said after a few seconds of internal debate.

'Maybe we could discuss how best to approach the situation,' Rachel suggested, knowing they would both have to present a united front if Ameera was to understand the lesson they were trying to teach her.

'I won't go blundering in,' the Sheikh said with a half-smile.

Rachel found herself momentarily unable to speak. The Sheikh didn't smile much—in fact, Rachel wasn't sure if she had ever seen anything more than an amused upturning of his lips before now—but when he did smile it was devastating. He was a handsome man, Sheikh Malik bin Jalal al-Mahrouky, but when he smiled he was more than handsome. Rachel felt her skin start to tingle and her lips felt unusually dry. Maybe it was a good thing he was so serious most of the time—if smiled at everyone then no one would ever get anything done.

She rallied, chastising herself. It was her first golden rule of being a governess: don't fall for your employer. Such thoughts had been the downfall of so many young governesses and Rachel was determined not to be one of them. Besides, whenever she conversed with the Sheikh they always seemed to end up butting heads over their differing opinions. It was just his smile that had put her a little off balance, nothing more.

'Wonderful,' Rachel said sunnily, trying to hide the slight tremor in her voice.

'Maybe you should take the lead,' the Sheikh said. 'I don't want to undermine your authority. You have to be with her every day.'

Rachel nodded her agreement. It was exactly what she would have suggested, but his reasons for letting her take the lead made Rachel a little sad. She knew things were different for royalty—the Sheikh had to focus on running his kingdom—but Rachel knew all too well how upsetting it was when your parents left decisions on your upbringing to others.

From a young age Rachel could remember realising her parents were much more interested in each other than they were in her. They had had a tempestuous relationship—blazing rows one minute, elaborate shows of affection another. She could recall many nights sitting at the top of the stairs listening to them shouting and throwing things at each other. The next day it would be back to kisses and pet names, all the while hardly remembering they had a daughter quietly taking it all in. By the age of eight Rachel had known she never wanted to marry if this was what it turned you into and, by the time she arrived at Madame Dubois's School for Young Ladies, she had decided she would much rather travel the world and make her own enjoyment than be stuck in a marriage such as her parents'. She felt she had always been destined to be a governess, but unlike many of her contemporaries, Rachel had looked forward to her chosen career with anticipation. She didn't want to be tied down, married to someone who made her miserable, not when she could be making a difference to young lives. Rachel knew many children experienced the same benign neglect as she had, and as a governess she could give these emotionally abandoned children the affection their parents couldn't. If she was completely honest with herself, the knowledge that she would never have children of her own made Rachel a little sad, but it was a sacrifice she had come to terms with.

Ameera's situation wasn't exactly like hers, but Rachel could empathise with the young girl. She was craving attention from her father, just like Rachel had from her parents, and he didn't know how to give it to her.

'Shall we?' The Sheikh motioned towards the door and Rachel found herself immediately moving that way. He was a man used to being obeyed without question and that was powerful all in itself.

They crossed the courtyard in silence, walking quickly to get out of the blazing sun, then ascended the stairs to Ameera's room. Rachel knocked on the door, but didn't wait for an answer before turning the handle and stepping inside.

It was dark in the room compared to the courtyard and Rachel's eyes took a moment to adjust. She glanced around the room and saw Ameera had pulled her books and her toys from the shelves in anger. For now Rachel would ignore the mess and instead she crossed to the bed where two wide, dark eyes were staring at her mutinously from out of the darkness.

Rachel sat, taking a moment to smooth her skirts and ensure she was comfortable. Ameera was a wilful little madam and they might be here for a while. She was pleased to see the Sheikh had hung back, standing by the door, silent but very much present in the room.

'Good afternoon, Ameera,' Rachel said.

The young girl stared back at her, lips firmly pressed together.

'Have you been having fun in here?' Rachel asked, looking around as if she genuinely didn't know that Ameera had been sent to her room for bad behaviour.

Still silence. Already Rachel could see a flicker of triumph in the young girl's eyes and she had to quash her own smile. The day Rachel was outmanoeuvred by a pupil was the day she gave up being a governess.

The Sheikh shifted his position behind them, but still remained silent.

'I would like you to apologise, Ameera, to myself and to your father.'

'No.'

'Very well.' Rachel stood and turned to leave. She counted the steps in her head and only got to four before Ameera's voice burst through the silence.

'That's it?' she asked. 'You're not going to force me to apologise?'

Rachel shook her head. 'I'm not going to force you to apologise, Ameera.' She continued walking to the door, stopping only when she was level with the Sheikh.

'It's a shame,' she said, 'but we tried.'

Rachel hoped the Sheikh would catch on and not spoil her little ruse.

'We tried,' he repeated, solemnly nodding his head.

Rachel had her hand on the door handle when she heard Ameera standing up.

'Why is it a shame?' she asked in a much-less-defiant voice than before.

'Well, we've baked biscuits,' Rachel said, 'and your father was telling me how you love sweet things, so we thought we'd come in and give you the chance to apologise and come and join us once the biscuits are out of the oven.'

'I can't be bribed,' the little Princess said in a voice that said she could quite easily be bribed.

'And then there was the little excursion next week…' Rachel let her sentence trail off. 'Hakim will be ever so disappointed, but I can't take your brothers and leave you here unsupervised.'

'Excursion?' Ameera asked.

Rachel nodded. 'Hakim was so looking forward to it.'

She knew it was important to give Ameera a way to save face. The little girl had declared she would never apologise and now Rachel was asking her to go back on that. She needed a way to justify it to herself.

Ameera fiddled with a strand of hair for a moment, twisting it round her finger. Just as she'd planned, Rachel could smell the first wafts of the scent of biscuits baking.

'I'm sorry,' Ameera mumbled.

'If you are going to apologise, Ameera, you need to do it properly, otherwise there's no point in doing it at all.'

The little Princess looked up at her and took a deep breath.

'I'm sorry, Miss Talbot, for being rude.'

Rachel smiled warmly. 'Thank you for apologising, Ameera, it was very big of you.'

For a moment they stood looking at each other. Then Ameera launched herself across the room, and gave Rachel a quick hug. Rachel stroked the young girl's hair and felt herself relax. Soon she would be able to start breaking down the walls these children had built to defend themselves from the pain of their mother's death. Soon she would be able to start to help them heal. She glanced briefly at the Sheikh, who had remained silent throughout. He was watching the interaction between her and his daughter almost wistfully and Rachel wondered if he was the one who needed the most help to heal.

'Why don't you choose a book for story time, then

go and find your brothers? We will test out the biscuits in ten minutes, I'll bring them to the table in the courtyard.'

Rachel stepped outside, followed closely by the Sheikh. To her surprise he caught her by the upper arm and gently spun her to face him.

'You were magnificent,' he murmured, looking directly into her eyes.

Rachel mumbled something incomprehensible under her breath, not able to string a coherent sentence together with his rich brown eyes locked on hers.

He was still touching her upper arm and Rachel could feel the heat of his skin against hers through the thin cotton of her dress. She felt herself sway towards him ever so slightly and found herself wondering for the first time in her life what it would be like to kiss a man.

Rachel's eyes flicked to his lips and she knew instantly what it would be like to kiss the Sheikh: sensuous and divine.

With a great effort she rallied. These thoughts were totally inappropriate. Not only was the Sheikh her employer, but she had sworn to herself long ago she would never let herself fall for a man and it would be all too easy to fall for the Sheikh. Sometimes his cool manner and distant demeanour irritated her, but she could already recognise the caring heart that beat under his icy façade.

Rachel stepped back, knowing she needed a little distance. Deep down she knew her attraction to this man was laughable really—he was royalty and she was the neglected daughter of a baron. Their gulf between their social statuses was so large it gaped before them, yet Rachel didn't feel uneasy when the Sheikh was around. At least as long as he didn't touch her and make her heart pound in her chest.

She had made her decision to always remain single and free years ago and she would not lose her head over this man who probably noticed her no more than he did his servants. Rachel had seen how love and relationships were more destructive than anything else. Her parents had always been somewhere in the cycle of vicious row or passionate reconciliation and Rachel knew she didn't want that in her life. She would be quite content to see the world, focus on the children in her care and never fall in love in her life. She would just have to work on maintaining a safe distance from the Sheikh and his seductive eyes, whilst of course getting him more involved in his children's lives.

'I would like to take the children on a little excursion out of the palace next week,' Rachel said, getting back to business.

'That sounds a wonderful idea. I'm keen for all of them to appreciate this country as a whole and not just the luxurious life they lead behind these walls. I will arrange for an escort to accompany you.'

Rachel took a deep breath before she continued. She knew her next suggestion wasn't going to help her maintain a safe distance from the Sheikh, but she also knew getting him involved with his children was more important than avoiding him because she felt a little tingle under her skin whenever he looked at her.

'I think it would be so good for the children if you came with us.'

Rachel thought he would refuse outright, cite some

important mediation or duty he had to attend to. To her surprise he seemed to deliberate her suggestion.

'I'll meet you out the front of the palace at nine o'clock Tuesday morning.'

They both seemed equally shocked by his agreement, but the Sheikh recovered first, giving a short bow and striding off, leaving Rachel to wonder what she had got herself into.

It was late before Rachel got any time to herself to sit down at the little writing desk in her room and lay out her paper and pen. She was an avid letter writer, and since arriving in Huria she had hardly had time to pen anything but short notes. But tonight she had decided to make time to write to her friends back in England, telling them about Huria, and maybe manage to get some of her thoughts straight at the same time.

It was times like these that she missed her parents. They had both died just over two years ago after contracting malaria on their travels. Despite not having a close relationship with them whilst she was growing up, Rachel had always wondered if things would have changed once she was an adult, once she was leading an interesting life of her own. She'd often imagined sending them postcards and letters whilst she was exploring the world, and when they were reunited for her parents to actually be interested in what she had been doing. Now she'd never know.

She started writing, addressing the top of the letters to Joanna, Isabel and Grace, her closest friends from the years she'd spent at Madame Dubois's School for Young Ladies. The three girls were like family to her and Rachel had found that leaving them all behind had been the hardest part of leaving England. The only consolation was that they all had been moving on to take up positions as governesses at different locations.

In her letters she described the beautiful desert and the verdant oasis and the luxurious palace. She told her friends of the three children in her care and how they were now beginning to blossom and allow her into their world. She even began to write about the Sheikh, carefully thinking about the words before she put them to paper. Rachel had never kept secrets from her friends, but she found herself unwilling to say much on the subject of the Sheikh. Just thinking about him made her face feel hot, and hurriedly she moved on to other matters.

As she signed her name at the bottom of the letters Rachel felt a sudden sadness at being so far away from her three friends. They had always been there for each other throughout their time at school and now Rachel wished she could sit with the three girls on one of their beds and just talk about nothing and everything. She wanted to laugh at Isabel's light-hearted exaggerations, pretend to be shocked at Grace's latest act of rebellion and listen to Joanna's quiet, soothing voice as she helped all three of her friends through their latest predicaments.

Rachel wondered how they were getting on in their new homes, whether they had been welcomed as they had all hoped and whether their employers were as infuriating and attractive as the cool, distant Sheikh. She worried about Grace's situation the most. Whereas she, Joanna and Isabel had all set off to make lives for themselves as governesses, Grace had set off in search of her young daughter, the baby born in secret and who Grace had regretted giving up every moment since. Rachel squeezed her eyes shut and wished Grace luck in her search, knowing her old friend would not be happy until she'd found her daughter.

Chapter Five

Malik wondered what he had got himself into for the hundredth time that morning. He had so many things he needed to do, decisions that needed making, disputes that needed settling, but instead he had agreed to spend the entire day with Miss Talbot and his children. The strangest thing was he was quite looking forward to it. Normally he avoided too much contact with his children. He had been raised by tutors and servants, seeing his father just once or twice a week, and he had turned out fine. He could remember the old man lecturing him on how children needed a firm hand and someone to look up to. He had cautioned Malik over becoming too involved in the day-to-day raising of the children, telling his son his first duty was to Huria and to set an example to the entire population. The fact that he sometimes caught himself wishing it was he his children ran to when they scraped their knees or he they wanted to read them a story at night was mere sentimentality and Malik knew he couldn't let that interfere with running his kingdom. His duty was to the people of Huria and he had never once shirked his duty, but today he was going to allow himself to show his children the kingdom he was so proud of.

Malik strode out into the blazing sunlight and surveyed the scene. Miss Talbot and the children had not yet arrived, but the horses were ready and waiting, as was Wahid.

'Nice day for an excursion,' Wahid said with a grin.

Malik had known Wahid since he had been a boy. The swarthy man was a few years older than him, and when the old Sheikh had sent Malik to Europe to study, it had been Wahid who had accompanied him. Now Wahid was more than a bodyguard. As well as being head of security for the palace, he was the closest thing Malik had to a confidant. It was a lonely business being Sheikh, with no one to share decisions with and no one really to talk to, and Wahid seemed to recognise that.

Malik turned back towards the palace as he heard a stampede of feet and saw all three children bursting through the doors and out into the sunlight. Walking calmly behind them, seeming cool and in control, was the unshakeable Miss Talbot.

Malik watched her for a few seconds. The half-dozen Englishmen who had visited Huria at one time or another always seemed red in the face and sweaty. They spent half their time mopping their brows or exclaiming about the heat of the sun and the other half fanning themselves with whatever they could lay their hands on. Miss Talbot was different, she seemed to enjoy the heat, as she seemed to enjoy everything, and take pleasure from the sun. She never appeared flustered or hot and her crisp cotton dresses remained a brilliant white in colour, unstained by sweat or the sands of the desert. Malik didn't know how she did it.

His gaze was drawn away from the governess by the sight of all three of his children stopping suddenly, mouths gaping open.

'Father?' Aahil said, as if he didn't quite believe what he was seeing.

Malik wasn't quite sure what the question was, but smiled encouragingly at his children.

'Come on and find your horses, we've got a busy day planned.'

None of the children moved.

'You're really coming with us?' Ameera asked.

Malik nodded.

'Really?' Ameera persisted. 'Miss Talbot said you were, but we didn't believe her.'

Malik felt a stab of sadness at his daughter's comment, but he understood his children's incredulity. He loved Aahil, Ameera and Hakim, but he didn't spend much time with them. Running the kingdom took so much of his time and energy and it wasn't as if he had ever taken them on an excursion before.

'Really. Now, who needs a hand mounting their horse?'

Malik knew in the year since his wife had died his children had most likely craved attention, but he had been too busy working through his own issues to even realise it. His children needed him, they needed him to give them the attention their mother once had and they needed him to help them understand her death, even if he didn't quite understand it himself. Throughout their young lives Malik knew he had kept his distance from his children and, looking at their beautiful faces assembled in front of him, he felt a pang of regret. As a boy it had been drummed into him that his place was running the kingdom and his wife would bring up any children, but now his children needed him to do both. Malik wondered whether he was capable of shouldering the responsibility for both Huria and the children and felt the weight of responsibility pressing heavily on him.

Malik watched as Aahil expertly mounted his large grey horse and a stab of regret coursed through him. He didn't know who had taught his son to ride, but it wasn't he.

Ameera was next. She placed a foot in Malik's hand and swung herself up on to the small mare that nuzzled her hand and preened under her touch.

All the while Hakim was standing with his hand firmly gripping Miss Talbot's, looking more than a little terrified.

'Hakim,' Malik said softly.

His youngest son looked at him with tears in his eyes.

'What's the matter?'

Hakim looked down at his feet.

Malik took a step towards him uncertainly. He glanced up to see Miss Talbot smiling encouragingly and all of a sudden he knew what to do. Malik knelt down in the sand in front of his son's feet and took the boy's hands in his own. Carefully he reached up and brushed the tears from his son's cheeks.

'Do you know I was seven when I first learnt to ride?' Malik said quietly.

Hakim's eyes flicked to his for just a second before returning to his feet.

'Before that I was rather scared of horses.'

Malik felt his heart soar as his son looked up again with an expression of doubtful hope on his face.

'I never thought I would ever be able to ride like my father or my uncles.'

Malik watched as his son glanced at Miss Talbot. She smiled at him encouragingly and gently let go of his hand.

'Maybe you'd like to ride with me today?' Malik suggested. 'And then next week we can choose a horse for you from the stables and I can teach you to ride.'

Malik surprised himself with the suggestion; he had never considered anything like it before. For a moment he felt a wave of panic and uncertainty, unsure whether his son might reject his offer, but before the feelings could take hold Hakim had launched himself into Malik's arms and was already chattering about what horse he might like.

As he led the boy towards his huge black stallion, Malik caught Miss Talbot's eye and saw the gleam of happiness there. He was inordinately pleased she cared so much for his children already and for a second wondered what it might be like to have her care for him in the same way.

Malik knew he had been blessed in life. He was Sheikh of this wonderful kingdom, he didn't want for any of life's necessities and he had three healthy children to carry on his line. He had once been married to one of the most beautiful women in Huria and time and time again other men had told him how lucky he was to have Aliyyah for his wife. But one thing he had never had was love. In childhood his father had cared for him in a distant kind of way, but never demonstrated any love, and his mother had died in childbirth. When he had married, Malik had done so to carry out his duty, not for love. Aliyyah had made her feelings on the matter quite clear and throughout their marriage he had never received a single look or touch laden with anything more than tolerance. Up until now Malik hadn't ever really thought too much of love, or having someone else's affections, but witnessing the way Miss Talbot looked at his children he wondered whether he was missing out.

Malik mounted his horse, bent down and pulled his son up in front of him. He could feel the small boy trembling slightly and Malik gently wrapped his arms around his son.

'Here's your first lesson,' he said, knowing that encouraging Hakim to concentrate on learning how to ride would take away at least some of the fear. Malik reached around, picked up the reins and positioned them in his son's hands. 'You hold the reins loosely, like this, allowing the horse to feel like they have some freedom. When you want to direct them one way or another, a gentle movement is all it takes.'

He demonstrated how to guide the horse, then let Hakim have a go.

The last person to mount a horse was Miss Talbot, and for a moment Malik wondered whether she knew how to ride. The idea of having her up on his horse, nestled between his thighs, was rather too appealing and he felt a surge of disappointment as she expertly settled on to the back of a headstrong mare. Malik watched as she rearranged her skirts, managing to look as composed as always, and felt the first stirrings of desire as he glimpsed a flash of her smooth calf before her dress settled into position.

Pushing such inappropriate thoughts away, Malik did a quick check that everyone was safe and comfortable, then they moved away from the palace. He'd decided to take only Wahid with them, not a formal full bodyguard, so they could move at their own pace and enjoy the outing. Most people in the surrounding villages would probably recognise him and the royal children, but there was a slight hope of a little more freedom if they travelled without a full escort. Sometimes Malik craved anonymity; he wanted to wander this kingdom he was so proud of incognito and enjoy some of the delights of the common man.

'This oasis is the largest in all of Huria,' Malik said to Miss Talbot as she drew her horse alongside his. Already Ameera and Aahil were out in front of their little group, talking animatedly to Wahid, leaving Malik with his youngest son and the pretty, young Englishwoman for company. 'When my ancestors became rulers of Huria they understood the most important resource for a desert kingdom was water. If you controlled the water you controlled the people.'

'That's why they built the palace around the oasis?' Miss Talbot asked.

Malik loved the way her eyes shone with genuine interest, he knew that she wasn't just asking the question to be polite.

'They built this settlement around the oasis and they built strongholds around the other sources of water in Huria.'

Malik's face darkened for a second as he thought of the less scrupulous of his ancestors, who had held the people of Huria hostage by withholding water over the centuries.

'Nowadays water belongs to every man, woman and child equally,' Malik said, 'but at certain points in our history the less principled of my ancestors used our most precious resource to hold the citizens of this kingdom hostage and enforce their rule.'

'Surely living in such an arid climate sometimes you have to ration the water so it does not run out completely.'

Malik was pleasantly surprised to see Miss Talbot take such an interest in his country. As he talked she listened to him attentively and did not let her concentration waver to other matters. It was rather enjoyable having someone to talk to who actually wanted to interact with him.

Although he and Aliyyah had been married for nine years he had never felt able to talk to his wife about anything other than routine matters. She had not once asked him about his plans for Huria, or wanted to discuss his wishes and dreams. Most of that indifference stemmed from the fact that she resented having to marry him. Malik had known her heart was lost to someone else long before they said their marriage vows, but he had never questioned his duty to marry her and assumed she had done the same. Once they had been married for two months and Aliyyah had only ever spoken the words *yes, husband* or *no, husband*, Malik had begun to suspect her feelings about their marriage did not mirror his own. He'd never expected love, but he'd hoped for pleasant companionship, a woman to be Shaykhah of the kingdom he loved so much. In the years that followed they had led completely separate lives, only coming together to fulfil the rest of their duty and conceive heirs to the throne of Huria.

He glanced again at Miss Talbot. She was the opposite of his late wife in so many ways. Whereas Aliyyah spent most of her life locked away in her rooms, Miss Talbot blossomed in the sunlight, and where Aliyyah's default expression was the frown, Miss Talbot's was a smile. It was refreshing to have someone so cheerful around the palace.

'At times of drought we do ration the water, prioritising drinking water above all else. We've had some tough years, but thankfully nothing too terrible in my lifetime.'

Malik watched as she digested the information, considering what he had just said. He liked how he could see her different thoughts as her expression changed.

Malik sat back in his saddle and contemplated another way Miss Talbot was different to his late wife: he was attracted to her. He could not deny Aliyyah had been beautiful; she was admired by everyone. But there had been no spark between her and Malik, no fire, no passion. Miss Talbot was a different matter. She was passionate about everything and her self-confidence and happy demeanour made her glow. Malik had found himself trying to catch glimpses of her over the past few days, wanting to see her as she walked across the courtyard or shielded her eyes from the sun. Although they disagreed on many aspects of how to raise his children, Malik loved the fire in her eyes when they argued and her determination to convince him she was right. All of these things made her attractive, qualities Malik had never paid attention to in anyone else, but when Miss Talbot looked him in the eye and smiled that genuinely happy smile, he couldn't deny the rise in his body temperature or the desire that flared inside him.

They rode at a comfortable pace, with Ameera and Aahil ahead, pestering Wahid with questions, and Malik and Hakim level with Rachel. She felt strangely contented, riding along with the Sheikh and his children. She knew she'd done a good thing here, asking him to accompany them. Already Hakim was appreciating all the attention from his father, and Rachel had seen the Sheikh's face as he swung his son up on to the horse in front of them. There was no questioning he cared for his children, he just needed to be shown how to demonstrate it.

They'd been riding for about half an hour when they emerged from the oasis and started into the desert proper. Although Rachel had crossed the arid terrain on her journey into Huria, she had mainly been secluded in the comfortable travelling chair, with only glimpses of the landscapes. As they mounted a rocky outcrop Rachel realised how easy it would be to get lost in the desert, even this close to the oasis. Red-orange dunes of sand spread out as far as the eye could see, gently undulating and shimmering in the early morning heat. Off in the distance she could see a rocky outcrop, but other than that the desert seemed impenetrable, and she began wondering where the first village they were going to visit was hiding.

Ever since she was a little girl Rachel had dreamed of the exotic and now she felt as though she were living the dream. She could never have imagined a place like Huria, despite her parents sending her detailed letters from their travels all over the world. They had described the deserts of Egypt and the rocky landscape of Morocco, but never had they told her of anything as beautiful as Huria. Never had they conjured images of vibrant reds and oranges, talked of lush oases, never had they stayed in such a sumptuous palace.

When she was young Rachel had begged her parents numerous times to take her with them when they set off for a new adventure. They'd always given empty, non-committal answers and always set off without her. Rachel had craved their attention, but she'd also desperately wanted to experience the excitement of exploring a new country.

Now here she was, living her life just as she wanted it, without having to rely on her parents for anything. With a wry smile Rachel admitted she'd stopped expecting much from her parents long ago. Not only had they always left her behind when they set off on their travels, the few times they had taken an interest it had ended in disaster. Rachel could remember one time when her parents had turned up at school unannounced. They had persuaded the teachers to let them take Rachel and her three friends on a trip to Sandhills, a sleepy coastal resort. It had been a wonderful day, full of ice cream and the pleasures of the seaside, but as it was getting dark her parents had decided to carry on their excursion and had left Rachel and her friends in Sandhills to fend for themselves whilst they continued to Brighton. With just money for a stagecoach and a brief note saying that they'd had to leave, Rachel had been abandoned again by her parents and the four girls had had to make their way back to school alone, eventually finding outside seats on a coach heading back to Salisbury. Isabelle, Grace and Joanna had thought it a grand adventure, but Rachel had felt embarrassed once again by her parents' lack of responsibility and upset that they would rather travel on to Brighton for a night of fun than see their daughter and her friends safely back to school.

As they came over the crest of a large sand dune Malik pointed out a faint track that was visible through the desert.

'That is the trade route from the east. We're lucky many merchants pass through this part of the world on their way to Europe,' the Sheikh told her as they rode further into the desert.

Rachel loved how animated he was when talking about his kingdom. It was rare to see such passion in a man. Even with her limited experience of society Rachel knew it was fashionable to be bored with everything. It was refreshing to find someone who cared so much about his duty to the people he ruled and his country.

An hour later Rachel was just starting to feel a little hot. She was blessed with a body that did not overheat and swoon like so many young ladies—in fact, she rather enjoyed the warmth of the sun on her—but even she had to admit it was more than a little warm in the desert. She was glad of the wide-brimmed hat one of the servants had dug out for her before they set off, otherwise she knew her nose would be peeling and her skin pink.

'Not far now,' the Sheikh said, seeming to sense her discomfort. 'And I promise we'll receive a warm welcome. Even the lowliest traveller can be certain of wonderful hospitality from Hurian people, it is something that we pride ourselves on.'

Their horses took them over a rocky hill and Rachel saw the small settlement beneath them in a narrow valley.

The Sheikh rode ahead and said something to his children, then pulled back so he was once again riding beside Rachel. Aahil and Ameera pulled their horses round as well and left Wahid up ahead alone.

'This is the village of Talir,' the Sheikh said once all his children were assembled together. 'Although small it is strategically important—does anyone know why that might be?'

Rachel had been looking at the small collection of whitewashed houses, but now she turned her attention back to the children. She could tell Ameera had been distracted by a procession of women and young girls walking up the hill towards them, chattering and carrying baskets on their heads.

'I'm sorry, sir, I don't know.' Aahil sounded dejected and was looking at his hands rather than meet his father's eye.

Rachel glanced at the Sheikh and wondered whether he would plough on with his lesson or pick up on the fact that Aahil so desperately wanted to please him, gain his approval, that it consumed the young boy every day.

The Sheikh's face softened and Rachel felt a smile of relief begin to blossom on her face.

'I was hoping no one would know so that I could explain,' the Sheikh said, with a trace of humour in his voice.

Rachel was impressed he had picked up that direct

words of commiseration for Aahil's lack of knowledge would probably have made the situation worse. Aahil needed to realise it was not a requirement of the Prince of Huria to know everything about his country at the age of eight.

'The trade route we've been following all morning passes through this village. Traders often rest here before proceeding on through the country. It means the villagers can exchange their wares and food for whatever the traders have to offer and a few have started buying in bulk and selling in the markets to other Hurians.' The Sheikh paused, looking at Aahil as if wondering how best to proceed. 'Aahil, maybe you could lead our procession into the village and greet the elders. I know you'll do a fantastic job.'

Aahil swelled with pride and Rachel was amazed to see him give his father a shy smile. She'd been working on giving the serious little boy more fun in his life, but she realised he also needed responsibility, to feel as though he was being useful in his role as Prince of Huria.

Aahil rode at the head of their party, allowing his horse to pick its own path down the winding track and entering the village just as a crowd of people emerged from their homes to greet them. An elderly man, dressed entirely in white robes, stepped forward and bowed his head.

Aahil spoke, his voice strong and confident. Malik quietly whispered a translation for Rachel's benefit.

'Blessings upon your village and the people of Talir.' The Sheikh translated Aahil's words for her quietly. 'We are privileged to stop in such a welcoming and beautiful village. I am Prince Aahil of Huria and

I am accompanied by my royal father and my brother and sister. We politely request refreshment and conversation with the village elders.'

There was a murmur among the crowd, which had grown even since Aahil had started speaking, and a few people peeled off and disappeared into various houses.

'You are very welcome here, Prince of Huria. We are honoured and delighted to provide hospitality for you and your family. Please follow me.'

Aahil glanced back at his father with a question in his eyes. In response the Sheikh slipped off his horse and lifted his youngest son off after him. Aahil looked grateful as he dismounted, handing the reins of his horse to a young boy in the crowd before following the elderly man into the village.

Rachel felt a swell of pride as Aahil led their procession into the village. Although he had only been in her care for a few weeks, already she loved him and the other two royal children. She wanted him to succeed in whatever he did and she wanted him to feel more at ease with himself.

They were taken into a small, whitewashed house in the middle of the village and shown into a cool room. After the heat of the desert Rachel was pleased to have a break from the unrelenting sun and immediately she felt her whole body begin to cool. The elderly man invited them to sit on the low cushions around the perimeter of the room and waited until they were all seated before he sat down himself.

Rachel was sitting on the Sheikh's left and Aahil was next to his father on the other side. As a younger woman entered the room with a tray of drinks, Rachel saw the Sheikh lean towards his son.

'I'm very proud of you, Aahil,' he said quietly. 'You are growing into a fine young man and one day you will make a wonderful ruler.'

Aahil smiled shyly and looked up at his father as if wondering whether the words could be true.

'I know I may be hard on you sometimes, but I just want you to be ready to be Sheikh when I'm gone.' Malik paused and for a second Rachel thought he was about to tell Aahil that he loved him, but in the end he just patted the young boy on the back.

Rachel had to suppress a sigh. Malik was a good man and undoubtedly a good ruler, but he was a little emotionally closed off. Aahil idolised his father and hearing that Malik loved him would bolster his confidence and remind the young boy it was all right to let your emotions show.

She wondered if Malik ever told his children he loved them. Those three little words were powerful and the more you heard them the more you were able to give love in return.

Rachel thought of the people in her life. She might have been an inconvenience to her parents, a barrier to the lifestyle that they wanted to lead, but they had loved her in their own way. Then there were her friends. Joanna, Isabel and Grace, three girls whom she loved and who loved her. They might be on the other side of the world right now, but Rachel still knew they loved her. They'd been through so much together, so many ups and downs of adolescence, their shared experiences at Madame Dubois's School for Young Ladies, even the secret they all kept for Grace, the secret that would ruin her if anyone found out, that bonded them and deepened their love for one another.

Rachel looked sadly at the Sheikh, wondering if his distant father or late wife had told him they loved him. Even the stern and serious Madame Dubois, headmistress and founder of their school, was rumoured to have been in love once. Every girl who had attended Madame Dubois's School for Young Ladies was told the story by one of the older girls. In her youth Madame Dubois had had a wealthy lover, his identity the subject of speculation—some said a duke, some an earl, and some even thought he could be a foreign prince. There was one point of the story there was no disagreement on, however; the man was forced to marry someone else and Madame Dubois had never seen him again. His parting gift had been the building for the school.

Rachel had dismissed the story as rumour, until the night before she had left the school for Huria, when she hadn't been able to sleep and had wandered downstairs for a glass of milk and had seen the normally unshakeable Madame Dubois reading a stack of old letters with tears in her eyes.

The older woman had looked up and caught Rachel's eye, and said, *'Par-dessus tout, garde votre coeur.' Above all else, guard your heart.*

Since then Rachel had known the truth: their headmistress had loved and lost.

The young woman hovering at the edge of the room stepped forward and served them glasses of cool, refreshing lemon and mint and bowls of sugared almonds, then sat down on one of the empty cushions and proceeded to stare at Rachel. Rachel smiled and slowly the woman started to smile back. On her other side Malik was now deep in conversation with the village elder and Rachel wished she understood more of the language to know what they were talking about.

The conversation between the Sheikh and the elderly man sounded serious. They spoke quietly and intently for a few minutes whilst everyone recovered from the heat, then suddenly the Sheikh was on his feet. He turned to Rachel and offered his hand. She took it and allowed him to gently pull her up, aware that her body brushed against his as she rose and even more aware of how she'd enjoyed the contact.

Rachel was an innocent; she'd never kissed a man, never been touched by a man, and up until now that was how she'd always wanted things to stay. She'd been sheltered and shielded most of her young life, but Rachel knew desire when it came up and overpowered her, and it was desire she was feeling right now. Her pulse was rising, her skin was tingling and every single part of her wanted the Sheikh to run his hands over her bare skin and cover her lips with his own.

When she was growing up Rachel had never thought she would want to give in to such primitive urges. Her friend Isabel had always been a romantic, talking about meeting and falling in love with the man of her dreams, but Rachel had never given the matter much thought. What she did know was that she didn't want a relationship like her parents. She had endured their tempestuous love for so many years she always thought she'd be happier without a man and all the complications that went with it. But with the Sheikh's body so close to hers Rachel was beginning to wonder if she had much choice in the matter.

Once she was on her feet the Sheikh didn't release

her hand immediately, instead he tucked it into the crook of his arm and led her back outside.

'The villagers want to put on a little entertainment,' he said into her ear, his breath tickling her neck and making her shiver.

Rachel managed a nod, but didn't trust herself to speak. Her arm was pressed up against his torso and she could feel the taut muscles through his thin shirt. She knew her reaction to him was entirely inappropriate, but she couldn't seem to control her thoughts.

They were taken to a small, open area in the middle of the village that was surrounded by bright, colourful canopies. Rachel realised there were no trees in this dry little settlement and the fabric shades were the only way for the villagers to be outside and still keep cool. They sat and waited for a few minutes as villagers trickled in behind them, some taking seats under the canopies whilst others took their places in the middle of the square.

Rachel watched with anticipation, glad to have something to take her mind off the man beside her. The villagers were mainly dressed in long, cool robes of either black or white, and many also had some intricate piece of fabric covering their heads to keep them cool. Around the perimeter of the square some men had placed stools and were perched with instruments Rachel had never seen before, waiting for some cue before they started. These men were dressed in baggy dark trousers and silky bright tops. Some were young, only a year or two older than Aahil, others strong-looking working men and still others grey and wrinkled.

The villagers began clapping as a procession of young women glided past the musicians and into the open space, taking up positions around the square. These women all had flowing dark hair and Rachel felt her eyes widen in response to their attire. They all had long skirts on, made of thin, gauzy material that floated around their bodies. Their midriffs were bare, strips of bronzed skin between the gauzy skirts and the tight tops. Silky material encased their breasts and upper arms and the overall effect was mesmerising. Rachel looked down at her rather conservative cotton dress, buttoned up to the neck, and felt decidedly frumpy. She would love to get her hands on such beautiful materials and try on such scandalous items of clothing, only for herself to see, of course. Although maybe in such an outfit the Sheikh might let his eyes linger on her for a little longer.

Rachel chastised herself again. He was her employer and she should be focusing on his children, not how much she wanted him to look at her semi-nude with those smouldering eyes of his.

The musicians began to play, a slow tune at first, stamping their feet to give a beat for the dancers and adding the melody with their assorted instruments. After a few seconds the dancers began and Rachel was entranced. The gauzy skirts billowed out in all directions as the young women spun in circles and their bare abdomens gyrated and moved their bodies in ways Rachel hadn't even thought possible.

It was exotic and sensual and so completely different to anything Rachel had ever seen before. Her friend Isabel had often put on performances at school, organising the girls and encouraging them to showcase their talents. She had an incredible singing voice and Rachel knew Isabel dreamed of being on the stage. As a result whenever a musician came to perform at the small theatre in Salisbury, Isabel was always there, often accompanied by her three friends if they could persuade one of the teachers at the school to chaperone them. Once they had even sneaked out to go to the annual Salisbury fair and had been awed by the singers and dancers that performed in tented auditoriums. Despite all this Rachel had seen nothing that could compare to the spectacle in front of her. Isabel would love to be here seated beside her, watching how the young girls moved, how they captured their audience's attention. Rachel wondered how her friend was coping with life as a governess. Isabel was a free spirit and Rachel hoped the routine and rules wouldn't break her friend.

As the dance ended the Sheikh leaned over to her, breaking the spell of the dancers.

'What did you think?' he asked.

'I don't think I've ever seen anything more wonderful in my life,' Rachel said.

The Sheikh levelled her with a long stare that made Rachel feel hot all over, and then briskly turned away.

Chapter Six

Malik forced himself to look away. He had been watching his children's governess during the dance, it was hard not to. He'd never known anyone take such joy in the world as Miss Talbot. She was mesmerised by the whirling dancers and the pounding music, and she didn't care if everyone knew it. All his life Malik had been surrounded by people who tried to keep their emotions and feelings to themselves, who would baulk at the idea of their expressions giving away exactly what they were thinking. It was refreshing to be with someone who allowed herself to enjoy new experiences.

As he stared out across the square Malik wondered what Miss Talbot would look like in one of the gauzy dancer's outfits. Her crisp, white cotton dresses were fitted to her figure, but hardly any skin peeked out of the material. He knew he shouldn't be thinking of the young woman like this, she was his employee, but there was something rather alluring about her. He'd been drawn to her the very first time he'd seen her, looking around the entrance chamber in the palace with wonder, but today there was something more. Malik wasn't going to deny she was attractive, but it wasn't her thick dark hair or warm brown eyes that incited his desire, it was her demeanour, her smile, her *joie de vivre*. She was the complete opposite to his late wife. Aliyyah had gone through life as a victim, always low in mood and not bothering to do anything about it. Malik knew if there was something Miss Talbot didn't like she would change it.

He sighed quietly. It was all very well imagining Miss Talbot in one of the revealing outfits, but that was as far as it could go. She was good with his children, better than anyone else had ever been, and they had to be his first priority. He couldn't jeopardise their education by seducing their governess and scaring her off, no matter how much he might want to.

Even if he didn't have his children to think about Malik knew a liaison between him and Miss Talbot was a bad idea. Deeper feelings between a man and a woman complicated things. He'd seen how love had made Aliyyah miserable and how a love lost could be the most devastating thing of all. Although Malik had never experienced that kind of love he was also certain he never wanted to. His duty was to Huria and to his children.

Malik turned to his other side where Ameera was sitting quietly beside him. As soon as the dancers had finished both his sons had been on their feet and engaged in some game or other, but Ameera still sat in the same position, staring wistfully at the women in the square.

Malik took in her slightly sad demeanour and large, doleful eyes and wondered when he had first started recognising his children for the little people they were. Each had their own fears and dreams, fears and dreams Malik realised he knew too little about. All his life he had been counselled to put Huria first, even before the needs of his own children, but his children were the future of Huria. Malik knew there was also a fear of rejection deep inside him. His wife had rejected him for so many years, he was afraid if he started to try and become more involved with his children now, they might reject him, too.

'What's wrong, my little Princess?' he asked his daughter.

Ameera just shook her head and continued to stare at the women in front of her.

Malik followed her gaze, saw her arms crossed over her body defensively and instinctively he knew what was troubling his little girl.

'You're beautiful, you know,' he said quietly.

Ameera finally turned to look at him, her eyes heavy with questions and a little bit of hope.

'Your mother was thought to be the most beautiful woman in the entire kingdom,' Malik said, taking Ameera's hand in his own, 'and I think you are growing up to be even more beautiful than her.'

Ameera still didn't speak and it was as if Malik could almost hear the thoughts running through her mind.

'I know it might feel as though you are never going to grow up, that you look at those young women and just want to be like them, but one day you will outshine every single one of them. Do you know how I know that?' Malik asked.

Ameera shook her head.

'Because you do already.'

Malik saw the hope and the doubt all mixed together in his daughter's eyes. He hadn't known she was so worried about her looks, so insecure. At the age of six he didn't think children thought like that, but seeing Ameera stare at the dancers he realised that probably no one had ever told her she was beautiful. He certainly hadn't—whilst Aliyyah had been alive he'd left raising their children to her, and Malik had to admit his late wife probably hadn't been in a fit state to compliment their little daughter. It made him feel sad to realise all the things his children had missed out on.

Malik knew he wasn't going to fix her self-doubt in one conversation, but he made a mental note to drop in the odd compliment every now and then to see if it would bolster her self-esteem.

Ameera shyly reached out and took his hand and Malik felt the love for her swell inside his heart. He wondered whether maybe he had been missing out on something important, focusing so much on running Huria and not on his children. He knew he would never be able to give more than his very best to the kingdom he loved so much, but he also knew his children deserved more of his time.

'I hope you enjoyed the entertainment, Your Majesty,' the village elder said as Malik stood to greet him.

'It was spectacular.'

'I wonder if I could raise a sensitive issue with you.'

Malik nodded, allowing the elder to steer him away from his family, pleased to see Miss Talbot had led Ameera over to where her brothers were playing.

'We have been troubled by bandits recently, Your Majesty. They will creep up on villagers who are trav-

elling alone or in small groups, often along the traders' route as they leave the village.'

Malik frowned. Huria had its share of crime like
any other country, but bandits could become a big
problem. They were often fast and fearless, spread-
ing terror through the villages they targeted, and they
were difficult to catch.

'They have beaten several men and they seem to be
getting bolder, edging closer to the village. I am worried about an all-out attack.'

'How many are there?'

'Five men, large and muscular. They are carrying
swords and are on horseback.'

'Have you heard of any other villages that are affected?'

The elder shook his head. 'So far I've had no word
from the local villages that they've had any attacks.'

Malik knew they needed to catch these bandits before they became a big problem. He beckoned Wahid
over and explained the situation.

'I can arrange for ten men to come and guard the
village if you can provide lodgings and food,' Malik
said. 'We will need to keep their presence as quiet as
possible, just in case anyone local is involved with
the bandits.'

The elder grasped Malik's hand in thanks.

'Once we return to the palace we will organise the
men. They should be with you by nightfall,' Wahid
said.

Malik glanced over at his children playing happily
with Miss Talbot and felt a stab of panic. He wasn't
afraid of confrontation and was an accomplished
swordsman, but normally on the occasions he'd had

to use his sword he'd not been accompanied by three children and a woman. If he'd known about the bandits they would have brought a larger guard. As it was he and Wahid would be able to protect themselves if they were attacked, but he wasn't sure if they would be able to protect the whole group. Wahid followed Malik's gaze, his eyes settling on the children.

'Maybe we should head back to the palace,' Wahid suggested.

Malik nodded his agreement. They would be upset their trip was to be cut short, but he'd much prefer disappointed children to them falling into the bandits' hands.

With much ceremony and many hand grasps and wishes of good fortune they eventually mounted the horses half an hour later. Malik once again had Hakim in front of him on his horse. This time the little boy had bounded up eagerly to be pulled up in front of his father.

'We need to return to the palace, I'm afraid,' Malik said as they set off out of the village.

Three disappointed faces looked up at him.

He wondered over the best approach to take and eventually decided on telling the truth. His three children were intelligent and would understand why they had to leave if he told them about the bandits.

'There have been some bandits on this road, and I want to get you safely back home,' he said, glancing at all of his children in turn. Aahil remained serious, his eyes darting from side to side as if checking for hidden dangers. Ameera looked a little excited and Hakim buried himself in closer to Malik. Miss Talbot remained remarkably calm. Malik knew when faced with the idea of bandits many women would swoon or twitter incessantly, but his children's governess just sat a little straighter in the saddle and pulled her horse closer to Ameera's as if she were ready to shield the young girl from whatever a bandit could throw at her.

Everyone seemed tense and Malik could feel the icy tingle of anticipation himself. His blood was pounding around his body and his senses on high alert.

They travelled for nearly an hour in silence. The tension was beginning to wane and one by one Malik could see his children begin to relax. In front of him Hakim was growing heavy and his body was beginning to slump. Even Malik was starting to relax. They were riding faster than the journey to the village, and at this pace Malik calculated they would be back at the palace within an hour. The further they got from the village, the less likely an attack from the bandits seemed.

Just as Malik was thinking he was certain they were out of danger, a figure on horseback appeared in front of them. He was clothed head-to-toe in black, most of his face obscured by fabric with only his eyes peeking out.

Quickly Malik looked behind them, knowing if this was an attack by the bandits then they would soon be surrounded. He needed to find a way to get his family to safety before the rest of the bandits got into position.

With a loud cry four more men appeared and galloped towards them, their horses kicking up sand and snorting into the dust cloud. Malik wheeled round a few times, keeping one arm looped around his son, the other controlling the reins and trying to brandish a sword. He could feel Hakim shaking with fear, his whole body stiffening in Malik's arms. Malik knew bandits such as these were often ruthless men who would think nothing of killing a child if it got them what they wanted. He felt sick at the prospect of one of his children being injured and he wondered if he should offer himself as a sacrifice, let the bandits have him if they let his children go.

'Stand still,' the head bandit ordered. Everyone gripped their reins tensely, nobody daring to move. 'Do exactly as I say and you'll stay alive.'

Malik glanced over at Wahid and saw his old friend eyeing up the two bandits closest to him. Wahid would be able to defeat both men, but that left three to deal with. Malik looked to his right. The two bandits there were nervous, their bodies stiff and their swords held at unnatural angles. He would bet his fortune that these men did not want to attack their party—that they had argued with their leader. All the attacks so far had been on people on foot, small groups or individuals that would not even think to put up a fight. Malik knew he would be able to disarm both men without too much trouble, but that left the leader. He was calm and confident, and was making sure he stayed well out of reach from both men.

'Give us your valuables,' the bandit said. 'Money and jewellery. Pass them to the lady and she will bring them to me.'

'What's he saying?' Miss Talbot asked.

Malik translated. Miss Talbot looked thoughtfully at the head bandit, then nodded.

'Do it,' she said.

Malik began to protest, but she silenced him with a steely look.

'Do it and be ready to act.'

'What are you saying?' the bandit shouted.

Malik motioned for Wahid to take out his coin purse.

'She's English,' Malik said. 'I was telling her what you want.'

Miss Talbot took the purse from Wahid, slipped a chain from her own neck and slowly started to ride towards the head bandit. Malik felt his entire body tense. He wanted to protect her, to sweep her up on to his horse and never let any harm come to her, but for the sake of his children he knew he couldn't.

'On foot,' the bandit commanded.

Malik reluctantly gave the order to Miss Talbot and watched as she slipped from her horse and proceeded on foot. He knew she must be nervous, but as she passed him there was only steely determination on her face.

She reached the bandit and Malik adjusted his grip on his sword slightly so he'd be ready to attack at the earliest opportunity. To his left he saw Wahid do the same.

Miss Talbot stopped just in front of the bandit, waiting for him to beckon her closer. As she came round the side of his horse the bandit leaned down and grabbed her hand, squeezing tightly and making her cry out in pain.

'Pretty ladies should know better than to wander through the desert with such a paltry escort,' he said.

Malik saw her start to cringe away from the bandit, as if she were truly scared of him and what he might do to her. Then, just as the bandit tensed his arm to pull her back towards him she launched herself at him, taking him completely by surprise. Malik just had time to see her grab the dagger that was resting in the bandit's belt and plunge it into his thigh. The bandit screamed, his horse rearing, and Miss Talbot stumbled backwards, her arms flailing as if trying to catch hold of something.

Malik didn't see any more. As the head bandit screamed Malik leapt into action, spurring his horse forward and thrusting his sword expertly at the two bandits to his right. One he slashed across the stomach, and the shriek of horror told him the man was completely out of action. The other bandit was a little faster. He'd seen what had happened to his comrade and raised his sword to mount a defence, but he was no match for Malik. The Sheikh pulled back and then lunged, catching the man across the wrist on his sword arm. With a wail of terror the bandit spun his horse around and fled.

Malik surveyed the scene. To his left Wahid had injured two bandits, both men fleeing in different directions. The first man Malik had attacked had fallen from his horse and was looking pleadingly up at everyone, blood pumping from his wound. The leader was still there, but as Malik turned to face him their eyes locked and the bandit snarled, but turned his horse and fled after the rest of his men, the dagger still sticking out of his thigh.

Malik quickly slid from his horse, plucked Hakim into his arms and hurried over to Miss Talbot. She was lying on the ground, not moving, and her face had an unnatural pallor to it. Tentatively Malik placed a hand on her chest and breathed a sigh of relief as he felt the pounding of her heart under the skin. Malik gently ran his hands over her head and found a large lump forming at the back of her skull.

'Father?' Ameera's worried voice spurred Malik into action.

'Miss Talbot has hit her head,' he said, trying not to let the children hear the worry in his voice. 'We need to get her back to the palace as quickly as possible.'

In an ideal world Malik would scoop the unconscious governess into his arms and gallop at full speed back to the palace, but he had his children to think about. He only hoped a slight delay in getting Miss Talbot back wouldn't affect her outcome.

'Aahil and Ameera, I need you to be brave. Do you think you can ride back to the palace?'

Both children continued to stare at their unconscious governess, but after a few seconds both nodded.

'Hakim, I have to carry Miss Talbot with me, will you be all right riding with Wahid?'

Malik looked down into his young son's face and was proud to see the little boy rally. He was only four years old and already Malik could see Hakim putting someone else's needs before his own.

Quickly Malik passed his son up to Wahid, who held on to Hakim tightly. Effortlessly Malik draped Miss Talbot over the front of his horse and vaulted up behind her. He had never ridden with an unconscious person as cargo before and he took a second to ensure she was well balanced before urging his horse forward.

'What about him?' Wahid asked as they all looked at the injured bandit lying in the dust. His eyes were fluttering as he slipped in and out of consciousness.

Normally Malik would have taken the injured man with them. It was no kind of end, dying in the unforgiving desert, no matter what his crime, but today they didn't have time to figure out how to transport the man back if they were going to get Miss Talbot to the palace and the palace doctor as quickly as possible.

'We will send out a troop of guards once we get back, but we cannot help him now. His fellow bandits might return for him. If not, the guards will bring him to the palace later.'

Pushing the unpleasant fate of the bandit from his mind, Malik spurred his horse into a canter and checked to see the rest of the group was keeping up. In front of him Miss Talbot had not stirred and Malik found himself wondering if her brave act was to be her last.

Chapter Seven

Rachel tried to open her eyes but it was too much effort. Even the slightest movement sent flashes of red hot pain through her head. For a few moments she lay absolutely still, gathering her strength and resolve for another try.

As she lay there she tried to recall what had happened and figure out why she was in so much pain. She wondered if she had fallen down the stairs at the school or been hit by an errant ball during their games session. Had she even been at school or was she back home for the holidays?

Rachel shifted in the bed slightly. She was hot, so hot she could feel little beads of perspiration forming at the base of her neck. Gently someone dabbed at her skin with a cool cloth, and Rachel felt some momentary relief.

This time she made a more concerted effort and her eyes flickered open. For a second the light blinded her, but she squinted for a few moments until the room came into focus.

As she looked up at the whitewashed ceiling and

became aware of the silky fabrics, the events of the last few weeks came flooding back. She was in Huria, not England; she was a governess to three beautiful and complex children, not a schoolgirl.

'Can you hear me?' The voice spoke softly, and with effort Rachel turned her head towards it.

The Sheikh was sitting by her bed, looking down at her with concern. Rachel gave him a shaky smile and looked around the room. There was no one else there, which meant he must have been the one dabbing her skin so gently with the cool cloth.

'How long?' Rachel managed to croak. Her throat felt like she had swallowed a whole desert of sand.

'You've been unconscious for nearly a day.'

She struggled to clear the fog in her head as she began remembering snippets of what had happened to knock her unconscious. She could clearly picture the trip to the village and the mesmerising dancing girls, and then their hurried departure. With difficulty Rachel focused her mind on their return journey and slowly the events with the bandits came back to her.

'The children,' she gasped, trying to sit up far too fast. Her head spun and for a second her vision went grey.

She felt a strong, cool hand on her shoulder, pressing her back into the bed.

'The children are all fine,' the Sheikh said. 'Worried about you, but fine.'

Rachel let herself relax a little, closing her eyes momentarily until she recovered from her sudden movement.

'And you, Your Majesty?' Rachel asked after a moment. She couldn't recall how the fight had gone after she'd plunged the dagger into the head bandit's thigh, but the Sheikh and Wahid were outnumbered two to one and it must have been close, even if they did have superior training and swordsmanship.

'I will live to fight another day,' he said with a trace of humour in his voice. 'Now, you must rest, Miss Talbot, get your strength back. I will send in the palace doctor and let him check you over.'

'Please call me Rachel,' Rachel said. It seemed absurd for him to be addressing her as Miss Talbot when they had been through so much together.

'Rachel,' the Sheikh said, as if trying it out on his tongue. With his hint of an accent her name sounded exotic, as if something alluring and exciting, not plain old Rachel from the south of England. 'And you must call me Malik.'

Rachel opened her eyes and looked at the Sheikh again. It seemed wrong to address him by anything other than his title, but she felt a thrill of pleasure at being able to use his name. Malik, it was strong and commanding, a name that suited him.

'Now rest, Rachel, I will bring the children in to see you later.'

Rachel watched his retreating form with a pang of regret. She wished she could call out, ask him to stay, but she knew that even with the recent subtle shift in their relationship she was in no position to ask a Sheikh to waste his day away sitting with her. She was amazed he had stayed with her whilst she was unconscious. He could just have easily asked one of the numerous palace servants to keep an eye on her and let the doctor know when she was awake.

She kept remembering the tender way he'd dabbed

her skin with the cool, damp cloth and couldn't help but wonder if he felt something more than responsibility towards her. She shook her head, stopping abruptly as pain shot through her skull, but still the thought lingered. She wondered if he viewed her only as the governess to his children, someone he was responsible for the safety of, but nothing more, or if she hadn't imagined the way he'd savoured her name on his tongue and the lingering look he'd given her before he'd left.

She felt a thrill of anticipation travel through her body and allowed herself to languish in it before trying to dismiss it. Of course, even if he was interested in her as anything more than his children's governess it didn't matter. Rachel loved her job here, she loved Aahil and Ameera and little Hakim, and she wouldn't jeopardise that for the sake of an attraction that couldn't lead anywhere.

Still, she couldn't deny Malik was an attractive man. He was handsome, but he was more than that. It was his confidence, his self-assurance and his love for the country he ruled that transformed his attractive features into something more mesmerising.

With a sigh Rachel sank further back into her pillows. She blamed the head injury; normally she wouldn't be taken with such fits of fancy. It was almost as bad as the fairy tales she had mocked when she was younger. Rachel didn't need a handsome prince to rescue her, her life was just fine as it was. She was carving out her own future.

The doctor bustled into the room and Rachel was grateful for a distraction from her thoughts. Quickly he checked the bump on her head, her vision and what seemed like a hundred other things before declaring that she needed to take things slowly, but there should be no lasting damage.

She must have slept, with fractured dreams in which Malik featured heavily. In one he was defending her from a whole army of bandits, slashing fiercely to protect her and her alone. Another was not quite so innocent and as Rachel woke with a start she felt every nerve in her body tingling with anticipation. Even though she was alone and no one would ever be able to guess what she'd been dreaming of she blushed.

There was a quiet rap on the door and hurriedly Rachel tried to regain her composure.

'Come in,' she called.

The door opened and Malik slipped into the room.

'The children are eager to see you, but if you're not up to it they'll understand.'

Rachel glanced at the door and could see three pairs of worried eyes peering in. Carefully she started to pull herself up in bed so she was sitting. Malik was immediately at her side, rearranging the pillows behind her so she could sit comfortably. As he did so his arm brushed against her shoulder and Rachel felt his touch linger for just a second. She knew she was being absurd, that he was just helping her sit up so she could reassure the children, but as he drew away their eyes met and Rachel was surprised to see the Sheikh give her a small smile. Normally he was so serious, so distant, but for a few moments he held her gaze and Rachel felt as though only the two of them existed.

'Come, children,' Malik said. 'But be very careful.'

The three of them slipped into the room and crept towards the bed, stopping when they were a few feet away.

'It's all right, you can come closer,' Rachel said gently. 'You won't hurt me.'

Hakim was the first to move. He softly climbed on to the bed and snuggled in against Rachel, burying his head in her chest. Ameera was next, she came and sat on Rachel's other side and didn't protest at all when Rachel slipped her arm around her shoulder and pulled her closer for a cuddle.

Aahil stood awkwardly for a few moments, before Malik put a hand on his shoulder and guided his eldest son to the edge of the bed. Father and son perched side by side halfway down the bed.

'Are you hurt, Miss Talbot?' Hakim asked, his voice muffled, as he didn't raise his head from her chest.

'I've got a bit of a sore head, but nothing that won't heal.'

'You were so brave,' Ameera said, looking up at her governess with a hint of awe in her eyes.

Rachel looked at the little family surrounding her on the bed and realised the truth in the words she was about to say.

'I know I've only been your governess for a short while, but I do care for you very much. When you care for someone you sometimes find bravery in yourself that you didn't even realise you had.'

Rachel thought back to when they'd been surrounded by the bandits, with the men demanding their money and valuables. She'd known they wouldn't be allowed to walk free, unharmed, and she'd also known that she would give her life to protect the three young children in her care. So when the bandit had told her to approach she'd found courage she'd never known she had.

'I was scared,' Hakim admitted, still not raising his head.

Rachel stroked his hair. 'It's all right to be scared in a situation like that. I was scared.'

'Were you?' Ameera asked. 'You didn't look scared.'

'I was scared,' Rachel said firmly, glancing at Aahil who had been sitting quietly the whole time. 'In fact, I think it would be foolish not to be scared when there is so much danger.'

Three little faces turned to their father to hear his opinion on this. Aahil in particular looked as though he really needed to know what his father was about to say.

Malik cleared his throat. 'Well, I think…' He trailed off as his eyes met Rachel's. A look of comprehension dawned on his face as he quickly glanced from her to Aahil. Addressing all three of his children, he started again.

'Sometimes a little bit of fear can be a good thing,' he confirmed. 'It focuses the mind and it is a sensible reaction to something that is dangerous or threatening.'

Aahil bit his lip, but still didn't say anything.

'I was afraid,' Malik continued. 'I was afraid that the bandits might hurt you children because you are the most precious things in the world to me.'

Rachel felt the tears well up in her eyes and hastily blinked them away. She could see by the quiet, intent way all three children were looking at Malik that they had never heard him tell them how important they were to him.

'There's nothing to be ashamed of if you felt scared,' Malik reiterated. 'I would be more worried if you didn't feel scared. You need to be able to recognise danger in this world and that is all fear is, your body's way of telling you something is dangerous.'

Aahil seemed to be digesting his father's words. Malik glanced at Rachel and she gave him a smile, pleased that he'd recognised what his eldest son had needed to hear. The boy was only eight, but he held himself to almost impossible standards. He also worshipped his father, so if Malik said it was fine to be scared, then he would believe it.

'Now we must let Miss Talbot rest,' Malik said firmly.

Obediently Ameera and Aahil stood, but Hakim didn't move.

'I'll still be here later,' Rachel said gently.

'You're not going to leave us?'

Rachel gently tilted Hakim's chin up and looked him in the eye. 'I'm not going to leave you. It takes a bit more than a few bandits to scare me away.'

Hakim threw his arms around her neck and hugged her, and although the movement made her head pound, Rachel sat up, motioned for the other two children to join them and held all three tightly to show them she wasn't going anywhere.

Chapter Eight

Malik paced nervously up and down. He felt like a young boy again, not a confident and powerful Sheikh of a beautiful desert kingdom.

He'd had a strange couple of days. It had been two days since the attack by the bandits and a day since Rachel had woken up. His children had been rather quiet and he'd felt an odd sense of listlessness, as if he was in limbo. Malik had tried to get on with things as normal, meeting chieftains and briefing guards on the bandit situation, but he'd been oddly distracted, his mind often wandering to the small bedroom where Rachel was recovering from her injury.

Malik didn't like the feeling of not being in charge, so this evening he'd decided to take his power back and had invited Rachel to join him for a stroll in one of the palace gardens. She had been out of bed that afternoon and he'd heard her comment that she wanted fresh air.

So here he was, inexplicably nervous, clutching a beautiful orchid in one hand, trying to tell himself he was just being a good employer, nothing more.

'Good evening, Your Majesty...' Rachel paused for a second. 'Malik.'

She looked at him questioningly as if to see whether he would withdraw his offer for things to be so informal between them.

'Good evening, Rachel. You're looking well.'

She was dressed in her normal white cotton dress, but her cheeks were a rosy pink and her eyes glittered in the moonlight.

'Thank you. I feel much better.'

Malik hesitated, then held out the orchid. 'This is for you.'

He was rewarded with a sunny smile and found himself suffused with pleasure that he'd been the one to make Rachel so happy. Carefully she took the delicate plant and inspected the beautiful petals and spindly stem.

'It's beautiful. No one's ever given me a flower before.'

Malik opened his mouth to disagree with her, surely a woman as good-natured and attractive as Rachel had received flowers before, but then he remembered her letter of introduction; until she'd travelled to Huria she'd been sequestered and shielded from the world at a girl's school. He felt inexplicably pleased that she'd never had an admirer before.

'It's an orchid, not native to Huria, but it thrives with a little love and attention.'

He offered her his arm and as she slipped her hand into the crook of his elbow he began to lead her slowly through the garden.

This was one of Malik's favourite places in the world. He loved coming into the sunken garden after dark, when the paths were lit by the silvery moonlight and the whole place looked magical. It had been a labour of love to cultivate, his father had told him, and his mother had spent all her spare time pruning and tending to the plants. Even though she had died giving birth to Malik, he still imagined he could picture her out here, bestowing love and patience on her garden.

'It's magical out here,' Rachel said after a few minutes of silence. She was looking around with an awed expression on her face and her eyes were lit up with pleasure.

'It was my mother's garden,' Malik said, surprising himself with the revelation. He'd never told anyone he still thought of the sunken bit of paradise as his mother's; it seemed indulgent and sentimental, but out here under the stars Malik thought Rachel would understand.

He saw her turn towards him, her expression full of questions, and Malik knew he wasn't ready to reveal his past to her yet, however much of a good listener Rachel might be. So instead he guided her forward and began to ask questions of his own.

'How are you finding Huria?' he asked, finding he genuinely wanted to know the answer. It had heartened him when she had assured his children that she would not be scared away from the country because of the bandit attack. Malik knew she was good for his children—they had blossomed in the short time she had been their governess—but he also knew there was more to his desire for her to stay.

He respected her; she was a talented governess despite being so young and fresh out of school herself. She understood his children's needs and wants and seemed to anticipate their questions and queries. More than that, she made him a better father.

Malik was too astute to fool himself that respect was all there was. Certainly that had been how it had started, but over the last few days he couldn't deny he had started looking at her with something more than respect in his eyes. He liked her, she was kind and fun and open-minded. Malik, who even as a child had been taught to keep his distance from people, felt himself wanting to draw closer to her, to get to know her better.

'I love it here,' she said simply. 'I love the country and I love the children and I love my job.'

He found himself smiling back at her. It was refreshing to have someone just come out and admit exactly how they were feeling. Many of the people he dealt with were skilled negotiators, people who held back and kept you guessing as to what they were thinking.

'You don't miss England too much?'

He saw her pause before answering and she considered the question carefully.

'I miss a lot of things,' she said slowly. 'I miss the feel of the rain on my face and the sound of a horse-drawn carriage on the cobbles. I miss the chatter of the other girls at school and I miss talking about my day with my friends. I miss the feel of grass between my toes and I miss having to pull a shawl across my shoulders on a chilly night.' She paused again and gave a self-deprecating laugh. 'Lots of things I never thought I would miss really, except for the other girls, of course.'

'But you don't regret your decision to come to Huria?'

Malik found he was holding his breath as he waited for her to answer. He wanted her to be pleased with her life out here in the desert kingdom, pleased with the niche she had carved for herself in the palace.

'No, I don't regret it.' There was no hesitation this time and Rachel's eyes met Malik's and held his gaze. 'There are things that I miss about England, but there was nothing keeping me there.'

Malik realised he knew next to nothing about Rachel's life before she had come to Huria. He knew where she was educated and he was in possession of a couple of praise-filled letters from her teachers at Madame Dubois's School for Young Ladies, but as to her private life, her family and friends he knew nothing.

'You must have family,' Malik said. 'I've seen you writing letters, I assumed they were to your parents.'

Rachel shook her head, looking a little surprised that he had noticed her prolific letter writing. Malik was a bit surprised himself. He was observant, but normally his observations were limited to things important to Huria.

'I write to my friends. The three girls I was at Madame Dubois's with. They're all the family I have now.'

She paused, looking out over the garden with a hint of sadness in her expression, and Malik knew immediately she had lost both her parents, just as he had.

'My parents died a couple of years ago,' she said, and although Malik could tell she was trying to be pragmatic, she couldn't keep all the emotion from her voice. 'Malaria.'

Malik frowned in surprise. Malaria was not what British people died of, at least not parents of a nice young lady like Rachel Talbot. Rachel must have noticed his surprise and smiled a sad smile.

'They were keen travellers, always setting sail for

different parts of the world. One day they left and never came back. They'd always written me such wonderful letters about their travels, but the letters suddenly stopped. A few months later I received word of their deaths.'

Malik found himself raising a hand and touching her gently on the upper arm. It was a gesture of sympathy and he saw her take strength from his touch.

'You must miss them very much,' he said, thinking of the hole left in his life when his father had died.

Rachel turned to look at him and a new expression crossed her face—guilt.

'Is it bad if I say some days go by when I don't think of them at all?' she asked. 'I loved them, of course I loved them, but they were hardly ever there, always travelling, always setting off to exotic locations, that sometimes I feel like they're not really gone.'

Malik saw the pain in her face as she confessed her feelings and not for the first time marvelled at how open and honest she was. Most people would have just said they missed their parents and left it at that, instead Rachel was baring her soul to him.

Malik moved in closer, knowing his next words were going to be important.

'It isn't bad,' he said. 'Just honest. If more people were honest about how they felt, the world would be a better and more simple place.'

He watched her as she searched his face for a few moments, then looked out across the garden.

'I have fond memories of them,' Rachel said. 'They were fun to be around, but sooner or later they would always leave again and I would be left behind, wondering when I would see them again.'

'It sounds like you were hurt by their desertion of you,' Malik said gently.

Rachel nodded. 'Every time they returned I thought it would be different, that if I was better, more interesting, they might stay or even take me with them. For years I cried and thought I would never be good enough.'

'What changed?' Malik knew something must have changed. Rachel was a confident young woman who did things her own way. She did not kowtow to anyone else and she obviously believed in herself.

'I went to school. I met Joanna, Isabel and Grace and I realised there was more to the world than my parents. They became my family, the ones that I turned to when I was upset or when I was celebrating.'

'They sound like wonderful young women,' Malik said quietly.

A smile blossomed across Rachel's face, a smile of true happiness. Malik knew in that instant he would move heaven and earth to see that smile directed at him. The thought hit him and he felt himself physically taking a step back. He hadn't expected to feel such strong emotions towards the pretty young woman. Physical attraction he could deal with, but deeper feelings were an abstract concept for him and he felt a bubble of panic.

'They're who I write the letters to,' Rachel said. 'I've told them all about Huria, all about the children...' she paused and turned to look at Malik '...all about you,' she finished quietly.

They stood no more than a foot apart, his hand still resting on her arm. It would take no effort at all to pull Rachel towards him, to cover her lips with his own.

Before Malik could act Rachel looked away, breaking the moment. Even in the moonlight he could see the blush creep across her cheeks and he found himself wanting to reach out and run a finger over the silky skin, to feel the warmth of her blush under his fingertips.

'I'm glad you want to stay,' Malik said, cursing himself for his words. This moment called for poetry, for a quotation from a book or an improvised compliment, but he'd never been one for poetry. He'd always preferred hard facts to flowery verses, favouring engineering and history to literature in his studies, and Aliyyah had never wanted him to woo her. She had shied away if he'd even tried to hold a conversation, he probably would have received stony silence if he'd recited a line of poetry at his late wife.

'Right now, right at this moment, I can't think of anywhere I'd rather be.'

Rachel felt dizzy with anticipation. It must be the head injury, she reasoned, normally she wasn't so forward and daring. There was something rather magical about this garden, though, as if they had entered another world, one where only she and Malik existed. The moonlight glinted from pools of water and the lovingly tended foliage cast deep shadows across the ground, and for a moment Rachel felt like a princess being wooed by a handsome and exotic prince.

She knew she needed to get a grip on reality again. Nothing could happen between them, at least nothing lasting and meaningful, and Rachel wasn't about to throw away her dream job for the sake of a man.

'Tell me about the children's mother,' Rachel said,

suggesting the one topic that was bound to put distance between them.

Malik turned away slightly and immediately Rachel regretted the question. She realised she wanted to bask in the Sheikh's undivided attention for a few moments longer and now she had instead brought up a topic that was bound to be painful for Malik. She felt selfish and unkind and placed a hand on Malik's arm to stop him from answering.

'I'm sorry,' she said, waiting for him to look at her before she continued. 'I don't want to pry. Let's talk of something else.'

For a moment Rachel thought Malik would agree, that her ill-timed question would be swept away and they could continue their pleasant walk through the gardens, but then Malik seemed to withdraw a little and Rachel knew his thoughts were in the past.

'It was an arranged marriage.' He chuckled softly. 'In fact, I can't remember a time when I wasn't betrothed to Aliyyah. On paper it was a perfect match, she was the daughter of the wealthiest family in Huria, but in reality it was a disaster.'

Malik turned away from her slightly as if he found it hard to confess his marriage had not been successful. Rachel supposed he was so good at everything in life, so used to succeeding, that it must hurt to admit his marriage hadn't been as perfect as it should.

'We both did our duty, married and produced children, heirs for the kingdom, but there wasn't really anything more to it.'

He fell silent and Rachel realised he probably had never told anyone about his marriage before. It wasn't as if he had lots of close friends or a brother to confide in. She felt strangely pleased that he had told her so much and felt as though she should give something back.

'I always wonder what makes a marriage work,' Rachel said slowly, not wanting to say anything to offend the Sheikh. 'My parents were madly in love, they didn't have eyes for anyone else but each other, but they had an awful marriage. One moment they were full of passion and devotion, the next they were shouting and throwing things at each other. I don't think either of them were truly happy.'

Malik turned back towards her and Rachel felt as though his eyes were inside her head, reading her innermost thoughts.

'And that is why you have decided to become a governess, to focus on the children in your care.'

Silently Rachel nodded, thinking it sounded a bit foolish when it was said out loud. It was why she had worked so hard at school. Whilst other girls had dreamed of husbands and families Rachel had always longed for an adventure and freedom. She couldn't deny the fact that she never would have children of her own didn't sadden her a little, but that was the price she had to pay. She would just have to love other people's children instead.

'I think the ways of our parents affect us more than we ever realise,' Malik said.

'When my parents sent me to school I think it was a way to pass on their responsibility for me. They never meant for me to be a governess.' She paused, wondering if Malik really wanted to hear all of the details of her unsatisfactory childhood. 'They always assumed I would marry a young man of a good family.'

'You didn't agree?'

'Secretly I always wanted to be a governess. I didn't want to be tied down in marriage and I wanted the freedom to choose my own path.' Rachel grimaced. 'It was a good job really—when my parents passed away they were in debt. What money was left over from the sale of our house just about covered my remaining school fees. I wasn't exactly a good match for a titled gentleman.'

They walked on wordlessly for a few minutes, both lost in their own thoughts, their own pasts. The garden was not large, but Malik was guiding her down winding paths and through miniature tree-lined avenues. He seemed to be walking with a purpose and after a few minutes they emerged from the foliage and started to climb some steps. Once at the top Malik directed her to a small bench and together they sat down.

As Rachel turned and looked over the garden they had just walked through she heard herself gasp with pleasure. From the elevated height the garden was magnificent. What seemed like a haphazard collection of plants, trees and water features whilst you were walking through was actually a meticulously planned pattern, swirling out from a central pool with a fountain. She understood now why the garden was sunk beneath the level of the palace—whilst you were in it you could enjoy a stroll through the foliage, but from above you could admire the majesty of the entire layout.

'It's beautiful,' Rachel said, unable to tear her eyes away from the garden beneath them.

'Many people see Huria as a country of dust and sand,' Malik said. 'When I picture my country I think of this; the beauty you can have in an arid climate if you put in a little work and a lot of love.'

Rachel turned towards him and studied his face. Malik was looking out over the garden with pride and happiness, the raw emotions obvious on his features. She thought back to the man she had first met on her arrival to the palace, the stiff and formal Sheikh who she had butted heads with over the education of his children. She had thought him severe and uptight, but she realised now she had been blind. Malik was a proud man and as Sheikh he had to keep his distance from people, but that didn't stop him from feeling happiness and sadness, love and grief the same as everyone else.

Hesitatingly Rachel reached out and took his hand in hers. She wondered if he would pull away, erect the invisible barrier that until recently had stood between them. Malik looked down at her hand and then at her.

Slowly, their bodies swayed closer together. Rachel felt Malik raise his free hand and run his fingers through her hair, down the nape of her neck and over her shoulders. The contact made her shiver with anticipation and lean even closer to Malik. For a few moments their eyes met and Rachel knew she would not be able to resist his kiss. She wanted to feel his lips on hers, his hands caressing her skin. She wanted it so much she allowed her eyes to flutter closed and her body to press against his.

Softly he brought his lips down on to hers, kissing her slowly, languorously, as if they had all night to enjoy each other. Rachel felt Malik's hand continue to travel down her back, caressing her skin through her thin dress and coming to rest in the small of her back. She arched her neck, pressing her lips more firmly on to his, and felt a thrill of pleasure as he gently ran the tip of his tongue along her lower lip.

Rachel moaned softly and the sound seemed to galvanise Malik into deepening the kiss. They were clinging on to one another now, as if both afraid the other would pull away, and Rachel raised a hand to cup Malik's cheek. She stroked the smooth skin, eliciting a deep groan from Malik, and then she felt him gently pull away.

For thirty seconds they just looked at one another, both their eyes glazed from the passion of the moment. Malik's hand was still resting on Rachel's lower back, but Rachel had let her fingers fall from his cheek.

Reality came crashing back for both of them at exactly the same moment. Gone was the heady passion and overwhelming excitement, leaving Rachel and Malik sitting side by side unsure of what to say to one another.

Slowly Malik shifted, turning back towards Rachel and taking her hand in his own. Rachel was surprised at the move and for a moment she wondered whether he was about to make some sort of declaration. Her heart began to pound in her chest and an unexpected surge of hope welled up inside her. Of course she found the Sheikh attractive and it was difficult to not be drawn in by his charisma and confidence, but she found herself holding her breath, as if she wanted him to say he wanted more from her.

'I admire you very much,' Malik said slowly, as if testing each individual word out first in his head. 'You are a beautiful and intelligent young woman, and I find I cannot regret our kiss.' He gave a small self-deprecating smile. 'In fact, I must confess I've had the urge to kiss you for some time.'

Rachel felt her hopes vanish. This was not a speech of someone declaring their undying love.

'But I'm sure you agree this can go no further.'

Rachel found herself nodding. She felt acute disappointment, but she did agree. Despite the lingering desire she felt as she looked up at Malik she knew he was right. They could have a relationship of employer and employee, admire each other's qualities objectively, even be friendly towards one another, but they could not become romantically involved. Malik was Sheikh, ruler of Huria, and Rachel was observant enough to notice that his marriage to his late wife had been damaging to him in some way or another. Rachel was his children's governess, and she knew they had to be her focus. She could not afford to become distracted by any man; she owed it to the three wonderful children in her care to focus on them.

'I agree,' she said quietly.

Inside she was already chastising herself for her unprofessional behaviour. She had always been so determined she would never let desire or lust overrule her head, had always been so resolved that she would remain in control at all times, and here she was upset because Malik had told her their kiss could go no further.

Carefully she moved away from Malik. He was sitting watching her with a mixture of concern and sadness on his face. For a moment Rachel wished for the severe, distant man she had first met, at least that man would be easy to walk away from.

'Let me take you back to the courtyard,' Malik said, standing and offering her his arm.

They walked in silence back down the steps and through the garden, past all the silvery pools of water and fragrant flowers. As they walked Rachel began to get her composure back. She'd been shaken by the kiss, more shaken than she cared to admit, but slowly she was beginning to think straight again.

'I don't want things to change,' she said as they reached the other edge of the sunken garden and began the climb back up to the courtyard. 'The children have enjoyed having you around these last couple of days and I could never forgive myself if you withdrew because of me.'

Malik paused halfway up the steps.

'Nothing will change,' he said firmly. 'We will put this moment down to the magic of the desert night and the sunken garden, and carry on as we were before.'

Rachel took one last look back at the garden over her shoulder, then felt her resolve harden and followed Malik back to reality.

Chapter Nine

Nothing will change, Malik thought with a grimace— who was he fooling? Everything had changed. He cursed himself for taking Rachel into the sunken garden. He'd known it would be beautiful, magical in the moonlight, and still he'd taken her there. And now, when he should be focusing on what Wahid was telling him, his mind kept wandering to his children's governess and the memory of the kiss they'd shared under the stars.

'Your Majesty?' Wahid asked, concern apparent in his voice.

'I'm sorry, Wahid, I'm rather distracted tonight, what did you say?'

'We've caught the bandits. The man you injured survived until the group of guards found him and he led us straight to the others. They're locked up for now, but I asked what you wanted to do with them.'

Huria had always been a country that prided itself on fairness and justice. If you were generous and helped others, then you would be recognised and rewarded by the community. If you committed a crime, if you stole or hurt someone, then you would be punished accordingly.

'They mainly targeted the people of Talir, is that right, Wahid?'

Wahid nodded. 'A few traders and people from other villages coming to see relatives were attacked, but mainly it was the people of Talir.'

'I think it is only fair to let them hold the trial and decide on the sentencing. Send word to the elders and we will escort the prisoners there tomorrow.'

'You want to oversee matters personally?'

Malik nodded. These men had threatened his family and seriously injured Rachel, but more than that, they had targeted his people, often beating and injuring them.

'You were about Aahil's age when you went to your first trial, Your Majesty,' Wahid said gently.

Malik could still remember every minute of it. His father had been keen for him to learn all about the justice system in Huria even from a young age. He had attended trials and watched and listened as criminals were sentenced. At the tender age of eight he had witnessed his first execution. When he closed his eyes Malik could still see the lifeless body of a thief hanging limply at the end of a rope.

'The children will attend the trial, it is important they understand about crime and punishment in Huria, but they will not stay while the sentence is carried out,' he said firmly.

Even Aahil, who was diligent in his studies and interested in all the traditions of the country he would one day rule, was too young to witness an execution. One day he would have to, one day he would likely have to take on the burden of sentencing someone to death himself, but for now Malik could shield his son from that.

'Very good, Your Majesty. I'll make all the arrangements.'

Wahid left the room and Malik stared after him for a moment. It was just getting dark outside and from across the courtyard he could hear the occasional squeal of pleasure as the children played some game before bed. Malik had a sudden urge to go and see them, to bask in their happiness for a while, and before he could talk himself out of it with thoughts of state business, he stood and strode out into the courtyard.

The laughter led him to Ameera's room, and for a moment he stood outside looking in, happy to watch his children play without being seen. Rachel was on the bed, tied up with a multitude of pieces of clothing and scarfs, and she was sighing most dramatically and kept pretending to swoon.

In front of her Hakim patrolled, dressed in green with a saucepan on his head. Every so often he growled or roared and Malik realised he was supposed to be a dragon. Quickly his eyes swept the room. Hiding behind the dressing table were Aahil and Ameera, both were brandishing wooden spoons, and as he watched they both surged forward, galloping as if they were riding horses, and let out a loud cry.

'Attack,' Ameera screeched.

His eldest two children charged at Hakim, who growled and batted out with his arms. Malik was proud to realise Aahil and Ameera were actually very gentle with their little brother, whilst still enjoying the game to the full. After a minute of attacking Hakim all three of his children collapsed on to the bed next to Rachel in fits of giggles.

Malik stepped into the room. Immediately Aahil straightened and stood, looking sheepish to be caught playing with his two younger siblings. He was so grown up, so sensible, and for the first time Malik realised his eldest son had never really been allowed a childhood. From a very young age Aahil had been told that one day he would have the responsibility of ruling Huria and had been expected to behave accordingly. He hadn't ever indulged in silliness or fun—at least not until Rachel had arrived and seen him for what he really was: a child like any other, even if one day he would have heavier responsibilities.

'Father—' Aahil began guiltily.

Malik quickly cut him off. 'This looks mightily unfair.'

Four sets of eyes looked at him with confusion.

'Two brave warriors, but only one dragon. You're outnumbered, Hakim.'

No one spoke. All three of his children were looking at him with such disbelief it almost broke his heart. Surely he had played with them before, Malik tried to recall, surely there had been at least one game, one afternoon of indulgence, but he knew despite all his wishing he hadn't. And he doubted their mother had ever played with them either.

'Come, Hakim, we've got a tasty governess to have for our supper.'

Quickly Malik swept his son back into position and

after a moment's hesitation Ameera moved as well. Only Aahil was left standing awkwardly by the bed.

'You'd better help your sister,' Malik prompted gently. 'Otherwise she'll be gobbled up by two hungry dragons.'

After a few more seconds Aahil smiled shyly and ran to join Ameera where she was hiding behind a chair. Malik turned to find Hakim offering him a saucepan for his head. Wondering what a saucepan had to do with dragons, Malik nevertheless put the pan on and started patrolling in front of the bed. Rachel smiled at him before starting to swoon and sigh dramatically again.

He heard whispers from behind the chair, his two eldest children planning their attack. They remained where they were for over a minute before charging out into the room. Both Aahil and Ameera went for Malik, knocking him back on to the bed and trying to pin him down. Out of the corner of his eye Malik saw Hakim hesitate, then launch himself on top of the pile. Malik started tickling all three of his children, making them all collapse in fits of giggles.

After a minute, when all four of them were panting from the exertion, Malik sat up. He felt light and carefree, and to him it was an odd sensation. He couldn't believe that for years he had held himself back from his children, not getting involved, as it wasn't proper for a Sheikh to show emotion or laugh with his sons and daughter. This felt right, natural, and he could also see his fear of rejection was unfounded, too. Aliyyah might have kept him at a distance through their long marriage, but his children were eager for his attention and his company.

'Well, I think we dragons won that round,' Malik said.

'It's all right, Miss Talbot,' Hakim said, turning to his governess. 'We won't really eat you.'

Malik watched as Rachel pulled Hakim in for a cuddle. She was so at ease around the children, always seeming to know what they wanted or what they needed. It came naturally to her and for a moment Malik wished he had the same talent. He loved his children more than anyone else in the world, but he still wasn't at ease with them. When he was making decisions on land disputes or negotiating trade deals he felt in his element, when he was faced with the three eager children he felt uneasy.

'Now it's nearly bedtime,' Rachel said. 'But I know I'll never sleep after all that excitement. Why don't we sneak down to the kitchen for some warm milk?'

A chorus of approval came from the children and quickly they hopped off the bed. Malik watched as Rachel led them out of the room, marvelling again at how easily she had slotted into their lives.

Hakim paused before he stepped through the door.

'Would you like some milk, Daddy?' he asked, holding out his hand.

Malik felt something shift inside him as he strode across the room and gently took his son's hand.

'I'd love some,' he said, his voice almost unrecognisable to his own ears.

They caught the others up just as they were peering into the darkened kitchen.

'We need to be very quiet,' Rachel was saying in a whisper. 'We don't want anyone knowing we're here.'

The children looked around excitedly and Malik had to smile. Of course they were allowed in the kitchen any time they wanted, he was Sheikh and they were the Royal Princes and Princess, but as ever Rachel was making this into a little adventure for them.

Quietly they crept inside and Malik watched as Rachel found a pan, lit the stove and started to heat some milk. In a few minutes they were all sipping the warm liquid, sweetened with sugar and cinnamon.

'Have I told you about the time I tried to make a birthday cake for my friend Grace?' Rachel asked the children. Three heads shook in unison. 'I'd been banned from the kitchen by the cook after forgetting I'd put a batch of biscuits in the oven and filling the whole school with smoke, but my friend Grace really needed cheering up.'

It had been soon after Grace had realised she was pregnant. All four friends had spent weeks trying to figure out what to do for the best, and as Grace's birthday loomed Rachel had decided they needed something to celebrate.

'I sneaked downstairs when everyone was in bed and very quietly made a cake for Grace's birthday. I made sure I cleaned everything and put it all away before morning, but when the cook came downstairs she found a few things out of place and for weeks was convinced the kitchen was haunted.'

'Did you get caught?' Ameera asked.

Rachel shook her head.

'I need to talk to you all about something,' Malik said as they drained their cups. 'Tomorrow we're going on a little trip.'

They looked at him expectantly and Malik wondered how best to phrase things.

'When we were coming back from Talir and we

were attacked by the bandits I know it was very scary,' Malik began. 'But the bandits have been caught and are going to be on trial tomorrow in Talir. We will all be there.'

Aahil nodded gravely, Ameera glanced at Rachel and Hakim started playing with his fingers nervously.

'Children, I think it's time for bed,' Rachel said. 'We will discuss tomorrow's plans in the morning. Go and get ready and I'll be up shortly to say goodnight.'

Even Hakim couldn't miss the steeliness to Rachel's voice and without a word of protest the three children filed out of the kitchen.

'I should get back,' Malik said, thinking already of the petitions from village elders he needed to read through before he retired for the night.

'We need to discuss tomorrow,' Rachel said.

Malik stopped and turned, ensuring he kept a good distance between him and Rachel, very aware that they were now alone in the palace kitchen.

'I will ensure you have a carrying chair to transport you to Talir,' Malik said.

'That's not what I wanted to discuss. And I will be perfectly fine on a horse, thank you.' Rachel paused and Malik wondered again what she could be asking of him. 'I do not think the children should attend the trial.'

Malik felt his hand start to rise up into the air, ready to give a dismissive gesture before he turned and walked out of the room. A week ago that would have been exactly how he would have reacted, but he valued Rachel's input with his children, so he tempered his response.

'Why not?' he asked brusquely.

'They are children. Hakim is four years old. They should be shielded from this sort of thing.'

'They need to be exposed to the real world.'

'Not like this. Visiting villages and touring the country is one thing, but they do not need to see the brutal reality of an execution,' Rachel said passionately.

'They will not be staying to view the execution.'

'It is still inappropriate. Wholly inappropriate.'

'One day Aahil will be ruling this kingdom. He will need to make difficult decisions and oversee events that make him uncomfortable.'

'We're talking about the distant future here.'

'What kind of father would I be if I didn't prepare my son for the harsh realities of the job he will take on? I saw my first execution when I was Aahil's age.'

'And how did that make you feel?'

Malik paused, transported back to that first execution he'd witnessed.

'That's not the point,' he persevered. 'I may not have felt very comfortable, but my father did his duty in preparing me to become Sheikh. I understood how a trial worked and what punishments lay in store for those who broke the law.'

'How did it make you feel?' Rachel repeated insistently.

Malik thought about the feelings of dread and fear he had experienced whilst sitting next to his father. He could still remember the condemned man's pleas, his shouts for mercy. Up until that point Malik had never seen true, unadulterated fear, but it was etched on the criminal's face as he was led to the gallows. And even now, over two decades later, Malik could hear the crack as the man's neck broke. He swallowed, he was never going to tell Rachel any of that.

'How did it make you feel?' she repeated a third time, softer now.

'I felt as if I were doing my duty to my father and my country,' Malik said stiffly. 'The children will be ready to depart at eight tomorrow morning.'

Before she could protest any further Malik gave her a curt nod and strode out of the room. He didn't want to discuss the matter any further and Rachel had a way of getting under his skin. He knew she was making a valid point, the children probably would be a little scared, but it was an important experience for them and it wasn't as though he was going to let them watch the actual execution.

Chapter Ten

The day was already hot as Rachel descended the steps of the palace towards the waiting convoy. Even the lush oasis seemed a little wilted this morning, as if all the water in the world couldn't make up for the scorching heat of the day to come.

Rachel gripped Ameera and Hakim firmly by the hands, leading them towards the plush carrying chair set at the bottom of the steps. Although she had insisted she ride the night before, Rachel had decided if the Sheikh was going to force his children to attend this trial the best thing she could do for them was to keep them close and safe and try to shield them from the worst. That meant having the safety of the carrying chair to retreat into.

Purposefully not looking at Malik, Rachel gave Wahid a short nod of acknowledgement before climbing into the plush carrying chair. She arranged her crisp cotton dress around her, then helped Hakim and Ameera in. Rachel knew Aahil wouldn't join them. The young boy was anxious for his father to be proud of him and despite his nerves wanted to be right by his father's side all day. Rachel had known trying to per-suade him otherwise would have been pointless. Aahil idolised his father, looked up to him and strove to be like him—Rachel's protestations would have made no difference at all.

Surreptitiously she watched as Aahil mounted his horse and Malik did the same. They looked impres-sive up on their strong desert horses, dressed in tradi-tional ceremonial robes. Most of the time in the palace Malik wore simple breeches and a shirt. Rachel sup-posed it was a habit from his days spent studying in Europe. When he had official business to oversee he donned the more traditional white robes, his status and wealth hinted at by a small band of coloured em-broidery around the hem, stitched in rich red-and-gold thread. Although she was annoyed with the Sheikh she couldn't deny he cut a fine figure today. He was handsome and confident and powerful, all the things a leader should be. She just wished he was a little more realistic about what an eight-year-old, a six-year-old and a four-year-old should be exposed to.

Suddenly Malik turned on his horse and through the gauzy curtains their eyes met for a moment. Rachel hastily looked away. She might be annoyed with him, but that didn't dampen the memory of the kiss they had shared. A wholly inappropriate kiss. A kiss that still made her skin tingle and her cheeks flush. Even when she was irritated by his behaviour she couldn't deny there was something rather mesmerising about Malik. She wasn't sure if it was his confidence or the rather heady mixture of good looks and authority, but she found herself secretly wanting to be alone with the

Sheikh again, even if the sensible part of her knew it was a terrible idea.

'How long until we get there?' Hakim asked, his little face white with worry.

Rachel pulled the small boy closer into her and cuddled him. Of all the children it was Hakim she was most worried about today. Not only was he the youngest, but he was the most sensitive as well, and since being told they were going to the trial Hakim had retreated into himself, hardly speaking at all.

'It will be a couple of hours in the carrying chair,' Rachel said. 'Why don't you lean against me and try to have a sleep?'

Eventually both children fell asleep in Rachel's arms and she enjoyed the surge of love she felt towards them. As they glided through the desert Rachel felt a pang of sadness that she would never have children of her own. The life of a governess could be quite a lonely one. Not quite a servant, not quite part of the family, Rachel had been warned many times she might feel isolated in her new job. So far she hadn't felt anything but joy and love for the children she was looking after, but she did wonder if one day she might become jealous. Governesses were not expected to marry or have their own families. They looked after other people's children, never their own. Rachel had always been very maternal, always loved children and even now she felt a little sad that she would never nurture her own baby through childhood and into adulthood. She'd always known she wasn't destined for love or marriage or motherhood, always welcomed the fact, knowing whatever happened she did not want to live life like her parents, but sometimes it felt unfair to give all her love to children who might not remember her in a few years' time.

Rachel allowed herself a few moments of silent sadness, then bent down and kissed the heads of Ameera and Hakim. In reality she was blessed. She loved her job and she loved these children. She would have to remember to be thankful for everything she did have. Burrowing a little deeper into the cushions, she closed her eyes and tried not to think of the trial ahead.

They arrived in the village of Talir mid-morning, and as the carrying chair was set down Rachel could already feel the heat of the sun trying to invade their cool sanctuary. Gently she shook the children awake and smiled at them warmly as they opened their bleary eyes.

The curtains on one side of the chair were pulled back and a hand thrust inside to assist her out. Rachel took it, allowing herself to be pulled up out of the chair and into the world. As she rose she realised the firm grip belonged to Malik and within a second they were standing face-to-face, their bodies far too close for two people trying to keep their distance from one another.

'Thank you, Your Majesty,' Rachel said quietly, pulling her hand from his and turning back to help Hakim and Ameera emerge from the chair.

Rachel felt his strong hands on her shoulders and firmly he turned her back to face him.

'I know you have your doubts about today, but the children will be shielded from anything unsavoury,' Malik said.

Rachel gave a short nod, acknowledging his olive

branch even if she still didn't agree the children should be here.

'Together we will protect them whilst ensuring they understand about the justice system of Huria.'

Hakim sidled in between them and Rachel felt his small hand slip into hers. She wondered whether Malik saw the frightened expression on his youngest son's face or whether he was too preoccupied thinking about the lesson his children would learn today.

To her surprise Malik crouched down in front of Hakim and tilted his son's face upwards.

'We will keep you safe, Hakim,' he said quietly. 'There is nothing to worry about.'

The village elder they had met on their previous visit stepped forward from the crowd to greet the royal family. Rachel listened to his welcome carefully. Since arriving in Huria she had been studying the language in her spare time, normally after the children had gone to bed. She was determined to master the language her young charges spoke naturally, but at present she only could understand a few words of the village elder's welcome.

After the lengthy speech the elderly man motioned for them to follow him to the village square. Rachel couldn't help but remember the last time they were here, the village had been filled with music and dancing and laughter, now they were assembled for an execution. The square was full; it seemed every inhabitant was present. Rachel was shocked to see so many children scattered throughout the crowd. It seemed that the Sheikh wasn't the only one who wanted his children to see justice prevail.

They were led to a row of plush cushions set out in

the shade and immediately Rachel gathered Ameera and Hakim to her side. Neither child protested, and she could feel the tension and worry emanating from her two young charges.

Rachel was surprised to see Malik sit down with them, she had assumed he would oversee the trial, but it appeared on this instance he was just there as a spectator like the rest of them. He came in close to his children, bringing Aahil with him, and Rachel felt the eyes of the crowd on the little family group.

'In a minute the bandits will be brought into the square,' Malik said as he helped his children get comfortable. 'There will probably be lots of shouting from the crowd, these men have stolen from and hurt a lot of people from Talir, but you have nothing to be afraid of. They will shout at the bandits, but they will not become violent.'

Rachel had to admit his words had a soothing effect on both her and the children. Even as the bandits were brought forward through the crowd and the shouting started none of the children flinched, but instead looked on curiously.

'The bandits will line up in front of the village and hear the crimes they have been accused of,' Malik explained. 'They will have a chance to speak in their defence before they are sentenced.'

Three of the four men stood with their eyes fixed to the ground. The fourth, the leader of the bandits, stared defiantly at the crowd, as if baiting them to attack. The fifth bandit, the one Malik had badly injured, was deemed too unwell to stand trial. If he ever recovered from his wounds he would be sentenced separately.

The village elder started to recite the men's crimes.

The list was long and every so often Malik would lean in and translate snippets for her. As he did so his breath tickled Rachel's neck and she felt her skin pucker and shiver. With Malik's unexpected gentle approach and careful explanations for the children, Rachel felt her previous misgivings about coming to the trial start to lessen. Although she still would prefer the children to be safely back at the palace, she couldn't deny Malik was handling the situation well.

After about twenty minutes the list of crimes the bandits were charged with petered out and immediately Rachel felt a change in the mood of the crowd. The bandits were now allowed to speak on their own behalf, but she suspected their victims were not going to be very sympathetic to their sob stories.

'This man is saying he joined the group in order to provide for his family,' Malik said softly.

The bandit was heckled by the crowd and soon he fell quiet.

'The people of Talir often struggle and go hungry if it is a hard year for farming, so they will not be sympathetic to such pleas,' Aahil said, glancing at his father for approval.

'That is very true, Aahil, although we must not forget that this man's family is in all likelihood innocent even if he is guilty. They will suffer for his crimes.' Rachel watched as Malik stared off into the distance, amazed again by how much Malik cared for the people he ruled, even the families of criminals.

The other men made similar pleas, all except the head bandit, who just spat on the ground in contempt when it was his turn to speak.

'The council of elders will now deliberate and decide on the sentence,' Malik explained as the noise from the crowd started to grow. People were chattering and taking the opportunity to discuss the trial whilst the elders deliberated.

A young woman approached from the square and offered them all refreshments, and Rachel gratefully sipped at the cool, sharp liquid. She was feeling a little nervous again, as if she could sense the crowd might turn at any moment, and she wondered when Malik would let her take the children home.

Suddenly there was silence. A village elder stepped forward and started to speak.

'He is pronouncing all the men guilty of banditry, of beating their victims and of having no regard for the lives of others.' Malik paused and Rachel found she was holding her breath. 'They are all sentenced to death.'

As the words were delivered Rachel felt Hakim's little body stiffen and burrow into her. Ameera seemed frozen and Aahil was valiantly trying to appear calm and collected.

'We need to leave,' Rachel said firmly. She stood, pulling the children up with her.

'They're going to stone them,' Ameera said as Rachel tried to pull her away.

Rachel felt sick. She knew about crime and punishment, knew that to live in a stable society you needed to have laws and people who broke them needed to be dealt with accordingly, but the idea of stoning someone to death made her shudder.

As the sentence was delivered there was a roar from the crowd and Rachel could only watch as the people of Talir surged forward. Hakim cried out in panic and even Aahil huddled closer to his family. There were shouts and cheers from the villagers as they pressed in towards the condemned men.

Rachel saw Malik glance at his family, huddled together and scared by the sudden change in atmosphere. Decisively he strode forward, motioning for Rachel to keep his children where they were, and he mounted the small platform the elders had sat on.

At the sight of their Sheikh the crowd fell silent and stopped in its tracks.

'People of Talir, you have been grievously wronged by these men,' Malik said calmly, 'but do not disgrace yourselves. Justice will be done, be patient and let it be done right.'

Without a single glance behind him Malik walked from the dais and back to his family. He picked Hakim up, took Ameera's hand and motioned for Rachel and Aahil to follow him. Quickly they left the village square, flanked by the palace guards. Still, there was silence from the crowd, and even as Malik helped Rachel into the carrying chair she could not hear a single villager whisper. Their Sheikh had spoken and they would obey.

Chapter Eleven

Malik paced backwards and forward across the courtyard, unsure of what to do. Never in his life before had he been struck with such uncertainty. No matter what decision needed making or steps taken, he had never hesitated, weighing the options calmly and deciding swiftly on the way forward, but tonight he was at a loss.

The ride back from Talir had been awful. Inside the carrying chair he had heard Rachel's soothing murmurs directed at Hakim and Ameera. The whole journey she had talked to them and sung to them, stopping only when both had drifted off to sleep. Malik only had to look at any one of his children's faces to realise how damaging it had been to take them to the trial.

It had all been going so well. With his calm explanation of what was occurring, his children had seemed interested and relaxed. Malik had felt pleased to be showing Aahil, Ameera and Hakim an example of Huria's justice system and they had not seemed fazed in the slightest. And then the crowd had turned ugly, surging forward towards the bandits, ready to draw blood. At that moment Malik had glanced at Hakim's face and seen pure terror. He hated that he was the reason his son had felt such fear, that any of his children had felt such fear.

As a young boy he could remember being summoned for one of the weekly audiences with his father. The older man had often used the hour a week they spent together to lecture Malik on qualities needed to rule a kingdom. On this particular occasion his father had told him how it was necessary for a Sheikh to keep his distance emotionally from everyone. He had to stand unshakeable and alone, a man people could look up to. A Sheikh could not show pleasure when he was happy or shed tears when he was sad, he must remain stony faced and detached.

Throughout his life Malik had tried to emulate his father and be true to the older man's teachings. He had not cried when his father had died, or shouted his joy from the rooftops when Aahil was born, he had quietly got on with doing his duty. But now, with the memory of Hakim turning to Rachel in his moment of distress, Malik wondered whether he had kept his distance from his children too much. He was never the one they turned to in moments of happiness or fear, and that hurt, but he only had himself to blame. For too long he had followed his father's teachings blindly, not assessing and adapting for his own situation. Yes, a Sheikh did need to be seen to be unflappable and constant to his subjects, but that didn't mean he couldn't laugh or cry with his children in the privacy of his own home. Slowly Malik was realising that although his father had been a good ruler of Huria, maybe he hadn't been the best role model as a parent.

Malik paused in his pacing as Rachel slipped out of the boys' room and closed the door quietly behind her. Silently she descended the steps to the courtyard and moved towards him. He braced himself for her tirade. She would be justified in chastising him, as she had warned him that the children were too young to go to the trial, but he had thought he knew best.

'They're all asleep now,' Rachel said, as she walked past him and perched on the low wall surrounding the fountain.

Without speaking Malik came and sat beside her. He watched as she absentmindedly trailed her fingers along the surface of the water in the pool and waited for a chastisement that never came.

She looked tired, Malik realised, and for a moment he felt guilty. He had employed her as a governess, but in reality she was doing two jobs: governess and nursemaid. She educated his children during the day, but she was also there for them with a kind word, loving cuddle or just her company, whatever the hour.

'I was wrong,' Malik said quietly.

He didn't often have to admit fault and he found the words hard to utter, but he knew that to move on they had to be said.

Rachel raised her head and met his gaze, smiling sadly.

'It's all right,' she said softly, taking his hand in her own.

Malik felt oddly comforted by her touch and he realised that hardly anyone ever dared to touch him. Of course his manservant shaved his beard every morning and he shook hands with visiting dignitaries and supplicants, but no one touched him like this.

'The children…' Malik began, but trailed off. He could still see the panic on Hakim's face and the way he had clung to Rachel even when they were back in the safety of the palace.

'The children will be fine,' Rachel said. 'They're very resilient and they will all bounce back.'

Malik wondered if she was speaking the truth or just trying to reassure him.

'You're not a bad father, you know,' she said quietly, getting to the root of his fears in one quick sentence.

He looked at her for a moment, wondering whether to deny that that was what was worrying him, and then realised there was no point. Rachel was observant and intuitive, she had got to know his children as if they were her own in the space of a few weeks, and Malik wondered if maybe she understood him a little, too.

'I shouldn't have insisted they attend the trial. You were right.'

Rachel shrugged. 'You weren't to know it would turn violent. Up until the sentencing I have to admit it was a good educational experience for them. And you calmed things down and got the children out when they needed it.'

She could be gloating that once again she had been right and he had been wrong when it came to decisions about his children, but instead she was trying to bolster his self-esteem when it came to parenting.

'The very fact that you care so much, that you're out here pacing up and down the courtyard worrying about them, shows that you're a good father.'

Malik felt her grip on his hand tighten and he wondered when such a young woman had become so wise. He had benefitted from the best education money could buy, first in Huria and then in Europe, but still this relatively sheltered young woman from England could make him see things in a different light.

'Sometimes we try our hardest do what we think is right, but still we make mistakes.'

Malik felt himself nod slowly. He did care about his children, but he felt so out of his depth with them. He knew how to run Huria, he was good at being the Sheikh, but when it came to his sons and daughter he felt like a complete novice and that wasn't a sensation that sat well with him.

Gently he raised Rachel's hand and brought the silky skin to his lips. He couldn't bring himself to admit out loud how right she was—Malik had never been good at admitting to his faults—but as he kissed the back of her hand and their eyes met he knew that she understood what he wasn't saying.

They sat with their fingers entwined for a few minutes, both lost in their own thoughts. The courtyard was empty and Malik knew someone could come across them at any time, but still he did not release Rachel's hand. Whilst their fingers were locked together Malik felt a little less lonely and for once he allowed himself to take strength from someone else, rather than insist he stand alone.

Malik was up at dawn the next morning. His personal set of rooms looked out over the palace gardens and in the early morning light the flowers and plants were bathed in golden rays. Further away the sands of the desert looked hazy in the already scorching heat.

Malik knew he needed to stop wallowing in self-pity and do something positive. He was very conscious that a few weeks previously he would have shied away from further interaction with his children, thinking that in all likelihood he would make things worse. But today he had an urge not only for his children to move on from the negative experience of the trial in Talir, but for it to be he who helped them to move on.

He knew it was Rachel's influence. He could see how she had masterfully taken him in hand alongside his children, using her considerable skill to show him what they all had been missing out on by him remaining distant. Malik still didn't agree with all her teaching methods—after all, Aahil wasn't going to learn how to rule a kingdom by play-acting knights and dragons—but he was man enough to admit they had all blossomed under Rachel's care, himself included.

The palace was quiet as he walked out into the courtyard and for a moment he savoured the peace. He allowed himself a minute just to look up at the brilliant blue sky and marvel at how the light reflected off the water from the fountain. Malik realised he didn't often just stop and appreciate the world, his life was a blur of meetings and negotiations, land disputes and hosting foreign and native dignitaries. In truth that was how he liked it. Ever since Aliyyah had died Malik had found himself taking on more and more, and deep down he knew it was so he didn't have time to think about his late wife or the manner of her death.

As he pondered how much his children had suffered as a result of his immersion in his duty Malik saw Rachel's door open and her slim figure slip out. She was already dressed, clad in one of her usual white-cotton gowns, and even at this early hour in the morning she looked refreshed and ready for the day. She hadn't seen him so Malik watched as she poked her head into first the boys' room and then Ameera's room. As if satisfied her charges were still asleep she descended the stairs into the courtyard and walked briskly to one of the archways.

Malik knew he should make his presence known, but something held him back. He wanted to see where she went and what she did.

He watched as finally Rachel reached one of the outer doors of the palace, turned the handle and slipped through. Malik stood frozen for a second, his curiosity turning to anger. She was leaving the palace. Not that she was a prisoner, but over the last few weeks surely she had realised it was not safe for a woman to venture into the streets alone, especially when she did not know the language or customs of the country well.

Quickly Malik pulled open the door and strode out after Rachel, intending to take her firmly by the arm and escort her back into the safety of the palace. He looked around, his heart pounding as he realised she had already disappeared. The door from the palace led out into the town of Pretia, a wealthy settlement centred around the oasis. The many palace servants, guards and advisors called Pretia their home, as well as some of the wealthier families in Huria. However, as with any town, there was an unsavoury element to the population and Malik knew Rachel, with her foreign looks and clothes, would be easy prey.

Purposefully he strode to the end of the street and looked in both directions. To his relief he saw the swish of white fabric round a corner and immediately he knew it was Rachel. She was walking fast and Malik realised she had covered her hair with a scarf, as was the custom of many Hurian women.

He followed her, curious as to what she could be doing out of the palace now he could see she was safe. The confident way she wove through the maze of streets made Malik suspect this was not her first excursion outside the safety of the palace walls and he wondered how many times she had put herself at risk to come into the town. He felt an unnatural stab of panic, knowing any one of those times she could have been attacked by a thief or lured into a deserted alleyway by less than scrupulous men.

With these disturbing thoughts in mind Malik quickened his pace, determined to catch up with Rachel and escort her safely back to the palace, where they would have a serious talk about her disregard for her own safety.

He was only a few feet behind her when Rachel stopped in front of a market stall displaying a multitude of beautiful fabrics. Silks and satins were draped seductively over each other, with brightly coloured gauze and richly embroidered cottons also vying for attention. Malik halted and watched as Rachel reverently ran her fingers over the luxurious materials and found himself wondering what it would feel like to have her fingers trailing over his skin in such a fashion.

She motioned to the stallholder, a stout, middle-aged woman, and Malik realised she was about to buy something.

He edged closer, curious to see how she would handle communicating in a language she could not speak, and was flabbergasted when a stream of slightly hesitant Hurian flowed from her lips.

The stallholder replied, having to repeat the prices twice before Rachel understood, and then money changed hands.

As Rachel turned, her newly purchased material clutched under one arm, Malik stepped forward. Her eyes widened and Malik saw she at least had the sense to look a little sheepish at being caught outside the palace all alone.

'Good morning, Your Majesty,' she said quietly when she had recovered from the shock of seeing him.

'Good morning, Rachel, so lovely to see you flagrantly disregarding your safety at such an early hour.'

She coloured, but defiantly held his eye.

'I wasn't aware I had to inform you of my movements.'

'Indeed you do not. You're not a prisoner, you're a governess.' Malik paused to take her arm firmly, he couldn't trust she wouldn't stalk away and try to return to the palace alone. 'Unfortunately you are a very beautiful woman in a foreign land who stands out to every thief and vagabond as an easy target.'

'Unfortunately?' Rachel asked quietly.

'Unfortunate that you are an easy target. Not unfortunate that you are beautiful.' Although Malik knew he would find it a lot easier not to care about Rachel's safety if she was the sort of governess with grey hair, a large nose and copious warts.

'Oh.'

'Do I take it this isn't your first trip out of the palace alone?'

Rachel shook her head, but had the good sense to keep quiet.

'And I'm guessing that you have never been sensible enough to take an escort on the previous occasions either.'

She shook her head again.

'Tell me, do you dislike your job?' Malik asked.

Rachel's eyes widened with surprise at this change in the direction of the conversation.

'Or maybe you dislike the palace. Or me. For surely if you were happy with your life, with being *alive*, you wouldn't so carelessly put it at risk.'

'I've never had even the slightest bit of trouble,' Rachel muttered mutinously.

'So I suppose you are aware of the two men following us, or the beggar child eyeing up your new purchase?' Malik asked.

Rachel tried to spin around, but Malik held her arm firmly.

'Just keep walking and we'll be fine,' he said calmly.

In fact, now that Rachel was safely on his arm Malik was rather enjoying himself. Of course there were no men following them and no beggar child ready to attack, but he did want to get his point across. Since becoming Sheikh all those years ago Malik realised he had never walked through the streets of his kingdom unguarded and unrecognised. There was a certain pleasure in the freedom he was now experiencing, a lightness in his step he didn't have when decked out in his ceremonial robes and waving to the gathered masses.

'So tell me, when did you learn our language?' Malik asked as they neared the palace.

'I've been studying ever since I left England,' Rachel said, looking slightly embarrassed.

Malik used his free hand to reach across and run his

fingers across her knuckles where they rested against his arm.

'You are a surprising woman,' he said softly. 'In all the years we have been welcoming foreign visitors to Huria, not a single one has ever bothered to learn a word of our language.'

'I want to be able to communicate with people and I am not so self-obsessed to think they should learn English to converse with me.'

'You plan on staying with us for a while, then?' Malik asked lightly, but found he was again holding his breath waiting for her reassurance.

Rachel turned and looked up at him, her eyes wide. 'As long as you'll have me.'

He wanted to kiss her. Every irrational fibre in his body wanted to gather her in his arms and kiss her, but as usual the rational parts of him won. He knew she was talking about her employment as his children's governess, but for a moment Malik wanted to keep her in Huria for much more selfish reasons.

'What is your purchase for?' he asked, forcing himself to return his thoughts to the more mundane and safe territory.

Rachel glanced at the roll of fabric under her arm before answering.

'I saw how Ameera looked at the dancing girls when we were in Talir last week. I thought we might fashion her a similar outfit and maybe if you are in agreement we could find someone to teach her how to dance.' Rachel paused and smiled ruefully. 'I don't think I could master those steps anywhere near well enough to teach her sufficiently.'

An image of Rachel clad in the gauzy material,

dancing just for him, popped into Malik's head and he found himself clearing his throat as he hastily tried to tear his thoughts away from such a tantalising prospect.

'Unless you think it would be inappropriate?'

It took Malik a moment to realise she was still talking about her proposal to find Ameera a dance teacher and not offering to perform for him personally herself.

'No, it's a lovely idea, just what Ameera needs.'

It was refreshing to agree with Rachel on something to do with his children for once. In fact, as they approached the palace entrance Malik realised it was pleasing to share a decision with someone else, for so long he had made every decision alone.

Rachel was reluctant to relinquish Malik's arm as they returned to the palace. She had been shocked to find him following her and even more surprised when he had shown such concern over her safety. She knew he now respected her as his children's governess and the kiss they had shared had hinted at some desire on his part, but Rachel thought she had detected a deeper level of concern, a level that might mean he cared for her more than just in a professional capacity.

Ruefully Rachel wondered whether she was projecting her own hopes on to Malik. Ever since their kiss she hadn't been able to keep the enigmatic Sheikh far from her mind. Even when they were disagreeing about the trip to Talir to witness the trial, Rachel had felt her eyes roam to his lips and wondered if she would ever kiss them again.

She needed to focus, she told herself. Malik had been right when he had said nothing more could happen between them. They were of differing stations, but that wasn't even the main reason—people had overcome much more in their quest for love. No, the main reason they couldn't be together was that neither of them was really ready for a relationship. Even though his marriage had not been one of love, Rachel sensed Malik was not truly over the death of his wife. And Rachel herself knew that despite the desire she felt for Malik she could never betray her principles. For years she had vowed not to let lust and love rule her as it had her parents. She had a good relationship with Malik now, one that benefitted the three children in her care. She would not jeopardise that for a few stolen kisses that could not lead to anything lasting.

Nevertheless, she could not deny her reluctance to let Malik go.

'I was coming to find you when I saw you sneak out,' Malik said as they reached the courtyard.

Rachel looked up at him, trying to read the expression on his face. Despite all her recent denials she wanted him to want her, to have come to find her because he just couldn't keep away.

'I thought it would be good to do something as a family, my way of apologising to the children for what happened in Talir.'

Rachel tried not to let the disappointment show on her face. She wondered what she would do without her three charges whilst they spent time with their father and whether she would be able to put the charismatic Sheikh from her mind whilst he was away.

'I am keen to show them their heritage, help them understand Huria is not a land of palaces and oases.' He paused, as if seeking her approval. 'I thought a camel trek with an overnight stay in one of the Bedouin tents.'

It sounded wonderful and Rachel knew the children would relish time spent with their father. Hakim would enjoy the adventure, Ameera would enjoy the camels and Aahil would feel proud to be travelling and staying in a traditional Hurian way.

'That sounds lovely. When were you thinking of going?'

'I have sent a messenger to sort out the details, but I think things should be ready by the day after tomorrow. If that suits you, of course.'

The surprise must have shown on Rachel's face for Malik flashed her one of his rare smiles.

'Me?'

'Well, I hoped you might accompany us.'

For a second Rachel saw the uncertainty in his expression and she realised Malik probably had never spent a night alone with his children, not away from all the servants in the palace. He couldn't come out and admit it, his pride wouldn't let him, but he needed her there.

Rachel felt a warm glow inside. She'd always wanted to be needed, to become indispensable, but she wondered now why she felt a little sad alongside the glow. She supposed it was one thing to be needed, but quite another to be wanted as well.

Chiding herself for not being pleased with what she had, Rachel smiled at Malik.

'Of course, I can't think of anything more delightful than a camel trek and a night in a Bedouin tent.'

'I thought I might tell the children myself.'

Rachel allowed Malik to guide her up the steps leading to the children's bedrooms. She was inordinately pleased that Malik wanted to tell the children his plan. When she had first arrived at the palace he hardly knew how to interact with his children, now he was actively seeking them out.

The sun set over the oasis early in Huria, staining the sky fiery reds and oranges before the purple dusk settled over the desert kingdom. Rachel had a rare moment to herself and was mesmerised by the beauty of the natural spectacle.

There was a tap on her door and after a few seconds Ameera poked her head round the frame and looked up at Rachel with guilty eyes. Rachel marvelled at the change in the girl over such a short time. Even though there were still times when Ameera could be surly or rude, mostly that was in response to things not going her way, and Rachel was slowly teaching the young Princess to accept defeat and to value the wants of others. She'd realised Ameera's surliness mainly sprang from the fact that she was insecure, insecure about herself and insecure about the love of the people around her. By showering the young girl with affection Rachel was hoping to help with some of that insecurity.

'Can I come in, miss?' Ameera asked, even though she was halfway into the room already.

Rachel stepped away from the window and motioned for Ameera to come and join her on the bed.

'Father said you might find me a dance teacher,' Ameera said once she was settled on the luxurious mattress.

Rachel smiled. She should have guessed Ameera wanted to talk about dancing—in the days since they had watched the young girls twirl and jump in Talir she had talked of little else.

'We will,' Rachel reassured her.

Ameera looked thoughtful, then nodded as if pleased to have got this reassurance.

'But for tonight I've got another treat in store for us,' Rachel said, standing and pulling out the bundle of material she had sneaked out of the palace to buy that morning.

Ameera looked on, perplexed, as Rachel undid the bundle and let her peek at the luxurious material. Rachel couldn't help but smile as the young girl's face lit up with pleasure as she realised what Rachel was suggesting.

'We can make costumes?' she asked, the hope and excitement mingling on her face.

Rachel nodded. 'Dancer's costumes.'

For a few seconds more Ameera sat running her fingers over the gauzy material, then suddenly she was on her feet.

'Wait there. Promise you won't move, Miss Talbot.'

Ameera darted from the room, disappearing from view within seconds, leaving Rachel to wonder what she could have thought of that was so important or exciting. She was back in two minutes, carrying a large bundle under her arm. Excitedly she held up the items she had run to fetch and Rachel realised they were thin cotton trousers, the sort many dancers wore underneath their flowing skirts to preserve a little of their modesty.

Carefully Rachel showed Ameera how to measure and cut the fabric, pin it into position and then delicately sew the edges together to fashion flowing skirts to be worn over the cotton trousers. The young Princess watched intently, then followed Rachel's lead, laughing and smiling when the outfit began to take shape.

The tops were a little more difficult to make. The dancers in Talir had left their midriffs bare, wearing skimpy tops that covered their breasts but not much else. Rachel knew this wasn't appropriate for Ameera, but she also knew the young girl wouldn't want something too different to what she had seen.

They worked together for two hours, Ameera concentrating hard on the task at hand, but opening up a little to Rachel, too. She talked of her mother, and her hopes and dreams, and Rachel realised the little Princess was lonely. With two brothers and no mother she was starved of female companionship and a role model. Rachel just hoped she could go a little way in making up for that.

For her part Rachel told Ameera of her time at school, of her three friends and some of their exploits.

'You remind me a lot of my friend Isabel,' Rachel told the young girl. 'She's headstrong and outspoken and would like nothing more than to be on the stage as a singer. We used to put on performances at school, some girls would play instruments, others would dance, but Isabel would always steal the show with her singing.'

'I wish I could be the best dancer in the world,' Ameera said.

'Work hard at it and anything is possible, little one.'

Finally the outfits had taken shape. It was fully dark outside and Rachel knew she should be ushering her young charge to bed, but Ameera was so excited about the prospect of trying her new outfit on Rachel couldn't bring herself to deny her.

'You try yours on, too,' Ameera instructed, as she wriggled into the trousers and started to step into the gauzy skirt.

Rachel had fashioned an outfit for herself alongside the one she had helped Ameera make, but she had thought only to try it on in private, to keep it as her little indulgence no one else would ever see.

'Maybe another time, Ameera,' Rachel said, helping the young girl fasten the skirt around her waist.

'Please, Miss Talbot, then we can pretend to be dancers together.'

Rachel looked into Ameera's eager face and relented. It would only be her and the six-year-old Princess who would ever see the slightly scandalous outfit—there couldn't be any harm in it.

Once Ameera was dressed Rachel unfastened her cotton dress and slipped on a pair of the trousers Ameera had brought for her. She wondered whose they had been. Luckily they more or less fit; the waistband was a little loose, but could be tightened with a piece of cord, and the legs were a little short, but under the flowing skirt it wouldn't be too obvious.

'Mother was a good dancer,' Ameera said quietly. 'Or at least that's what Mrs Fitt said. I never saw her dance.'

So the trousers had likely once been Ameera's mother's.

'I never saw her do much at all.'

Rachel moved towards Ameera, thinking to comfort her, but the young Princess turned away slightly, gath-

ering up the material of her new skirt in her hands. Not
for the first time Rachel wondered what their mother
had been like. All three children hardly spoke of her
and when they did their comments hinted that they did
not know their mother well. Rachel couldn't imagine
being blessed with three such wonderful children and
wanting to keep your distance. If she were a mother,
she would want to be involved in every aspect of her
children's lives.

Rachel wriggled into the rest of the costume and
turned to survey herself in the full-length mirror. For
a few seconds she just stared, running her hands over
her body, not quite believing it was her she was seeing
in the reflection. Gone was the prim white dress, with
buttons all the way up to the neck, and in its place was
a scandalously revealing outfit that showed off more
skin than Rachel's underclothes.

'You look nice, Miss Talbot,' Ameera said, coming
to stand beside her.

'You look lovely,' Rachel said, turning to face
Ameera. 'You look as though you're about to go and
join a troupe of dancing girls.'

Ameera swayed from side to side, swishing her skirt
around her knees and running her fingers over the soft
material. Rachel knew she'd done a good thing today,
despite Malik's words of warning over risking her own
safety. The smile on Ameera's face, and the confi-
dences she had begun to share, were worth a little risk.

'I never want to take it off.'

Rachel smiled indulgently. 'I think maybe it would
be a good idea to take it off before you go to sleep, otherwise the whole outfit might become ruined.'

Ameera looked up at Rachel and seemed to hesitate

for a second, then she leaned forward and wrapped her arms around Rachel's hips, hugging her close. Rachel felt a swell of contentment inside. She was slowly and surely breaking down these children's walls and finding a way to help them blossom and grow.

'Thank you,' Ameera said, her face buried in Rachel's tummy.

'Thank you, Ameera, I had a lovely evening.'

Rachel watched as the young girl skipped from the room, swishing her skirt backwards and forward as she went, twirling and pirouetting and leaping from side to side.

Rachel turned back to the mirror. She had chosen the purple material to complement Ameera's colouring, but she could see it was a shade that also sat well on her own honeyed skin tones and looked good against her dark hair. Tentatively Rachel raised a hand and trailed her fingers across the bare skin of her abdomen. Never had she worn anything that left so much skin scandalously bare, not even as a small child. She could not tell if so much skin was alluring or if it didn't leave enough to the imagination. Although the dancers in Talir had held everyone's attention with similar outfits.

A soft knock on the door roused her from her perusal of her body and her outfit. She thought it was likely Ameera returning for something she had forgotten, but just in case Rachel hurriedly pulled a sheet from the bed and wrapped it around her body, hiding the outfit underneath.

She opened the door to find Mallik standing on the other side, leaning casually against the wall. He raised an eyebrow at her attire, taking in the voluminous sheets that covered her from neck to toe.

'I thought I'd let you know the trek is arranged for the beginning of next week,' Malik said.

Rachel knew he didn't have to come and tell her this information this evening, it would have been much more appropriate to seek her out tomorrow when she was with the children.

'I just saw Ameera leaving your room,' Malik continued. 'She was dressed like a dancer.'

'We made costumes,' Rachel said, feeling the colour start to rise in her cheeks. Malik was studying her intently, as if he were trying to see through the sheet to what lay beneath.

'I know, I spoke to her.'

Rachel nodded, her mouth feeling suddenly too dry to speak.

'She said you had *both* made costumes.'

Rachel nodded again.

'I see.'

Malik seemed to be wrestling with himself and Rachel wasn't sure which side of him she wanted to win.

'Maybe I…' He trailed off, straightened and took a step back. 'Goodnight Rachel,' he said firmly.

Rachel watched as Malik walked away, undeniable disappointment blossoming inside her. It wasn't as though she ever meant for him to see her in the outfit, but a small part of her wanted to observe his reaction as his eyes swept over her body, taking in every inch of bare skin and every curve.

Chapter Twelve

Malik rose early, favouring a quick trip to his private *hammam* to an extra hour's sleep. He was going to be spending the majority of the day on the back of a camel and the night on the desert floor, so he wanted his muscles to be as relaxed as possible before the trek ahead. It wasn't as though he would have slept well anyway, his dreams had been invaded the last few nights by images of Rachel dressed as a scantily clad dancer. Every time Malik imagined something slightly different and after nights of interrupted sleep he was aching to know the truth. He wished he hadn't tried to be so noble, so self-controlled, and had pulled Rachel's covering sheet down and seen what lay beneath when he had had the chance.

Damn his sense of chivalry and honour, for once Malik just wanted to be a man.

He allowed himself thirty blissful minutes in the sweltering steam room, and after a dip in the cold pool he felt refreshed and revitalised.

'Father, Ameera said I can't ride my own camel,'

Hakim accosted him as soon as he exited his private rooms.

Malik smiled indulgently and felt a sense of well-being wash over him. A few weeks ago he would have stormed off to find his daughter and reprimanded her for dashing her brother's hopes.

'I don't see why you can't ride a camel,' Malik said, ruffling Hakim's dark hair.

Hopeful eyes looked up into his own.

'All by myself?'

'All by yourself.'

When planning the trip Malik had realised his youngest son would probably like a taste of independence, especially because they would encounter nomadic children even younger than Hakim who were more confident on camelback than walking on their own two feet. He had instructed one of the stable masters to find a saddle Hakim could be safely strapped into and to ensure the little boy's camel was always tethered to his own. That way Hakim would feel like he was in control without things actually being dangerous.

Hakim scampered off, no doubt to find Ameera and correct her. Malik made his way to the entrance of the palace to see how the preparations were coming along.

At nine exactly Rachel emerged with all three of his children in tow. Their faces broke out into beams of pleasure as they saw the assembled camels and they ran towards him chattering excitedly. Malik couldn't help but glance at Rachel and saw for once she was looking a little apprehensive.

'There's nothing to worry about,' Malik said softly to

her as she came to stand by his side. 'Camels are gentle beasts. They will not try to throw you or hurt you.'

Rachel's eyes met his own and for a few moments it was as though it was just the two of them. Malik was tempted to sweep Rachel up on to one of the camels and show her there was nothing to be afraid of, but he knew the proximity wouldn't be good for them. He'd spent far too much time recently thinking about his children's governess, he didn't need any more close encounters to fuel his dreams.

'You might find it a little difficult to ride in that dress, though,' Malik said, looking Rachel up and down.

He had never really considered suitable camel-riding attire before. He had donned the traditional loose trousers and white tunic top that the nomads of Huria had been wearing for centuries, whether riding their camels or trekking through the desert on foot. The thin garments gave protection from the sun, but let you remain cool at the same time.

Rachel looked up at the camel standing before her uncertainly.

'What else can I wear?'

Malik considered the question carefully. When he came to think about it you didn't see many women riding camels in Huria. They were expected to stay at home, raise the children and run the house, not trek through the desert on camelback. If they did need to travel most women either walked if they were poor or sat in front of their husbands on horseback.

'Come with me, *sayeda*, I have just the thing,' Wahid said, stepping forward.

Malik busied himself helping each of his children mount their camels, ensuring each was securely strapped into the saddles before the servants ushered the large beasts to their feet. Hakim and Ameera squealed in pleasure as the camels rocked backwards and forward as they rose, and even Aahil could not stop himself grinning at the ungainly movements.

After a few minutes Malik heard Rachel's voice from the entrance chamber of the palace. She sounded as if she were disagreeing with Wahid and he was trying his best to reassure her. Reluctantly Rachel stepped out into the daylight.

Malik stared in disbelief. Wahid had certainly found clothes Rachel would be able to ride a camel in: Malik's clothes.

'I'm not sure that's appropriate,' Malik began as Wahid led Rachel down the steps.

'See, it's not appropriate,' Rachel protested.

'Nonsense,' Wahid said with a wave of his hand. 'His Majesty is just worried he won't be able to keep his eyes on the camels.'

Rachel's eyes widened and rose to meet Malik's. For his part Malik couldn't deny Wahid was right. His old friend had raided Malik's own wardrobe and clothed Rachel in his European riding trousers. They were skintight and hugged every curve. Admittedly Rachel was also wearing a tunic over the top of the trousers, but that only covered so much, and Malik could make out enough of her figure below to distract him from the trek ahead.

'But what if we meet people on the road?' Rachel asked.

'They will just think you are an eccentric English woman, *sayeda*, you've nothing to worry about,' Wahid said cheerfully. 'Now, why don't you help Miss Talbot on to her camel, Your Majesty?'

Malik stepped forward, trying to pretend he wasn't still a little mesmerised by the shape of Rachel's legs under the skintight riding breeches.

'I'm guessing you've never done this before?' Malik asked.

Rachel shook her head. She was nervous, he realised, the woman who took everything in her stride was nervous of riding a camel.

'They're gentle beasts,' Malik repeated his assurance from earlier. 'But it is very different riding a camel to riding a horse.'

Malik held out his hand and steadied Rachel as she swung one leg over her camel's back. Already he could see Wahid was right, Rachel wouldn't get far at all trying to ride in her voluminous dress.

'Now make sure you're comfortable, then hold tight.'

He arranged her hands on the pommel in front of her.

'Really tight.' He pressed his hands on top of hers to ensure she had a good grip on the wood. 'Are you ready?'

For a moment he wondered if she was going to say no, to ask him to saddle a horse for her and have done with it, but he doubted Rachel had ever shied away from any new experience in her life.

'I'm ready,' she said, a slight tremor in her voice.

'Up,' Malik gave the command and swatted the camel on the rump.

The camel lurched upwards, throwing Rachel first forward, then backwards. Malik saw the fear on her face, but once the camel was on its feet he could see her muscles relaxing a little as she got used to the new sensation.

Malik had been riding camels since he was a boy. He loved the ungainly looking beasts. They looked as though they could only move at a slow pace, but once camels got going they could cover large distances surprising quickly and their movements were much more graceful than their appearances suggested. He hopped on to the back of his camel, issued the command and hung on tight as he rose from the ground.

Now that they were all mounted Malik rode to the front of their small group and waited for Rachel and the children to gather round him.

'The rest of the group will meet us on the route east, but first we have a stop to make.'

Aahil's eyes widened and Malik turned to his eldest son.

'Pay attention to the route we take. One day you will be the guardian of the high place and you will need to know how to get there.'

'You're taking us to the high place?' Aahil asked, his voice husky with anticipation.

'It's time,' Malik said simply.

All three children remained quiet for the next few minutes—even Hakim was aware of the enormity of the moment. Malik led their little party through the oasis and out into the desert to the north-east. This route was rocky and wound through long-dried-up gorges and riverbeds. The rocks were a beautiful amber colour out here and the sand beneath their feet had a similar vibrancy. This was the true Huria that Malik loved, these rocky hills and jagged pathways. Centu-

ries earlier his ancestors had made this area their home
and as a young boy Malik's father had brought him on
a similar journey to the one they were doing now. It
had been one of the few times they had done something together, just father and son, with no servants or
advisors accompanying them. Malik remembered the
weight of responsibility as his father had explained
the purpose of their trip, and now he felt proud to be
passing the tradition on to his own son.

'Long ago this is where our ancestors settled when
they first made Huria their home. They had been nomadic people, but the beauty of this land inspired them
to put down roots and build a kingdom here.'

Malik swivelled his head round as he spoke so he
could see his children. They were all looking around
in awe and at the back of the group Rachel was visibly
enthralled by the experience.

'For many years our ancestors lived as one with
the landscape, slowly turning the many caves in the
cliffs into homes and adding small additions made
from wood and fabric.'

As they rode Malik pointed out the caves in the
cliffs and showed his children the roughly hewn steps
their ancestors had carved into the rocks to reach their
dwellings. All three children were enthralled and once
again Malik could not believe only a few short weeks
ago he had been afraid to reach out in case they rejected him.

'They kept many of their nomadic ways, relying
on livestock for food, but after a few years of living
here they realised the oasis gave them the opportunity
to grow crops and it was then their community really
began to thrive.'

Malik told the story of his ancestors just as his father had, with a mixture of pride and awe. It would take hardy people to first settle the barren lands of Huria and make them prosper.

'Over the years many tribes became jealous of what they had here and attacked to try and gain control of the oasis, but our ancestors always stood firm and defended their fledgling kingdom.'

As the camels picked a path over the rocky ground Malik slowed slightly so Aahil would have chance to catch up with him. They rode side by side, Malik pointing out the markers that identified the route as they went, and Aahil taking in everything his father said with wide eyes.

After twenty minutes of riding through the gorge Malik stopped and slid off his camel. Quickly he secured it to a small tree that was growing out of the rock face.

He went first to Hakim's camel, uttering the command that made it lurch forward and backwards to sit, and helped his youngest son off. He repeated the process with Ameera and Aahil. Only Rachel was left on her camel and she was looking decidedly nervous at the idea of getting off.

'Hold on tight and you'll be fine,' Malik said, gripping her camel by the bridle.

Rachel gave a short nod, but Malik could tell she was apprehensive. For a woman so in control, so on top of things, it was strange to see her nervous of a beast Malik had grown up with. He could ride a camel better than he could ride a horse, but he supposed Rachel had only set eyes on the strange-looking creatures for the first time a few weeks previously, it was natural for her to be afraid.

Gently Malik commanded the camel to sit and he had to hide a smile when Rachel let out a strangled squeal of panic as she lurched towards the ground. Once the beast was seated Malik offered Rachel his hand, pulling her out of the saddle and trying not to look too hard at the way his trousers clung to the curve of her thighs.

He led Rachel over to where his children were gathered, feeling the undercurrent of excitement buzzing through their little group.

'What now, Father?' Ameera asked.

'Now we climb.'

Rachel looked up at the sheer rock face and wondered whether she had misheard.

'Climb?' she asked.

There was no staircase hewn into the rock, no handholds or ledges to scramble up. The rock face was smooth and insurmountable to Rachel's eye.

'If it were obvious then the way to the high place wouldn't be a secret,' Malik said, teasingly. His mood seemed lighter out here in the desert, as if just being away from the palace and the weight of responsibility that bore down on him was enough to bring out his mischievous side. 'Follow me.'

They left the camels behind them, tracing their way along the gorge for about a hundred yards before Malik stopped and motioned to the rock face.

'Do you see the sign?' he asked, directing the question at Aahil.

The Prince studied the rock and then suddenly

grinned. He looked triumphant and although Rachel felt as though she were walking through a bizarre dream where she didn't quite understand anything, she was pleased he and Malik were finally bonding over something.

After a few seconds Malik put her out of her misery by tracing his fingers across a set of grooves in the rock. They were three horizontal lines bisected by one vertical line. Once you knew it was there the marks did look man-made, but to the casual observer they could just be another set of cracks made by time and the elements.

'The sign of the high place,' Malik explained. 'Left as a marker to guide us to the high place.'

'I still can't see where we climb,' Rachel said, studying the walls of the gorge.

'Aahil, would you like to guide us?'

Aahil turned to his father, his eyes wide. 'Really, Father?'

'Really. I know you can do it.'

Malik stepped back beside Rachel as together they watched Aahil start his search. Rachel felt proud at the systematic way he studied the rock face, running his hand over the amber-coloured rock, taking a step back to observe the different cracks and crannies.

'Are you sure he'll find it?' Rachel whispered, knowing Aahil would be devastated if he thought he had failed.

'He'll find it,' Malik said confidently, turning to her briefly to give her a reassuring smile before refocusing his attention back on his son.

Rachel tried to concentrate on Aahil's search as well, but she felt distracted by the man beside her. He had so many sides to him, so many hidden depths. To see him now, encouraging his son to grasp a piece of his heritage, bolstering the young boy's confidence at the same time, you would never believe a few weeks ago he barely spent any time with his children. The transformation was incredible and Rachel knew that she had played some part in that.

The only problem was she couldn't help feeling as though Malik's transformation was a double-edged sword. She loved that he was taking an interest in his children, but this trait, this man he was now, was a man it was difficult not to be attracted to. He was powerful and confident, handsome and charming, and he was turning into a good father. In reality he didn't even have to be the best father ever, it was the fact that he was trying so hard to give his children what they needed. It didn't matter if he made a few mistakes along the way.

The cold and distant Sheikh Rachel had met a few weeks ago might have been handsome and confident, but Rachel would have had no trouble resisting a smouldering look from that man. But if Malik turned to her now and moved towards her in that possessive way of his, she doubted she'd have the strength to push him away, whatever her best intentions.

Not for the first time since they'd shared their kiss in the sunken garden Rachel considered her position. She questioned whether it really would be so bad to fall for the Sheikh, whether any romance would truly be doomed.

With an inner sigh she knew it would. She loved the three children in her care, even after just a few short weeks, and she knew that if she and Malik became romantically entangled she would not be able to focus her attention on Aahil, Ameera and Hakim. Her childhood had been marred by the adults in her life arguing and putting their needs first, and the royal children didn't deserve the same. They'd already lost their mother; they needed stability from her and Malik, not a passionate affair with a painful aftermath.

Rachel found herself blushing at the idea of an affair with Malik. She wasn't naive enough to think there could be anything more between them. Malik's first wife had been from the second most powerful family of Huria, a woman brought up to be Queen. Rachel had been brought up to be a governess and in real life governesses did not get the powerful and charismatic man for more than a short affair. Still, as she watched Malik encouraging his son, Rachel couldn't help wondering what even a short affair with this surprising man might be like.

'Here. It's here!' Aahil exclaimed after a few minutes. He'd walked a few paces to the left, rounding a natural curve in the rock face and almost disappearing from view.

'Brilliant,' Malik said, grabbing Rachel's hand and pulling her forward. Hakim and Ameera were already crowding behind their older brother trying to see what he had seen.

As Rachel slipped into the crevice in the gorge wall, her body dangerously close to Malik's, she saw what Aahil had seen. Carved into the rock face, carefully hidden from view, was a roughly hewn set of stairs zig-zagging steeply upwards.

Malik regarded their little group as if trying to decide the best way to proceed.

'Aahil, you will go first. I will go behind you, then Hakim, then Ameera and then Miss Talbot at the back.'

Rachel saw Ameera pull a face, but before she could say anything Malik held up a placating hand.

'The stairs are steep and worn in places, Ameera, and Hakim is still quite small. I will need to help him over the rough areas. You can help Miss Talbot, she isn't used to the desert terrain.'

As Ameera lost her defiant look Malik caught Rachel's eye and quickly winked at her. Rachel couldn't help but smile in return, wondering whether the royal advisors and palace secretaries would recognise the Sheikh with his current demeanour.

They began to climb, slowly rising up the edge of the gorge, tracing a path backwards and forward along the cliff edge. Their progress was steady, although a few times the group had to stop when the path became a little too uneven for Hakim to keep his balance and Malik had to effortlessly hoist him on to his shoulders.

They had been climbing for nearly twenty minutes when Aahil at the front of the group paused.

'Father,' he called out, sounding unsure.

Rachel watched as Malik set Hakim down on the path and moved forward. She wondered how many times he had climbed this same route. He seemed confident on the rocky terrain, never stumbling or missing a step, but she wasn't sure if that was because he was a frequent visitor or if a childhood spent in the desert meant he had traversed many routes like this one.

For her part Rachel climbed slowly but surely, never looking back. Luckily she wasn't afraid of heights. Sometimes at school, when the chatter of the other girls had got too much for her, Rachel had climbed up to the attic, pushed open one of the rickety windows and sat on the ledge looking out over the Wiltshire country-side. She had found the height and the small sense of danger refreshing and when she climbed back down she always felt renewed. After Grace had gone through the trauma of giving birth and having to give her baby away, Rachel had shown her friend her special place and often the two girls had sat up there together, hold-ing hands and taking solace from the peace.

'Ah,' Malik said. 'We have a small problem.'

Rachel craned her neck to try and see what had caused them to halt. Ahead of Aahil the path seemed to have completely disappeared, instead there was a mound of rocks blocking their path.

'Do we have to turn back?' Aahil asked, looking devastated.

Malik shook his head. 'It'll just take us a little lon-ger. I'll go first. Aahil, you come with me. Once we've mapped out a route I'll come back for Hakim, Ameera and Miss Talbot.'

Father and son began their scramble over the rocks. They were only out of view for a minute before Malik returned without Aahil.

'It's only a short distance,' he reassured them. 'Climb on, Hakim.'

Rachel watched as Malik ferried his two younger children across the rockfall. He seemed so at ease with them, and they with him, it was lovely to watch. Once all three royal children were safe on the other side Malik reappeared.

'Your turn,' he said.

Rachel didn't move, wondering what he had planned. She thought she could probably manage the scramble over, especially if Aahil had, but Malik looked as though he were preparing to carry her.

Malik held out a hand and Rachel stepped forward uncertainly.

'I can carry you if you're nervous,' he said quietly, his strong hand gripping hers reassuringly.

Rachel hesitated only a moment before shaking her head. She didn't need to be carried, however tempting the thought.

'Shame,' she thought she heard Malik mutter, but before she could react he was guiding her up over the rockfall.

They reached the top of the collapsed cliff within a minute and Rachel looked around her with awe. Although half the horizon was blocked by the gently sloping rock rising up ahead of them, the view behind was spectacular. She peered down into the gorge they had left the camels waiting in and marvelled at the vibrant rock face they had just climbed. In the distance she could make out the rolling sand dunes, shimmering in the heat of the morning.

'One last scramble and we're there,' Malik said, his eyes flashing with excitement.

Rachel had never seen him so animated, so enthusiastic, and she could tell the children were loving this side of their father, too.

They set off up the gently sloping, smooth rock, and not for the first time Rachel was glad she was wearing Malik's breeches. There was no way she would have made it this far in her cumbersome dress and she would have been devastated if she'd had to stay at the bottom of the gorge.

Carefully Rachel followed Malik, gripping Ameera's

hand tightly in case the young girl should slip. Up ahead Malik had hoisted Hakim on to his shoulders and in front of them Aahil was proudly leading the way.

As they mounted the crest of the rock Rachel couldn't help but draw in a sharp breath; the view from up here was incredible. She could see for miles in every direction, only the haze from the heat obscuring the far horizon.

'It's beautiful,' Rachel murmured to herself.

Quickly she caught up with Malik and the children, to see them all gathered around a large, flat stone.

'The high place,' whispered Aahil, as if he couldn't quite believe he was there.

Malik drew his children to him, and motioned for Rachel to draw closer as well.

'The high place of sacrifice,' Malik said reverently.

Rachel felt a chill travel down here spine. The large, flat stone did look like it could be a sacrificial altar. Its position, so high above the desert, certainly meant they were closer to any gods in the heavens.

'Many, many years ago our ancestors likely sacrificed animals and left offerings of food here to gain the blessing of the gods,' Malik said. 'But for centuries our family has been the sole guardians of the location of this sacred place. We come here to ask for our ancestors' blessing and guidance for any journey we are to make.'

He motioned for them all to join hands, then spoke a few sentences in Hurian.

Rachel felt the tears begin to well in her eyes at the sentimentality of the moment. Malik had included her in this trip to his most sacred place, an honour indeed for someone who wasn't part of the family. Just standing here, looking out over the rolling orange sands, Rachel could feel the centuries of tradition bearing down on her and wondered what it felt like to be part of something that was bigger than yourself. She could see much of Malik's self-assurance sprang from the fact that he had a strong sense of belonging. Rachel had never really experienced that. Home had always been lonely without her parents and, despite her wonderful friends, school wasn't a place where you really felt as though you belonged. She'd always wanted to travel, to see the world and not be tied down by the normal constraints of a young lady's existence, but right now Rachel wondered whether she was missing out on something. A place to call home, somewhere she truly belonged.

She was shaken from her reverie by Malik stepping back to stand beside her.

'Thank you,' she said softly.

'What for?'

'For including me.'

A puzzled look dawned on Malik's face and he said, more to himself than to her, 'I didn't ever consider not bringing you here with us.'

The climb back down into the bed of the gorge was quick now Rachel and the children had grown in confidence and their steps over the uneven terrain were surer.

Malik allowed Aahil to lead the way again. He could see how much it meant to his eldest son to be given the responsibility and honour of leading their party, and Malik realised that he needed to encourage this aspect of his son's personality. Aahil would make a wonderful Sheikh one day and already he was eager to learn everything he could about his country and his heritage.

Malik was quiet on the descent from the high place, his mind preoccupied with Rachel's words and his response to them. He supposed he should have considered bringing his children here alone, but somehow that didn't seem right. In just a few weeks Rachel had become such an integral part of their lives, and Malik knew all three of his children followed him with confidence because Rachel was smiling her encouragement behind them.

He knew he had to address the consequences of this realisation, but something held him back. He didn't want to examine his feelings too closely—he was afraid of what he might discover.

Malik glanced back over his shoulder, watching as Rachel held Ameera's hand over a particularly uneven set of steps, and realised he had never once contemplated bringing his late wife to the high place. Not that she would have deigned to accompany him on a trip like this. In the nine years they were married Malik could count on one hand the number of times she had left her set of rooms at the palace. But the fact remained he had never wanted to bring her here either. The high place was special, sacred, and only a select few knew of its location. He hadn't wanted his thoughts of a place so dear to him to be marred by his wife's unavoidable low mood, but he'd had no qualms with Rachel.

He doubted that Rachel had ever had a truly depressing thought in her whole life. Her entire outlook was sunny, optimistic, and cheerfulness was woven through her personality. She didn't mar his positive thoughts of the high place, she enhanced them.

There was the temptation to build his relationship with Rachel into something much more. Already he desired her, but more than that he admired her. He admired her self-confidence, her happy demeanour and her ability to bring out the best in his children. She had all the qualities of a good governess, but Malik knew some part of him wanted her to be more than that.

With an exhalation of frustration Malik shook his head. He'd tried to build a relationship once before and look what that had got him: nine years of misery and a wife who had barely spoken to him. If he pursued something more with Rachel he might satisfy his short-term desire for intimacy and affection, but he could not see a future for them. He would just succeed in driving Rachel away, and his children would suffer because he could not keep control of his urges.

It would be difficult to live side by side with her in the palace, seeing her every day, noticing every one of her different smiles and feeling a quickening of desire inside when she directed those smiles at him, but that would be better than acting on those desires and driving away the best thing that had happened to his children in years.

For a moment Malik's mind rebelled. It asked him why he could not have Rachel without ultimately driving her away, but reason soon prevailed. Malik knew someone in his position was not destined for love. He would focus on his duty, as his father had before him, and his grandfather before him.

As they reached the bottom of the gorge and Malik

held up his hand to help Rachel down the last big step, his eyes flickered down to the tight riding breeches and the curve of her thighs just visible underneath her tunic. Silently he cursed Wahid—his old friend had made it that much more difficult to focus on his duty right now.

'Let's get you all remounted,' Malik said, trying to pull his attention away from Rachel and her curvaceous anatomy.

One by one he helped his children back into their saddles and made sure they were all secure. Once the three camels were standing he turned to Rachel.

'Are you ready?' he asked.

Already she was eyeing the camel less nervously than she had done on their outward trip.

Gently Malik boosted her up, watching as Rachel threw her leg over the camel's back and settled herself in the saddle.

'We'll have you racing in no time,' he said, keeping his expression serious.

'Racing?' Rachel asked, her voice quivering slightly.

'Yes, the camels go rather fast, they can outrun even a desert-bred horse.'

He broke out into a grin as she gripped the pommel tighter and after a few seconds was rewarded with a reciprocal smile.

'You're teasing me.'

Malik shrugged. 'It's true, the camels can outrun a horse over the desert terrain, but I promise I won't make you race on your first day. Maybe tomorrow.'

As Malik swung himself up on to the camel's back he felt a little giddy and carefree. It wasn't often he managed to get out of the palace and when he did it was normally for official visits. He couldn't remember the last time he had been out in the desert without any escort at all. It was rather liberating and for a few moments he felt like a normal family man, taking his children on a regular trip.

Malik loved Huria and he loved his role as leader of the small desert kingdom, but he had to admit sometimes it was a little stifling. He knew he had let his responsibilities as a father slide because of his determination to do the best for Huria, but he hoped he was beginning to balance the needs of his children with the needs of his country.

A little mutinous voice in his head asked what about *his* needs, but Malik quashed the thought before it could get hold. He was a father and a Sheikh, he didn't have time for anything else. Especially anything as distracting as Rachel.

They met up with the rest of their travelling party after about an hour's ride. Malik had been content to listen to his children chatter on about the high place, the excitement of the climb and the thrill of trekking through the desert on camelback. Every so often he glanced at Rachel and saw she was watching the three children indulgently, too. Only once did their eyes meet and a mutual understanding passed between them. Today was Aahil, Ameera and Hakim's day. It was about showing them their heritage, but most of all showing them they were loved and cherished.

'Let's stop for refreshments before we set out into the desert proper,' Malik suggested.

The servants had set up a small tent, scattered with

comfortable pillows, for refreshments to be served in out of the sun.

Carefully Malik helped each of his children down from their camels, and then turned to Rachel. Already she was more confident, sitting straighter in the saddle and relaxing her grip on the reins. She must have been listening to the commands Malik used to control the beasts, for before Malik could instruct her camel to lower to the ground, she had uttered the word and was lurching forward and backwards before slipping out of the saddle.

'You have a talent for languages,' Malik said, taking her arm and escorting her into the tent.

He ensured Rachel and his three children were settled on the cushions before taking his seat beside them.

'Miss Talbot is studying our language,' he said to his children, 'so we must help her.'

Rachel smiled and Malik wondered when he had begun to feel so at ease in this situation. He was comfortable and happy, and it was lovely not to want to pass his children back to someone else when he ran out of things to say to them. He wondered how he could have ever run out of things to say to them in the first place.

'Why don't we all pick a word to teach Miss Talbot, something important to each of you, or something you want to say to her?' he suggested.

All three children fell silent, pondering which word they would choose to teach their governess.

'Dragon,' Hakim said, repeating the word in Hurian.

Rachel ruffled his hair, but carefully repeated his chosen word.

'Dancer,' Ameera chose next.

'Tradition,' Aahil said.

Rachel carefully repeated the three words before turning to Malik.

'Your turn,' she said.

'Thank you,' he said in Hurian, holding her gaze.

Chapter Thirteen

Rachel's body ached all over. She felt as though she had spent the day being beaten with a club, but she didn't regret one moment of it. Their camel ride through the desert had been an incredible experience, something she had only dreamed of when she had been in England not so many months ago. The camels were gentle but stubborn beasts, difficult to control if they sensed you were nervous, but once you relaxed into their loping gait they were fun to ride. Rachel had even allowed Malik to goad her into a short race across the sand dunes and, although she had lost terribly, she hadn't fallen off.

Now it was late afternoon and she was eager to stretch her legs and relax with a refreshing drink.

'Our camp will be set up just over the next dune,' Malik said, as if reading her mind.

Rachel sat a little straighter in the saddle and strained to see over the top of the rolling sand dune. As they reached the top she could make out the fluttering of the tents in the distance.

'We should be there before sundown,' Malik said.

Night came early in the desert, bringing with it the darkness and unexpected chill. Rachel knew Malik would have prepared for the drop in temperature, but was curious to see how they did it. She wondered if they would spend the evening sitting round a fire, or wrapped up in blankets. As they neared the camp Rachel felt herself smiling; this was just the sort of adventure she had always dreamed of.

'Careful,' Malik warned as they stopped in front of the largest tent. 'Your legs will be stiff after the day's ride.'

Rachel heeded his warning and waited a moment after her camel had sunk to the ground to get off. As she swung her legs over the animal's back Malik was at her side, taking her arm and guiding her towards the tent.

'Your Majesty,' Wahid said, appearing beside them before they had even taken a few steps. 'We may have a problem.'

Immediately Rachel let go of Malik's arm and gathered the children to her. She wasn't sure of the nature of this problem, but Wahid wasn't easily flustered and right now he looked worried.

'It's a little sensitive,' Wahid said, taking the Sheikh's arm and guiding him away from the tents.

Looking back over her shoulder, Rachel could not hear the words that passed between the two men, but she saw some of the colour drain from Malik's face and watched him run a hand distractedly through his hair. He stood still for a few seconds, as if deciding on the best course of action, then Rachel was surprised to see a flash of anger cross his face. He issued an order to Wahid, who looked a little surprised, then Malik strode back towards the tents with a determined air about him.

'Is there a problem?' Rachel asked.

Malik shook his head, his every movement short and sharp, and tinged with irritation.

'Family,' he snorted in exasperation.

Without any further explanation Malik ushered them into the largest tent where a spacious sitting area was set up, strewn with comfortable cushions, thick woollen blankets and an assortment of animal furs. Rachel felt as though she had walked into the most luxurious tent in the world.

The children were all quiet, as if picking up on their father's tension, and they instinctively huddled in closer to Rachel. As they sat Hakim snuggled into one side and Ameera her other, both children watching their father warily.

A servant appeared, bringing refreshing glasses of lemon and mint, and set down plates of sweet biscuits and dried fruit in front of them. Before anyone could reach for any of the delicious-looking display a man in his thirties was led into the tent by Wahid. He was well dressed and pristinely groomed, but there was something a little wild-looking about him that made Rachel instinctively pull Ameera and Hakim closer to her.

Rachel watched as Malik took a long sip of his drink before greeting the man.

'Omar,' Malik said eventually, 'what a pleasant surprise. It must be ten months since we last saw each other.' To Rachel's surprise Malik addressed the man called Omar in English and she wondered if it was a technique he employed to put his visitor on the back foot.

'Your Majesty,' Omar responded with a deep bow. However, his demeanour belied the animosity between the two men.

'Please sit, share a drink with us,' Malik said.

Rachel remembered what Malik had told her of Hurian hospitality before their trip to Talir; he was almost honour-bound to offer this man some refreshments after his journey.

'I wish to speak with you,' Omar said, ignoring the offer to sit.

Malik spread his arms in a show of openness. 'Go ahead.'

Omar shot a glance at Rachel and she found she had to make an effort not to squirm under his stony glare. Instead she adopted a demeanour of serenity and smiled sweetly at this rude man.

'In private.'

'We are in private, there are no advisors or guards to overhear us.'

Omar glanced at Rachel again.

'Miss Talbot is my children's governess. She is an important part of my household. My children stay and Miss Talbot stays.' Rachel could tell Malik was beginning to lose patience with this interloper and knew it wouldn't be long until he was ordered away.

'I would like a word in private,' Omar repeated stubbornly.

Malik's entire body went still and the smile faded from his face.

'Omar, I am making many concessions for you because of our connection, but I am on a private family trip and want to focus on my children. I will order you to leave and as your Sheikh you would be law-bound to obey me. Do not underestimate me.' Malik spoke with steely confidence and Rachel could see the other man diminish in size as Malik spoke.

'A great insult is being felt by my family. The people of Huria are talking, and the subject of the rumours sullies the memory of my sister.'

Rachel watched with interest as the man spoke. She wondered who he was, what connection he had to Malik and what insult he was talking about.

'I am sorry your family is being hurt by rumours.'

Omar shot a look of contempt at the Sheikh before composing himself again.

'You are the subject of the rumours.'

Rachel saw Malik's lips curve up into a measured smile and wondered whether he'd had to practise to get the right amount of amusement and disinterest to show on his face, or whether it came naturally.

'The people will always talk about their rulers,' he said indulgently.

'My sister has been dead for barely a year and you have already taken up with this English hussy. It defiles her memory and it insults our family.'

Rachel felt as though she had been slapped in the face as Omar's finger pointed at her. He was shaking with indignation, his face red and his eyes bulging with the force of his accusation.

'Children,' Malik said calmly, 'go and find Wahid and ask him to start building a campfire outside. We will dine under the stars tonight.'

Warily Ameera and Hakim stood and hurried out of the tent. Aahil stayed where he was beside his father.

'Hello, Uncle,' he said quietly.

'Aahil, I need to speak to your uncle, and I would

rather you were not here whilst I did it. I'm afraid I would not set a good example to you. Go and find your brother and sister.'

Aahil nodded and left.

'Would you like me to…?' Rachel began to offer to leave, but Malik shook his head.

'I think this matter concerns you, so stay, please.'

When Malik spoke in such a commanding voice Rachel knew she didn't really have a choice in the matter.

'So there are rumours about me and Miss Talbot?' Malik asked mildly. 'What do they say?'

Omar looked from Malik to Rachel and back again.

'Please, tell us. You were so eager a moment ago.'

'They say you have taken an English whore as your concubine and that you sully the memory of my sister with a woman of ill repute.'

Malik turned to Rachel and raised an eyebrow.

'*They* have been saying quite a lot, it would seem,' he said, his tone still jovial.

Omar's lips pressed together until they formed a thin pink line.

'There is no need to mock me, Your Highness.'

Rachel saw the moment Malik froze and she felt her own blood turn to ice. She knew then that Malik's brother-in-law would not leave the tent unscathed.

'I thought more of you, Omar,' Malik said, his voice still low and soft. 'I respected you, but it seems I was wrong.'

Omar flushed a little, but held the Sheikh's eye.

'Miss Talbot is my children's governess, she is a cherished and integral part of our family, and your comments concerning her virtue have offended me deeply.'

'I was only repeating rumours, Your Highness.'

'You uttered the words, Omar, take responsibility for them.'

Omar was starting to sag a little as if he had realised his outburst could only have a bad outcome for him.

'It is small-minded and petty to believe rumours about Miss Talbot's moral character. In my mind that is as great an insult as if I called your mother or sister a whore. I have selected Miss Talbot carefully as the person to guide my children through their young lives and into adulthood. To suggest that I would choose someone who had anything less than an impeccable reputation also insults me.'

Omar took a step back as Malik continued.

'I was greatly honoured by the joining of our ancient and noble families when I married your sister, but she is dead, which weakens our link considerably. Do not think we are close enough for you to insult me in such a way and for our relationship to remain unscathed.'

Rachel watched as the blood drained from Omar's face and the man held out his hands in supplication.

'I will not sever all connection with you and your family for the sake of my children, but let me be clear, I will not forget what you said here today.'

Malik stood and strode to the entrance to the tent, holding open one flap.

'I am offended and hurt by your accusations and your actions today, Omar, but frankly I'm more shocked at your impudence. Whilst I was married to your sister I took my marriage vows very seriously, even if she did not, but now she is gone I am free to do as I choose. If I wish, I could import concubines from every continent and it would be none of your business.'

Omar nodded, wringing his hands.

'Now leave, and think very carefully before coming to me again.'

Malik's ex-brother-in-law shuffled out of the tent backwards, bowing as he went.

Rachel watched as Malik let out a long breath and allowed his shoulders to sag.

'I'm sorry if he offended you,' he said softly.

Rachel shook her head. 'You were magnificent.'

Malik stood for a few moments, then returned to the cushions and sank down beside her.

'I have never been able to see eye to eye with Omar. He is a righteous, pompous man who acts before he thinks and then runs away from the consequences. He is a hard man to respect.'

'He was your wife's brother.'

Malik nodded. 'He's the head of the family now her father is dead. I pity the rest of them, with Omar at the helm the Saddiqi family's power and riches will likely dwindle.'

'Do you think there really are rumours?' Rachel asked.

Malik turned to her and smiled, and Rachel sensed him relax a little.

'Of course. There will be rumours that we are lovers. There will be rumours that you are the wife of the English King and have run away to be with me. There will be rumours that you are my secret love child even though we are not of such a dissimilar age. There will be rumours that you are English, French, Italian, African.'

Rachel smiled as he ticked off each rumour on his fingers.

'People love to gossip and they love to gossip most about their rulers. You have brought the people of Huria an endless supply of possibilities and speculation.'

Rachel smiled. She supposed it wasn't truly a bad thing, although the thought of having people talk about her, speculate about her relationship with the Sheikh, felt a little surreal. She'd never been anyone important, never been interesting enough to be the subject of anyone's gossip before.

'You don't mind?' Rachel asked.

Malik shrugged. 'Speculation and rumour had been part of my life for so long I barely even notice it.'

Rachel was suddenly struck by how different Malik's life had been to hers. He had never known anonymity, every trip he took had to be pre-planned and every place he visited he was surrounded by a group of guards. He couldn't just pop out to the market if something took his fancy, or stop to talk to an interesting old lady on the street. Despite his riches and his power Rachel felt a little sorry for him. Malik might be Sheikh of Huria, but he didn't have true freedom.

Chapter Fourteen

The sun was just beginning to dip lower in the sky as Malik rounded up his children and escorted them to the small campfire Wahid was building. Rachel was sitting on the ground, passing pieces of wood to Wahid when he needed them and talking quietly to the older man. For a moment Malik was struck by Rachel's serenity and he wondered how many women would be as calm as she was after hearing the rumours Omar had been repeating.

Inside Malik was still a maelstrom of emotions from his confrontation with his ex-brother-in-law. Everything he had told Rachel was true—Omar was a fool and an impetuous one at that, but even so Malik didn't want the rest of Aliyyah's family hurt by the rumours. More importantly he didn't want this trip with his children to be spoiled by Omar's rude interruption.

'Come and sit down,' Wahid said. 'Pick a spot close to the fire, it'll get cold once the sun goes down.'

Immediately Hakim went and cuddled in next to Rachel, and Malik was struck by a sudden wave of sentimentality as she pulled the small boy in closer to her. She'd make a good mother; she had so much love for his children and they weren't even her own blood. Malik knew governesses generally didn't marry and have families of their own, but for Rachel to stay single and not be someone's mother would be a great shame.

He was surprised at his thoughts, but he knew they were driven by images of his wife with their children. Aliyyah had loved Aahil, Ameera and Hakim, Malik was sure of it, but she hadn't really been in a position to demonstrate her love. So much of her life had been consumed by the blackness that crept over her mood, she'd never picked Hakim up for a cuddle or danced around the courtyard with Ameera. Sometimes Malik wondered if he could have made things better, but deep down he knew Aliyyah's sadness sprung from something even he could not fix. He could have been a better husband, more attentive, but after years of trying to coax his wife out of her rooms Malik had given up. He'd focused on running Huria, on devoting his life to his kingdom, and Aliyyah had hardly noticed when he had stopped visiting her bedchamber or when the invitations to dine with him had dried up. There were only so many years a man could take rejection before he hardened his heart and turned to other things to occupy him.

Malik knew that some of his undeniable attraction for Rachel sprung from the fact that she was always happy. It was hard to imagine her sobbing in her bedchamber or refusing to get dressed for days on end. For Malik it was refreshing to have someone living in the palace who cherished life as much as he did.

'I'm sorry you had to leave,' Malik said to his children. He knew his next words, how he handled this entire situation, were important. As much as he disliked Omar, he didn't want to separate his children from their family. He needed to reassure them whilst explaining a little about why their uncle had been so upset.

'Why was Uncle Omar angry?' Ameera asked. She had remained standing whilst her brothers sat. Malik couldn't help but smile to himself. Even at the age of six Ameera was a force to be reckoned with. He loved how his daughter spat fire if she thought something was unfair and was never content to lay down and let someone deceive her.

'Uncle Omar is still very upset about your mother's death,' Malik said, choosing his words carefully.

He glanced at Rachel and found her looking at him with her wide, encouraging eyes and immediately he knew what he had to do.

'Come here, all of you,' Malik said, pulling his children in towards him as he sat. Even Rachel moved closer, which pleased Malik more than it should. 'I know in the past few months I haven't spoken much about your mother, but it has been a difficult time for all of us and maybe it would make us all feel better if we remembered her a little tonight.'

All his children looked up at him in surprised silence, and Malik realised that since Aliyyah's death he hadn't spoken to his children once about their mother. They must have so many questions, so many unspoken emotions, and he'd left them to deal with it on their own.

'Do you have any questions about your mother?' he asked.

There was silence. Eventually Rachel shifted and spoke.

'I'd like to know how you met,' she said. 'Did you always know you were to be married, what did you think when you first saw her?'

Malik caught Rachel's eye and smiled gratefully. He wondered how she always knew what to say. Her question was innocuous, unlikely to dredge up any bad memories, and a good way to help his children understand a little more about their mother.

'We met when I was eight years old and Aliyyah was six. Our fathers had just signed the betrothal contract and we had a dinner with all the noble families of Huria to celebrate. Your mother was beautiful even then. She looked very much like you, Ameera, although she was a little taller.'

'Were you angry your father had decided who you would marry?' Ameera asked.

Malik looked at his daughter's mutinous expression and had to hold back a laugh. He wondered what his little warrior Princess would do if she was betrothed to a boy she barely knew. He didn't think the outcome would be positive.

'I didn't know any different. All my life my father had told me I would marry a daughter of one of the noble families, I just accepted it as part of my life.'

'I wouldn't just accept it if someone told me who to marry,' Ameera said, making sure her views on the matter were clear.

'I wouldn't dream of forcing you to marry anyone, Princess,' Malik said, planting a kiss on the top of her head.

'Why was Mama sad all the time?' Aahil asked quietly.

Malik turned to his eldest son and saw the pain and confusion behind his eyes. Ameera and Hakim had only been five and three when their mother had died and probably already many of their memories of her were slipping away. However, Aahil had lived for seven years with his mother's mood swings and unintentional neglect. He remembered his mother as she'd actually been, not the rose-tinted caricature Ameera and Hakim had spun in their minds.

He wondered how best to answer his son, knowing all his children were far too young to know the full truth, but also realising he did not want to lie to them. Aliyyah had been their mother—in a way she meant more to them than she had ever done to him.

'Your mother was very often sad,' Malik said, choosing his words carefully. 'Even as a young girl I don't remember her laughing or playing much, not like the three of you.'

It was something Malik had watched for carefully in his children, this tendency towards melancholy, but thankfully he had not detected it in any of them so far.

'But when we got older, when it was time to marry and move to the palace, your mother missed her family very much.'

There was so much more to it than that, but his children did not need to know their mother had pined for another man. Malik himself hadn't known the depth of Aliyyah's feelings, otherwise he wouldn't have gone through with the marriage, but as time passed it had become apparent Aliyyah's heart and mind were fully occupied elsewhere. By then it had been too late, of course, Malik and Aliyyah were married and Aliyyah had to give up on the man she loved, which had eventually proved impossible.

Malik caught Rachel's eye and felt a surge of confidence. Although she remained silent Malik could sense her approval at how he was handling the situation. This was what it must feel like not to have to deal with everything on your own, to have someone to back you up through the important moments in life.

'Will we get a new mummy?' Hakim asked, his voice thick with exhaustion after the long day's ride.

The question startled Malik, who had been poised to answer the most awkward and difficult queries about their mother, but not about himself.

'Well…' Malik started, not sure what to say.

'I'd like a mummy. Someone to kiss me at night. Someone like Miss Talbot.'

Rachel and Malik's eyes locked over Hakim's sleepy head and a spark flared between them. Suddenly Malik was reminded of all the reasons he admired his children's governess and couldn't remember any of his arguments for keeping his distance.

In the slightly awkward silence that followed Malik found himself considering Hakim's question. It was just over a year since Aliyyah had died and he was officially out of mourning. If he wished to he could get married tomorrow, but every time one of his advisors brought up the subject, suggesting some political match or other, Malik had shaken his head and put an end to any speculation.

The truth was he was still reeling from Aliyyah's

death. Even a year on, despite not being particularly close to his wife, he was still mourning. He wasn't sure if he was still mourning Aliyyah, or if in fact he was mourning the loss of his innocence and hopes she took with her. If Malik was honest with himself he felt angry and betrayed at the circumstances surrounding his late wife's death and he wasn't sure if he could ever trust anyone to allow them into his life and his heart.

He risked another glance at Rachel, who was gazing into the dancing flames of the fire and stroking Hakim's hair absentmindedly. Malik felt the all-too-familiar surge of desire as he watched her and he wondered if this was a sign that he had been without a female companion for too long. Maybe he did need a wife, someone to share his bed and share his burdens, someone to stop him from fantasising about his children's governess.

'Why did Mama die?' Ameera asked, shaking him from his reverie.

Malik found himself clearing his throat nervously and studying his daughter. He wanted to make sure the question was innocent, that there was no deeper probing behind it. He hoped none of his children were old enough to begin to understand what he suspected, but he knew sometimes a child could be especially intuitive.

'Your mother got lost in the desert,' Malik said softly, 'and she couldn't find her way home.'

'What was she doing in the desert all alone?' Ameera persisted.

'She liked to walk alone to gather her thoughts,' Malik lied. Despite wanting to be honest with his children there were some things they just didn't need to know.

'You won't ever leave me in the desert, will you?' Hakim asked, his voice slurring with tiredness.

'I won't ever leave any of you in the desert,' Malik said firmly.

Chapter Fifteen

Rachel shifted under the heap of blankets and moved carefully away from Ameera's sleeping body. She didn't want to wake the young girl with her tossing and turning, but she knew she would struggle to get to sleep.

The conversation from the campfire earlier that evening kept floating into her head and an image of Malik's pained face as he talked about his late wife was seared into her mind. Something terrible had happened to this little family, something they hadn't recovered from even a year on. Rachel realised the children had been shielded from the worst by their age, but the events of the past year had caused Malik to retreat into himself and strengthen his defences so no one could penetrate easily.

Sitting up, Rachel wondered what life would have been like for Malik, living with a wife who didn't want to be married to him. Although he had never come out and said Aliyyah was unhappy in the marriage, Rachel only had to look at Malik to know he had never been properly loved.

It was heartbreaking, really. Malik was a good man, he was principled and generous, but he had never known the warmth love could bring. From his comments about his parents Rachel knew his father had been distant and formal, even if he cared for his son, and his mother had died giving birth to Malik. Rachel knew the pain from having distant parents, but she had been loved. She loved her friends Joanna, Isabel and Grace as though they were her sisters and they had loved her back. She doubted Malik had anyone like that.

It was hard to fathom, though, because Malik would be an easy man to love. Behind the formal exterior and serious demeanour was a kind heart and a man who could admit his mistakes, which was a rare quality indeed. Rachel only had to look at the progress he'd made with his children over the last few weeks to know he was a man unafraid to address his weaknesses.

Malik would certainly be an easy man to love, an easy man for her to love.

Rachel stiffened as she mulled over this latest thought. Surely she didn't love Malik. She respected him, liked him and would even go so far as to say she desired him, but love was too big a step. Love implied either settling down into a married life or tremendous heartbreak, or most likely both. Rachel had always vowed she would protect herself from heartbreak by not opening herself up to love, but sitting here, in the middle of the desert with only a fabric tent between her and the stars, Rachel wondered whether she had been naive, whether she didn't have much choice in the matter after all.

Careful not to disturb Ameera, Rachel stood and

made her way out of the tent. She needed some water and she needed some fresh air. Hopefully that would help her gain control of her thoughts and work out what she really felt.

It was dark out, darker than she had ever known a night in England, but after a few moments her eyes adjusted and she could just about see the ground in front of her by the soft light of the moon. She picked her way over to the main tent, away from the sleeping tents, and was just about to lift the flap to enter when a warm body collided with hers.

'Rachel.' Malik's deep voice rumbled in her ear.

She looked up, but couldn't make out his expression in the darkness.

'I was just getting some water,' she said, trying to hide the fact that her heart was beating double its normal speed.

Malik held something up in the air. 'So was I.'

They stood in silence for almost a minute, neither knowing what to say, but neither wanting to leave the other and return to their tent.

'Will you come and sit with me by the fire?' Malik asked eventually. 'I'm finding it difficult to sleep.'

Rachel took his proffered arm and allowed him to lead the way to the smouldering fire. Only the embers were left now, but it still leant some warmth to the chilly night air. She felt nervous, on edge, as if something momentous was about to happen. She wondered if Malik could feel her pounding heart through her skin, but knew he was likely to be oblivious to her heightened sensitivity.

They sat for some moments, side by side, staring into the glowing embers. Malik, always quiet, seemed particularly contemplative this evening. Rachel wondered whether she should say something, try and reassure him he had done the right thing by allowing his children some insight into their mother's life, but she sensed he would begin speaking when he was ready.

'I've never spoken to you about Aliyyah, have I?' Malik asked eventually.

Rachel shook her head. She had heard snippets of rumour and chatter from the palace servants, but Malik had been understandably close-lipped about his late wife.

'I don't often speak of her. I wonder if the children notice.'

Rachel remembered Aahil's wide eyes as he asked why his mother was always sad and Ameera's probing questions as she quizzed her father about why her mother had died. She thought that despite their young age the children knew something had been wrong in the palace. They would have noticed Malik's reluctance to remember the years he spent married and the lack of emotion as he spoke of her death.

'I think they realise it was a great loss for you as well as them,' Rachel said diplomatically.

Malik shook his head sadly. 'Is it bad if I say I don't miss Aliyyah?'

Rachel wondered how you could be married to someone for nine years and not miss them when they were gone. She knew Malik had a soft heart under his stern exterior—how could he not mourn his wife?

'I never really had her in the first place.' Malik sighed and Rachel felt his body sag under the weight of his emotional baggage. She realised he had probably not spoken to anyone about his feelings since Aliy-yah's death—he didn't have anyone he could speak to.

Tentatively Rachel reached out and took Malik's hand. He stiffened for a moment, then allowed himself to relax, entwining his fingers with hers and pulling her forearm to rest on his leg. They sat there for a few moments, both contemplating the secrets Malik was holding close to him, and Rachel knew she wanted to understand what he was thinking and feeling. She could tell herself it was for selfless reasons—that he needed to let go of all his pent-up anger so he could properly connect with his children—but deep down Rachel knew that it wasn't true. She wanted to under-stand him for herself, to reassure herself she hadn't misjudged this man…that he was capable of real emo-tions and wasn't sailing through life without his rela-tionships affecting him one bit.

'Talk to me,' she said softly. 'Tell me about your wife.'

Malik grunted softly, seeming to consider the offer. 'Where to begin?'

'Start at the beginning and tell me everything,' Ra-chel said. 'We've got all night.'

Malik began talking. He told her about his arranged betrothal, the first time he'd set eyes on his wife-to-be, and he told her of the half-a-dozen times they had met during their teenage years.

'Then I went to Europe, of course,' Malik said, a smile dancing over his lips at the memories. 'I for-got about Aliyyah, stuck back here. I knew she'd be waiting when I returned, but I have to admit I didn't spare her a single thought as I sampled what Europe had to offer.'

The idea of Malik enjoying himself during his university years seemed strange to Rachel. She couldn't imagine him as a carefree youth and she had a sneaking suspicion he hadn't been all that carefree with his constant thoughts of bettering himself for the good of his kingdom, but all the same he must have experienced some of the pleasures of student life.

'Whilst I was enjoying myself in Europe, Aliyyah was having an adventure of her own.' Malik paused, as if uncomfortable with what he was about to say next. 'She fell in love. She met a tradesman when her father was having part of his house renovated and they ran away together.'

Rachel felt her eyes widen in surprise. Whatever she had imagined to have happened between Malik and Aliyyah, this hadn't been it.

'Her father found her and brought her home before there was too much of a scandal, and he forbade them to see each other ever again.'

Rachel squeezed Malik's hand and felt him lean towards her slightly. She wondered whether he had ever loved his wife; if so it would be difficult to talk of her affection for another man.

'I returned to Huria and not long after my father passed away. I became Sheikh, took the reins of the kingdom and I felt like it was time to marry and fulfil the next bit of my duty.'

'You didn't know about Aliyyah and this man?' Rachel asked.

Malik shook his head. 'Her father and my father agreed it would be best if the marriage still went ahead. I was never told.' He paused, staring into the glowing embers of the fire. 'I don't know if it would have made a difference if I had known. Marrying Aliyyah was my duty and I assumed she felt the same.'

Rachel wondered what it must be like to be so resigned to your duty. Aliyyah had obviously not taken to it well, but it must have been a burden for Malik as well.

'We married and I knew we were not in love. I never contemplated a love match, but I'd hoped for companionship and mutual support. I'd hoped for a Shaykhah to help me run the kingdom.'

Malik's complete self-sufficiency and isolation must have sprung from this, Rachel realised. For years he had to run the Kingdom of Huria on his own, it would make you used to getting your own way.

'That didn't happen?'

He shook his head. 'Aliyyah barely left her rooms for the nine years we were married. I would visit her at first, sometimes to talk, to try and draw her out, sometimes because I was conscious of my need for an heir.'

Rachel sensed how difficult this was for Malik to admit. He was a Sheikh, a powerful man, irresistible to many, but his wife had chosen to ignore him and lock herself away rather than enjoy his company.

'From the very beginning she was often melancholy, but years of barely leaving the palace made things so much worse.'

'What about when the children were born?' Rachel asked. She could not fathom how someone could not celebrate the birth of their own child, but she did know some women seemed to withdraw into themselves more and found it hard to bond with their newborns.

Malik shook his head sadly. 'I hoped that might be a new start for us, a shared interest, someone for us both to love, but Aliyyah was as distant with me as ever.' He paused before continuing. 'She wasn't a bad mother, in her own way she doted on the children, but she was a little inconsistent. Some days she would play with them, read them their bedtime stories, and other days she would barricade her door and you could hear her sobbing in her room.'

Rachel wondered what it must have been like for him, living with Aliyyah for so long but barely knowing her, being shut out of her life despite all that they shared.

'I tried,' Malik said quietly. 'I tried so many times to make her happy, but after a while I gave up.'

She could sense his feelings of failure and his frustration at not being able to succeed at one of the most important aspects in his life. For such a charismatic and powerful man it must be hard to stomach.

'After years of sending her flowers with an invitation to dinner, just to dine alone, or trying to engage her in talk about the children to be greeted with monosyllabic answers, I moved on. I let Aliyyah wallow deeper in her black moods and I gave up.'

'No,' Rachel said forcefully, 'you can't blame yourself for Aliyyah's moods. Many people seem predisposed to these sorts of depressing thoughts and isolating behaviours. It sounds as though you tried your hardest to engage her, it is only human nature to give up eventually when you don't receive any interaction.'

Malik smiled at her and raised a hand to her cheek, gently running his thumb over her skin.

'My warrior governess,' he said. 'Defending me from myself.'

Rachel reached up and placed her hand over his

own. 'You are your own harshest critic,' she said. 'You're a good man, Malik, and sometimes even the most powerful of us need someone to come out and say nice things about us.'

He held her gaze for a moment, staring into her eyes as if they held all the answers in the world, and for a few seconds Rachel felt powerful herself. Then Malik shook his head and the moment was broken.

'Save making up your mind on your opinion of me until you've heard the rest of the story.'

Rachel sat back and watched as Malik steeled himself to continue. He was finding this difficult, airing his relationship failures to her, but she also sensed it was a little cathartic for him, too. As he spoke he was relaxing a little, allowing his shoulder to roll back and some of the familiar gleam to return to his eyes.

'The next part I've never told anyone.'

Malik wondered why it was so easy to open up to Rachel. He had never had a confidant before. With no brothers or sisters and no close friends whilst he was growing up he'd become accustomed to dealing with his problems on his own. Talking to Rachel, watching as she became indignant on his behalf, defended his actions and did not judge him, was liberating. All the feelings he had kept inside were just spilling out, and it felt good.

'Just over a year ago Aliyyah found out the man she loved died in an accident. I had no idea.'

Malik always wondered if he should have kept a closer eye on Aliyyah's correspondence, but he reasoned he was her husband, not her gaoler. After her death he had found out that she had been in contact with this man for many years, that they had exchanged promises to love one another for eternity even if they were physically kept apart. Sometimes Malik tried to understand how his wife had viewed him, the man she had been forced to marry. If he had known she was in love with someone else, that marriage would make her whole life miserable, Malik liked to think he wouldn't have gone through with the wedding. But he hadn't known and they had married and to him the only thing to do was make the best of it.

'One morning one of her attendants came and found me. She was in a state and at first I could barely understand what she was saying.'

Malik heard the emotion in his own voice and he felt Rachel shift towards him. Her body was pressed up against his and he took comfort from her close presence.

'It turned out Aliyyah had crept out in the night—she'd disappeared.'

Rachel brought a hand to her mouth to stifle a murmur of horror as she foresaw what he was going to say next.

'She'd wandered out into the desert, without any food or water, all alone, dressed only in her nightclothes.' Malik felt the emotion leave his body and his voice become flat. 'We sent out search parties, we searched for days.'

He always felt numb when he thought about how Aliyyah had died. They hadn't been close—in fact, even after nine years of marriage Malik hardly knew anything about his wife—but they had still lived under the same roof, were parents to the same children. Aliyyah would have died in pain and Malik hated that maybe he could have prevented it, if he'd just taken a bit more notice of what his wife was doing.

'After four days we found her, half buried in a sand dune. She'd died of dehydration.'

Malik fell silent. He'd never voiced what he was about to say next, never let the thought leave his head, even though many people knew the truth deep in their hearts.

'We told the world it was a terrible accident—that she'd got lost in the desert and hadn't been able to find her way home...' Malik trailed off, then took a deep breath. 'But deep down I don't think that's true.'

Rachel shifted beside him, raising a hand up to his cheek and turning his head so he was looking at her.

'I think she was so unhappy she didn't want to live any longer.'

Malik felt all the tension he had been carrying start to drain out of him. He'd never admitted out loud that he thought Aliyyah had killed herself, for some reason it had felt like a betrayal of her and a judgement on him, but with Rachel sitting beside him, looking up at him with her understanding eyes, it just felt like the truth. A nasty truth that had been allowed to fester, but the truth all the same.

'You've coped with this all on your own, haven't you?' Rachel asked softly.

Malik nodded. There hadn't been anyone else to confide in. He was sure Aliyyah's family knew the circumstances surrounding her death, but they had been eager to hide the truth, to preserve her memory and avoid the shame that was associated with a suicide.

'You're a strong man, Malik. The strongest I know.'

Suddenly Malik needed to possess her. He wanted

to kiss her and claim her as his own. Rachel's soft words and understanding heart triggered something inside him that made him want to wrap his arms around her and never let her go.

Without saying another word, Malik turned his body and looped his arms around Rachel. Firmly he pulled her towards him, noting how she melted into his body with no resistance whatsoever. In the soft light from the moon he could just make out the curve of her lips and the tilt of her face as she looked up at him.

With a groan of surrender Malik kissed her. He couldn't have resisted if his whole life had depended on it. He covered her lips with his own and felt a surge of desire as she kissed him back. Feverishly he ran his hands over her back, up her neck and tangled his fingers in her hair, pulling at the grips that secured it. He wanted to possess her, to kiss every inch of her body and trail his fingers over her silky smooth skin.

A soft moan escaped Rachel's lips and Malik felt her clutch at his arms, trying to pull him closer. Rachel wasn't a woman who did things in half measures, he thought, wondering what it would be like to strip her naked and lay her down in front of the fire.

Malik pulled away, just enough to start kissing Rachel down the angle of her jaw and on to her neck. He felt her shiver with anticipation as he reached her collarbone, his hands all the time dancing over her back and neck, wishing he could feel more of her bare skin.

'Malik,' she moaned as he kissed the hollow at the base of her throat.

He wanted to strip off her clothes, devour every bit of her body with his eyes, claim her for himself.

Rachel looked at him, her eyes glazed with desire.

It took every bit of Malik's legendary self-control not to scoop her up in his arms and make her his right here in the desert. For a few seconds they both just sat, their breathing heavy and erratic, and looked at one another. Then Rachel pulled further away and shook her head.

'We can't do this,' Rachel said, her voice heavy with uncertainty.

He wanted her badly and he could tell she wanted him. Malik would enjoy nothing more than to lose control and take what he wanted, but he knew he would not let himself. If Rachel could find it in herself to be strong, then so could he. Kissing Rachel again had been unforgivable enough, if he took things further their relationship would be ruined and he would lose her.

Malik knew that part of him was scared of losing Rachel the governess, the woman who in just a few short weeks had made his children blossom and grow. He had a sneaking feeling that he also didn't want to lose Rachel the woman, the one person he could talk to, open up to. If he drove her away, he would go back to having nothing, no one.

'We can't do this,' Rachel repeated quietly before Malik could speak. 'We can't.'

She sounded dejected and sad, and Malik wondered whether they were making the right decision. Surely if they both wanted it so much it couldn't be wrong.

'I need to focus on Huria, on the children,' Malik said, trying to convince himself.

All his life he had been brought up to put his duty before his desires, but right now Malik was questioning that. He kept reminding himself how destructive love and relationships were—he only had to think of

Aliyyah to recognise how her life had been ruined by love. Malik knew his wife would have been happier if she'd never fallen in love, if she'd put her duty to her country and her children before her own wants and desires.

'It's all right,' Rachel said, patting his hand. 'It was only a kiss.'

Suddenly Malik wondered what was giving Rachel such a resigned air. He had Huria and his duty to think of, but he realised something was holding her back as well.

'It's not that I'm not attracted to you,' Malik said, trying to make things better, all the time knowing he was making it worse.

'It's just not meant to be,' Rachel said, more firmly.

They stood, both looking awkwardly, neither knowing whether to say any more or to go their separate ways.

'You would make a fine companion for any man,' Malik said.

Rachel turned to him, a fiery look flaring in her eyes. 'I don't need to be a companion to any man,' she said firmly. 'And you don't need to keep trying to reassure me. I'm a grown woman, I know when something is a bad idea, just like I can take responsibility for my own actions.'

Malik was pleased to see some of Rachel's customary confidence come flooding back. He had to suppress a smile as he realised no one else had ever spoken to him so directly and honestly as Rachel.

'We kissed. Thousands of people do it. Hundreds of thousands. It doesn't mean I'm expecting a marriage proposal and it doesn't mean I'm going to swoon every time I see you.'

Malik nodded gravely, wondering whether he could get away with kissing her one more time. He loved it when she was aroused like this, the passion and self-confidence so many lacked making her into an incredible woman.

'In fact, I plan on returning to my tent and getting some sleep. I suggest you do the same.'

Malik wondered what his advisors and the noblemen of Huria would say if they heard how Rachel spoke to him. Many were very old-fashioned and traditional in their views on women and marriage; they thought their wives existed to make their lives more comfortable, but not to have opinions on anything other than running the household or occasionally on raising the children.

'Tell me one thing before you go,' Malik said, catching hold of Rachel's arm.

She looked at him expectantly.

'If I kissed you again, would you resist?'

Chapter Sixteen

Rachel firmly pulled her arm out of Malik's grasp before she answered his question. Just the heat of his skin against hers made it hard for her to think, but she could never tell him that. She needed to preserve some dignity, to walk away with a modicum of self-respect.

If I kissed you again, would you resist?

'I suggest we don't find out,' Rachel said more coolly than she had imagined was possible.

Holding her head up high, she walked away. She felt the tears begin to well in her eyes and was glad her back was to Malik. She'd hate for him to see her cry, to see that she wasn't as strong as she made out.

The distressing thing was that she didn't even know why she was upset. The kiss had been lovely. No, it had been more than that. It had been passionate and heart-melting and all-encompassing, but then it had ended and Rachel had known that it couldn't happen again. Theirs was not to be a happy ending, she was not destined to marry a prince, or a Sheikh as it might be. She should be glad that Malik was so level-headed about it and that they agreed they should just put the moment behind them, but part of her cried out for something more. All her life she had promised herself she would not get carried away with the notion of love and romance; all her life she had vowed not to let passion make her as selfish and volatile as it had her parents. It had been easy to stick to that vow before Malik, but when he looked at her with his serious eyes and just a flicker of a smile, or when she watched him bend down to talk to one of his children, her heart screamed out in protest. She might have promised herself not to fall in love, but she was having a hard time obeying her own command.

Rachel stopped walking and looked up at the stars. She wished she had someone to talk to, to help her sort her thoughts and feelings out and untangle the raging emotions that kept colliding inside her. She wished Joanna was here with her quiet sensibility and soothing words. Or Grace, indignant on her behalf and spitting fire. Or Isabel, ready to distract her and occupy her mind with something else. Rachel wished for any one of her friends right now, just someone to put their arms around her and tell her she would be all right.

She wasn't even sure what to label the feelings she had for Malik. Sometimes he infuriated her with his self-assured ways, sometimes he humbled her with his ability to admit his faults. Her heart quickened when he looked at her and her skin tingled when he touched her. Rachel knew she liked Malik and that she enjoyed spending time in his company, but she also knew there was more to it than that. There was a deeper, more primal emotion present and Rachel wondered if it could be love. She'd only seen the volatile, destructive love her parents had shared, but could there be a different sort? Something that didn't require you to argue and fight the entire time.

Rachel knew she should try to put their kisses behind her, try to forget how Malik's lips felt against her skin, but she knew that would be close to impossible. She might have been able to walk away with dignity, but she knew she would struggle not to imagine Malik leaning in towards her, the flame of desire burning in his eyes, the next time they were alone together.

Standing in the darkness of the desert, looking up at the stars, Rachel suddenly felt very small and alone. She had never considered her path in life might make her lonely—after all, she would be surrounded by the children she taught and the interesting and diverse people she met on her travels—but she was beginning to realise that might not be enough. She could see the appeal of having someone to hold at night, to curl up beside and share the ups and downs of the day with. Someone constant, someone who wanted her as much as she wanted him.

Rachel sighed. That was the problem—even if she did decide she felt more for Malik than respect and friendship, he could not love her back. Rachel had a sneaking feeling that Malik didn't really know what love was. He certainly hadn't been close to anyone in his life. From his stories his father was stern and distant, his mother had passed away when he was born and his wife had been cold and unloving. He'd even needed Rachel to show him how to love his children properly, or at least how to demonstrate that love. His role as Sheikh meant that he didn't even have any close friends to care for. He might desire her and enjoy her company, but how could Malik love her if he didn't even know what love was?

She knew she was being self-indulgent and unnecessarily melancholy. She had a good life here in Huria. She loved the children and loved her job, and the exotic location was more than she had ever hoped for, but all of a sudden Rachel felt as though maybe travelling and seeing the world weren't as important as she'd thought if you had no one to share it with.

Slipping back into her tent, she lay down and looked up at the fabric ceiling in the darkness. She tried to imagine the advice her friends would give her, but she found the images of their faces blurring and she felt properly homesick for the first time since she'd arrived in Huria. Closing her eyes, Rachel willed sleep to come, knowing that if she stayed awake through the long hours of the night only one man would occupy her thoughts.

As the morning sun filtered into the tent Rachel allowed her eyes to flutter open slowly. She'd slept fitfully, often awaking to find herself imagining Malik's lithe body slipping under the blankets beside her. In the pale light of the morning Rachel tried to think about things rationally. They'd shared a few kisses, a few sublime, shivers-down-the-spine kisses, but that was all. There hadn't been any further indiscretion and no one but the two of them knew about the kisses. Rachel was almost certain she would be able to act as if nothing had happened when she saw Malik, even if her insides were churning and her heart pounding at the thought. She'd just have to obey a couple of simple rules.

Number one was that on no account could she ever be alone with him. There had to be at least one child between them at all times and preferably three. Number two was that she could not look into his eyes for more than five seconds at a time, or maybe she should just aim to avoid eye contact completely. She did feel decidedly distracted when he looked at her with those serious eyes. Number three, and this was the most important, if she had somehow forgotten about rules one and two and they were alone and staring into one another's eyes, on no account was she to kiss him again. Once was a mistake, twice she could just about excuse herself, but three times really couldn't be put down to being caught in the moment. Rachel knew if she kissed Malik again she was at high risk of blurting out something she would regret, something that might make Malik send her back to England and replace her with a grey-haired old governess who didn't fancy herself in love with the Sheikh.

I'm not in love with him, Rachel reminded herself. Although she knew she was in trouble when she had to remind herself not to be in love with Malik.

Carefully she sat up, looking down at Ameera's peaceful face beside her. The young girl had slept deeply and hadn't noticed Rachel tossing and turning in the night. Without waking her, Rachel slipped into her dress and left the tent, stretching as she emerged into the sunlight.

'Good morning,' Malik said from somewhere behind her.

Rachel yelped, stifling the noise with her hand. She hadn't expected to be ambushed this soon after getting up. Slowly she turned around and looked into Malik's eyes. Silently she cursed—already she was breaking both rules one and two. She'd probably be kissing him within seconds at this rate.

'Sleep well?' he asked innocuously.

'Very.' Rachel refused to let him see the effect he had on her. 'Like the dead.'

'I'm glad.' He smiled and Rachel wondered how he could be quite so calm and collected when her heart was hammering inside her chest as if it wanted to escape her body.

'Would you like an orange juice?' he offered politely.

Rachel wondered when he had started acting as a footman as he escorted her to the main tent and poured her a glass of freshly squeezed juice.

She sipped it, closed her eyes and smiled. The flavour was tangy and refreshing and as she drank Rachel felt her nerves settling and her confidence returning.

'I like watching you eat and drink,' Malik said.

Rachel's eyes flew open and she stared at him. Malik looked startled, as if he hadn't meant to say anything out loud, and then he gave a lazy grin.

'You enjoy everything so much.'

She didn't know what to say.

'It's a good thing. Not many people show their pleasure with the world as openly as you do.'

'This is good,' Rachel said, brandishing her glass of orange juice. 'But I would grin like a Cheshire cat if I could get my hands on a proper cup of tea.'

'Ah, tea, yes. I remember it from my time in England.' Malik pulled a face. 'Bit insipid and watery.'

'It reminds me of home.'

Malik looked at her carefully. 'You're homesick.'

Rachel suddenly felt the tears well in her eyes and she realised she was. She had never thought she would be homesick—after all, her parents were dead and her childhood home lived in by some other family by now—but she missed other things. She missed her friends and she missed the familiarity of Madame Dubois's School for Young Ladies. She even missed the stern head teacher herself and the kindlier Miss Fanworth, Rachel's favourite teacher. She missed the cool mist of autumn mornings and she missed curling up by a fire with a proper cup of tea.

Malik took her hand, stroking it gently. All Rachel's earlier resolve disappeared and she rested her head on his shoulder as he pulled her in closer.

'I don't want you to leave us,' he said after a few minutes.

'I'm not going to leave,' Rachel said. 'I love it here. I love the children. I love…' She trailed off, frightened of what might slip from her lips. 'I love everything about Huria,' she continued, injecting a cheerful note into her voice, 'except that you can't get a decent cup of tea for love or money.'

Malik pulled away a little, his expression suggesting he hadn't missed her pause. 'I'm glad you want to stay. The children would be devastated to lose you.'

And you? Rachel wanted to ask, but didn't have the courage.

'I would hate to think I'd driven you away.'

Rachel took a step back. She'd been expecting this topic of conversation ever since she'd found Malik waiting for her outside her tent.

'Last night we were both emotional,' Rachel said slowly, hoping the blush that was burning her cheeks was less obvious in the dim light of the tent. 'We were emotional and lonely, and we got carried away in the moment.'

Malik looked as though he wanted to say something, but Rachel pressed on, knowing she didn't want to hear his rejection.

'I very much enjoy your company and I would hate for this to come between us,' she said, trying to sound efficient and emotionless.

'Me, too,' Malik murmured.

'So shall we agree to forget about last night and resume our normal relationship?'

'I would very much like to resume our normal relationship.' He looked at Rachel with his serious eyes. 'And I will try my utmost to forget about last night.'

She felt a thrill of excitement course through her as he said the words, implying that he would not forget their kiss easily. She wondered what he would do if she came out and admitted she cared for him, that she had greater feelings than a governess should for her employer.

Rachel had never been shy or run from confrontation, but right now she decided it was best to keep her feelings to herself. She wasn't sure how she would cope if Malik came out and rejected her completely. At least this way, with her emotions kept locked up safe inside her, she had the fantasy that he might feel the same about her.

Rachel had barely had time to change out of her dusty clothes when a palace servant knocked quietly on her door. The young girl stood outside nervously, brandishing a letter, which Rachel took eagerly. She recognised the handwriting immediately; the letter was from Joanna.

Quickly Rachel tore open the envelope and clutched at the pages of paper inside. She hadn't realised quite how eager she was to hear from one of her friends, to know what was happening to them on the other side of the world.

Dearest Rachel,

What a long time it seems since we all stood together at school, wishing each other well for our onward journeys. So much has happened in the past few weeks I barely know where to start, but I suppose I should just come out and tell you my big news. I know who my parents were! In fact, as I write this, I'm sitting in the drawing room of my grandfather's house.

I should explain. After taking up my position with the Huntfords—I know I shouldn't gossip, but they're not a particularly nice family—my grandfather tracked me down. It turns out my father and my mother had a short affair many years ago and I was the result.

After my mother died my grandfather never gave up hope of finding me. He's a sweet man, kinder than I could ever have hoped for, and he's eager to try and make up for the time we have lost.

Rachel, I can't tell you how wonderful it feels to finally know the circumstances of my birth. Ever since I was a young girl my greatest wish has been to find my family and now I have.

Rachel found herself smiling. Joanna had never complained about her lot in life. Abandoned on the steps of Madame Dubois's School for Young Ladies when she was a baby, Joanna had been raised by the various teachers at the school. It had been a lonely existence, at least until some girls her own age had arrived, and Rachel knew Joanna would have done anything to find her family.

> *Here's the most shocking part of it all: Grand-father is a marquis! He doesn't have any other family so he is eager for me to be introduced to society as his granddaughter and heir. Grandfather is keen to see me settled and has arranged my marriage to a good friend of his, who he promises is kind and will make a good husband. I have to admit I'm a little nervous at the prospect, but I owe it to my grandfather to at least consider the man.*
>
> *I do have a small confession, Rachel. Whilst I was in Hertfordshire I met someone. He makes my heart pound when I look at him, but I'm not sure we're meant to be. Grandfather would be disappointed and I don't think I can upset him like that. I have someone else to think of now besides myself.*

Rachel read between the lines to all the words her friend hadn't written. She wondered if she was in love. She knew all about relationships that weren't meant to be, but even from the letter she could tell Joanna would be unhappy if she married the man her grand-father intended.

Anyway, enough about me. Have you heard from Isabel? She penned me a quick note a few weeks ago and dropped in the fact that she was married. It is all very hush-hush, but I'm determined to find out all the details soon. Isabel always manages to surprise us!

I hope things are going well in Huria and that you're settling in. I can't wait to hear your news. Yours with love,
Joanna

Rachel flopped back on to her bed. Isabel was married. And Joanna was in love, if she wasn't very much mistaken. She'd missed so much in the short time she'd been away. Then Rachel reflected on the changes in her life during that time. Within a few months she'd travelled to Huria, become the governess of three wonderful children and was trying very hard not to fall for her employer. It sounded as though it had been an eventful few months for her friends, too. As Rachel read back through the letter she wondered whether Grace was having any luck finding her daughter and if Isabel was happy in her marriage. She wanted to reply immediately, to tell Joanna all her news, but she wasn't quite sure what she should write about Malik. She couldn't stop thinking about him, but she knew nothing could come of their relationship.

Rachel folded the letter up and decided she would reply tomorrow. Maybe by then she would have interpreted her feelings for Malik.

Chapter Seventeen

Malik strode across the courtyard and swept Hakim up into his arms. Ever since the camel trek and the night they had spent in the Bedouin tents his youngest son had been asking Malik to teach him to ride and today was the day Malik had put aside some time to fulfil his promise.

'Daddy, I've chosen a horse and I practised sitting up straight all day yesterday and I think I know how to hold the reins just right and I want to gallop.' Hakim's words came out in such a rush Malik had to take a moment to decipher them. 'Miss Talbot's coming to watch.'

Ah. Miss Talbot. Rachel. Malik wasn't sure how to feel about this latest development. Since their kiss under the stars in the desert Malik had tried to act normal around his children's governess, but he had to admit he was failing quite stupendously. He either found himself acting with exaggerated politeness, to a degree even Hakim noticed he was behaving strangely, or was far too familiar for his own good. Sometimes he caught himself just staring at her lips, wondering when they would next stretch into her bewitching smile, or lightly brushing his fingertips over the skin of her hand, enjoying the feel of her silky smooth skin under his fingertips.

'She said Aahil and Ameera could pick some books to read because my first time on a horse was far too important for her to miss.'

Malik nodded solemnly. Part of him wondered if Rachel was doing what he had done so many times this past week and was finding any excuse to see him. The idea sent a thrill of excitement through his body, but he quickly reined it in. Rachel probably was just eager to support Hakim. She loved his children as if they were her own and she seemed to know exactly what they needed at any given time.

'Let's go find this horse,' Malik said, refocusing his attention on his son. Today was about Hakim and helping the little Prince get over his fear of horses.

'May I watch?' Rachel's familiar voice stopped Malik in his tracks.

Hakim immediately wriggled from his father's arms and skipped across the courtyard to his governess. Chattering away, he grabbed her hand and began to pull her along. Malik had to smile at his excitement, it was infectious, and he knew that part of his own excitement was the prospect of spending the morning with Rachel.

Out in the stables a groom was waiting with Malik's own horse and a small, friendly looking pony who was chewing away on a handful of hay. As they entered Hakim let go of both Malik's and Rachel's hands and ran towards his pony.

'I'm going to call him Dragon,' Hakim said.

Malik looked at the docile beast and ruffled his son's hair.

'Dragon it is. Now it is very important that your horse trusts you before you get on.'

Hakim nodded seriously and gently began to stroke his pony on the nose.

'Hello, Dragon,' he said. 'I'm Hakim. I promise I'll be gentle with you.'

Malik caught the look of love that passed over Rachel's face as she watched Hakim and realised just how lucky his children were to have a governess who cared for them as much as she did.

'Good. Let's get you mounted and safe in the saddle, then we can start with a gentle walk.'

Malik boosted Hakim up into the saddle and quickly placed his feet in the stirrups. Hakim held on to the reins tightly and gently Malik was able to coax him to relax a little with some soothing words.

'Shall we go for a walk?'

Malik took hold of the front of Dragon's bridle and started to lead the pony out of the stable and into the small yard that lay beyond. Hakim sat stiffly at first, but after a few minutes he started to relax.

'You look like a natural,' Rachel said, making Hakim beam with pride.

'Are you ready to have a go on your own?' Malik asked. 'I'll be right here beside you.'

Hakim looked nervous, but he nodded anyway and Malik let go of the bridle. The docile pony continued to walk at the same pace, steadily plodding along.

'I'm doing it,' Hakim whispered. 'I'm actually riding a horse.

They continued with the lesson for another half an

hour until Malik could see his son was starting to tire. As he lifted Hakim down from the saddle the young boy clung on to him, giving him a tight hug.

'Thank you, Daddy. That was the best day ever.'

Malik realised he had never spent time with just one of his children before now; they'd always had to share his attention. He wondered whether it would be a good idea to try to carve out some time with each one of them, to make them feel special and show them they were loved.

'You did a good thing today,' Rachel said quietly as Malik began to take the saddle and bridle off the pony. He'd sent Hakim back to the palace to wash for lunch and apart from him and Rachel the stables were deserted.

'I don't know why I never thought to teach him to ride before.'

Rachel took a brush and started to rub down the appreciative pony as Malik finished tidying away the riding equipment. They worked in silence for a few minutes, but there was a tension in the air, an electrical charge that fizzled and sparked between them.

Malik glanced at Rachel, trying to figure out what made him so attracted to her. She was beautiful, with her thick, dark hair and warm brown eyes, and he longed to run his hands over the curves of her body. And she was kind and caring, towards him and towards his children. He respected her confidence and her positive attitude. But there was something else, something deep and primal, something he couldn't describe or explain, that made him want to claim her as his own, to make sure no man ever looked at her ever again.

Which was ridiculous. He had no right to claim

her, no right to insist no man ever looked at her again. He couldn't give her love and marriage. He'd tried to be a husband before and that had been an unmitigated disaster. As for love, he didn't really believe in it. He believed in duty and honour, but he found it hard to believe in love. Aliyyah had believed in love and she had only years of heartache and an early death to show for it.

Malik knew this meant he and Rachel could never be together, could never share even one more kiss. He respected her too much to ask her to be his mistress or his lover. He and his children needed her too much for him to even risk suggesting those things. But he wanted her, even though there was no way he could ever have her.

Once the pony was rubbed down and the equipment stored away they walked out of the stable side by side, neither saying a word. Malik relished these few moments he got to spend just with Rachel, when it was just the two of them. They didn't even need to speak for him to enjoy her company.

'Meet me this evening,' he said impulsively.

Malik couldn't quite believe he'd just uttered the invitation. He knew all the reasons he had to keep his distance from Rachel, he'd just recited them all again to himself inside his head, but still he found himself going against reason and finding excuses to spend time with her.

Rachel turned to look at him, her expression wary.

'I've got a surprise for you. Meet me at the entrance to the sunken garden once the children are in bed.'

He realised he was holding his breath as he waited for her to reply.

Rachel eventually nodded and Malik exhaled, not quite able to regret his spontaneous invitation, but knowing he would have to keep reciting all the reasons they could not be together over and over to remind himself not to lean in and kiss her.

'I wasn't sure if you would come,' Malik said as he led Rachel into the sunken garden.

'I don't think I had a choice,' Rachel said quietly. Malik knew how she felt, he found it hard to say no to any situation that might bring them closer together.

'I remember you telling me about some of the things you missed from back home,' Malik said as they walked. 'I wasn't able to arrange everything, but I hope it is enough.'

They emerged into a little courtyard that had a small table covered in mosaic pieces in the centre of it. Laid out on the table were a couple of cups, a pot of tea and two slices of fruit cake. For a moment Rachel stood frozen, not saying a word.

'I'm sorry if it is not accurate,' Malik said.

Rachel turned to him with tears in her eyes. 'This is the nicest thing anyone has ever done for me.'

Malik took her hand and led her over to the small table, pulling out her chair and waiting for her to sit before taking a seat himself. He watched as Rachel's fingers danced across the bone china of the dainty cups and rested on the delicate handle of the silver forks set out for the fruit cake.

'I remember my parents taking me for tea once in this cosy little teahouse in the middle of Brighton. We'd gone there for a day trip and I felt like the luckiest girl on earth.'

'It's difficult being away from home, apart from everyone you know,' Malik said.

Rachel picked up the teapot and poured two cups of the fragrant amber liquid, adding milk and stirring until she had got them just the right shade.

'I know when I was studying in Europe I used to yearn for the deserts and the heat of Huria. Sometimes I felt that if I ate one more Western meal or drank one more cup of tea I might scream.'

Rachel smiled at him, as if she were trying to picture him losing control but was unable to do so.

'This is very kind of you. No one has ever done anything like this for me before.'

Malik held her gaze and he knew right then something more was going to happen between them. They might currently be sitting having an innocuous cup of tea, but Rachel was looking at him as though he were the kindest and best man in the world, and Malik knew he wasn't strong enough to resist her.

They ate the cake and sipped their cups of tea, and when it was all gone Malik offered Rachel his arm and led her further into the sunken garden. He was very aware this was where they had shared their first kiss and he knew the entire garden was romantic at night. He wasn't sure what he had hoped to achieve by setting out the table of tea, but after realising that Rachel was a little homesick he'd been determined to give her a little taste of home. Now he knew that small act was spiralling into something much more momentous.

As they walked he glanced at Rachel's profile, and wondered if he could just give in to his desires. He wanted to kiss her, to take her to his bed and claim her, but then he wanted to wake up the next morning with Rachel by his side, to have her smile at him as they discussed their days and their future. To him that sounded like a marriage and Malik knew he wasn't ready for another one of those. He was still reeling from his disastrous marriage to Aliyyah and her awful death, and he didn't need a further complication in his life. The problem was Rachel wasn't the sort of woman he could just have a dalliance with. He liked her too much, respected her too much and he didn't want to lose her because he couldn't keep his desire in check.

Malik felt the pressure building inside him. The situation was impossible. He wanted Rachel, but there was no way he could have her. And if he wasn't very much mistaken she was falling for him, too. He'd seen the way she looked at him, noticed the warmth behind her smiles, and Malik knew he couldn't give her what she wanted, what she deserved. A woman like Rachel needed to be loved completely and utterly, she deserved no less than a man's entire heart. Malik couldn't give her that, he wasn't sure if he was capable of loving at all, and he wasn't going to destroy Rachel the way Aliyyah had been destroyed and turn this happy contented woman sad with disappointment.

They reached a little fountain and Rachel paused in front of it. In the moonlight she looked beautiful, with the soft light dancing across her features and making her eyes shine. Malik knew he had to kiss her, just one last time. He'd kiss her once more and then he would never touch her again. He knew it was an empty promise to himself, but he needed an excuse, any excuse, to dip his head and cover her lips with his own.

Malik felt a surge of desire as Rachel tilted her head back and met his kiss with passion of her own. She laced her fingers through his hair and he felt her warm body pressing up against his. All his promises to himself, all his resolutions after their kiss in the desert, melted away and all he could think about was Rachel. He ran his hands over her arms, down her back, stopping to cup her bottom and pull her in even closer. He wanted to possess every part of her, to run his hands over every inch of her skin, to strip her of every item of clothing and see every bit of her in the moonlight.

Rachel moaned softly and the sound cut through the haze of Malik's desire and shook his very core. In that moment he wanted Rachel more than he wanted anything else. He could picture them running away together, spending their days lounging in bed and their nights locked in passionate embraces. In this fantasy Malik didn't have a kingdom to think about, no responsibilities or cares. His life consisted of purely the woman in front of him and solely satisfying both their needs.

He froze, then pulled away, looking at Rachel's face searchingly, wondering how one woman could make him feel all of this. Then he felt the weight of responsibility come crashing back down and he realised just how dangerous his feelings for Rachel actually were. If one kiss could make him want to abandon his country, he dreaded to think what a night in her arms would do.

'Malik, what's wrong?' Rachel asked softly, her face clouded with concern.

He realised he was backing away from her, his hands held out protectively in front of him as if he were trying to ward off some evil spirit.

'This is wrong,' he managed to whisper. 'Selfish.'

In all his years as Sheikh of Huria Malik had never

once complained about the responsibilities of the role, or how isolating his position was. Never before had he wanted to leave it all behind, to hand over the reins of power and live a normal life, but Rachel was making him yearn for something else: a life without the burden of a kingdom to put first.

He couldn't allow those thoughts to multiply and flourish. His duty was to Huria and he could not allow anything or anyone to change his priorities. Not even kind, caring Rachel with her soft lips and infectious smile. Malik was a Sheikh before he was a man and he knew he needed to start acting accordingly.

Malik began to reach out, then let his hand fall to his side. If he weakened in his resolve it would only be Rachel who suffered in the long run. Better for their relationship to fizzle and fail now than for there to be more heartache further down the line.

'I'm sorry,' he said, and left the garden before he could see the expression of devastation that was sure to be on Rachel's face.

Chapter Eighteen

Malik was avoiding her, Rachel was sure of it. There was no other explanation. In the last two weeks Rachel had seen the Sheikh for a total of five minutes. Whenever they bumped into one another he had to hurry off to some meeting or event and they hadn't exchanged more than pleasantries since their kiss in the garden.

Rachel was disappointed, of course, and she missed Malik's company, but part of her could reason that the new distance he was keeping between them at least made it easier for her not to do or say something she might regret. Some days she even went for half an hour without thinking about the serious Sheikh, although other times she still found herself remembering their kisses far too often.

What Rachel was really annoyed about was Malik's regression with his children. He'd made so much progress with them and they'd begun to relax around him. Hakim had started to trust his father, Ameera had started to believe his confidence-boosting compliments and Aahil had just enjoyed spending time with the man he looked up to so much.

That had been two weeks ago. Now the children saw their father as little as she did. Malik no longer came to tuck them into bed at night, he didn't slip out of meetings to ask them what they were doing with their day. There had been no more trips out into the desert and no more lessons for Hakim. The children were devastated, and Rachel was furious. It was bad enough not interacting with your children in the first place, but to build that relationship only to desert them was heinous.

Rachel had been bubbling with anger the last couple of days and she'd been eager to confront Malik and tell him in no uncertain terms that his behaviour was not good enough. The only problem was she hadn't caught even a glimpse of him. She'd even resorted to teaching the children outside for the entire day, not leaving the courtyard and always keeping one eye fixed on the doors from the public rooms to the outside space, but still Malik had not appeared.

'Do you think Father will give me another lesson tomorrow?' Hakim asked as Rachel brushed the hair from his forehead.

The young boy had asked the same question for almost a week and now Rachel sensed he was losing hope.

'I'll ask him,' she said, bending down and placing a kiss on Hakim's head.

'Father's too busy,' Aahil said.

Rachel heard the note of resignation in Aahil's voice and she knew tonight would be the night she finally confronted Malik. Even if she had to break down the door of his private chamber herself, she was going to talk to the Sheikh.

'I'll ask him,' Rachel repeated soothingly.

She sat on the edge of Hakim's bed until his breathing slowed and deepened and she was sure he was asleep, then she said goodnight to Aahil, blew out the candle and slipped from the room.

Before setting out on her crusade Rachel returned to her own room to prepare herself. She checked her appearance in the mirror, straightening her dress and patting down her hair, checking that any stray strands were in place, and then she rolled back her shoulders and raised her chin a notch. This was a fight Malik was not going to win.

Purposefully Rachel strode across the courtyard, heading straight for Malik's private rooms. She had never been inside them, but she knew where most places were in the palace now and Malik's rooms had a very distinctive, heavy set of doors leading to them.

'The Sheikh has asked to see me, regarding the children,' Rachel said to the guard standing outside the doors.

He looked unsure, but he didn't stop her as Rachel opened the door and slipped through. She made sure she closed it quietly behind her and for a second she didn't move, allowing her eyes to adjust to the darkness in the corridor.

Before her was a long, wide corridor, the walls whitewashed like the rest of the palace and the floor lined with exotic plants in mosaic pots. Along one side were the windows that looked out to the courtyard and on the other were three doors.

Rachel gathered her confidence and walked forward. She didn't know what lay behind the doors and she didn't particularly want to surprise Malik in his bedroom, but her priority was finding the man. She wasn't going to let the fact that these were his private rooms deter her. It was his fault that she was here, sneaking about after dark. If he'd made an appearance in daylight hours she wouldn't have to resort to this.

Rachel reached the first door, gripped the handle and pushed it open. She could see immediately it was his private study, a functional room with a large desk and maps of Huria on the walls. Rachel noticed the large portrait of a couple behind his desk and she wondered if the subjects of the painting were Malik's parents.

Seeing that the room was empty, Rachel quickly moved on. Behind the second door was Malik's bedroom. It was large and richly decorated, with ornate furniture and luxurious fabrics draped over the bed and hanging in front of the windows. There was a comfortable sitting area, with plump cushions and inviting blankets, although Rachel doubted Malik got much time to relax. A door led off his bedroom to a private bathroom and Rachel could see the largest bath she had ever set eyes on standing in the middle of the room. She found her mouth becoming dry as she involuntarily pictured Malik sitting in the bath and pulling her in there to join him.

Rachel swiftly retreated. She didn't need any more fuel for her inappropriate thoughts about Malik and she didn't want to pry into his private space, even though she was interested in what the enigmatic Sheikh did with his free time.

Emerging back into the corridor, Rachel carried on to the final door. She knew Malik was in his private set of rooms somewhere and, seeing that the other two rooms were empty, he must be behind this door. Summoning up all her confidence and righteous outrage, Rachel gripped the handle, then flung open the door.

Malik was nowhere to be seen. In fact, there wasn't even a room behind this door, just a corridor and a set of steps at the end of it. The entire corridor was tiled, even the ceiling, and there were recesses in the wall every few feet with candles set in them.

Rachel hesitated for a moment, wondering what could be down the steps, not knowing whether to turn back or not, but then she heard Hakim's hopeful voice in her head asking if Malik was going to give him another riding lesson and she stepped into the corridor.

As she descended Rachel felt the air getting warmer, and she could hear a trickle of water coming from the room at the bottom of the steps. Slowly Rachel passed through an ornate archway and into a little chamber with a fountain in the middle of it. The water that was bubbling over the stone was clear and crisp and Rachel had the urge to dip her fingers in the little pool to cool herself down.

Still, there was no sign of Malik. Rachel was now moving as if she were in a trance, being drawn forward by some invisible force. She knew she was invading Malik's private space, but the anger inside her drove her on.

The next room contained a small pool set into the floor and a stone bench around the edge. Rachel was just beginning to realise what this place was when she heard someone shifting in the next room. Summoning her courage, she stalked through the archway.

Rachel froze. Malik was lying on a raised table in the middle of the room with his eyes closed. His entire body was naked except for a towel draped over his midsection. Rachel felt the heat begin to rise in her body as her eyes travelled over his broad chest, chiselled muscles and powerful thighs. She knew she should look away, knew she should quietly retreat, but she was mesmerised.

The room was warm and Rachel watched in fascination as a bead of sweat trickled from the base of Malik's throat over his torso. She wished she could trail her fingers over its course, feel Malik's hard muscles under his smooth skin.

Without warning Malik's eyes jolted open and for a few seconds he stared at Rachel in surprise. Rachel found herself backing away as Malik swung his legs off the stone table, tucking the towel round his waist.

'What an unexpected visit,' he murmured. 'I never took you for a voyeur.'

As he spoke Rachel felt all of her anger and disappointment in his behaviour rise to the surface. She forgot he was nearly naked, forgot how difficult it was to focus when there was so much her eyes wanted to look at.

'You've been avoiding me,' Rachel said.

'So you thought you'd come into my private *hammam* to seek me out. You must have really wanted to see me.' His voice was low and dangerous.

'Your children are asking what they've done wrong. They want to know why you've abandoned them.'

'I haven't abandoned them. I've just been very busy with state business,' Malik said, but Rachel caught the fleeting expression of guilt that crossed Malik's face before he regained his haughty poised composure.

'The children aren't playthings that you can lavish with attention when it suits you and then ignore when it doesn't. They're living, breathing people whose feelings get hurt if you ignore them.'

Malik narrowed his eyes and took a step towards Rachel. She stepped back. Suddenly the chamber felt very small, and Malik's presence felt very large.

'I know my children aren't playthings. Do not presume to lecture me about my children.'

'Someone has to speak for them, stand up for them. They can't tell you how they feel themselves because they haven't seen you.'

'And at least they have more manners than to break into a man's private *hammam*.'

'If you deigned to speak to me in the last two weeks, I wouldn't have had to come in here.'

Rachel saw the black look cross Malik's face and she tried to take another step back, but her back was already against the wall. She sensed she was about to see something not many people had ever witnessed; she was about to see Malik get properly angry.

'Would you like to know the reason I've been avoiding my children the last two weeks? Why I've missed out on giving them a kiss goodnight, of hearing the stories about their days? Why I haven't encouraged Ameera to dance, or given Hakim another riding lesson?'

Rachel pressed herself into the wall as Malik stalked closer. His body was mere inches away from hers now and she thought she could feel the pure power and heat radiating from his skin.

'Would you like to know?' His voice dropped to a growl as he placed a hand on the wall beside her head.

Rachel felt compelled to nod her head. She wanted

to know, she needed to know, even though part of her already knew the truth.

Instead of answering Malik leaned in and kissed her roughly on the lips. He was full of pent-up anger and passion, and the kiss was firm, but Rachel realised despite all this he was careful not to hurt her.

'You. You are the reason. I can't bear to be around you.'

Malik leaned in again and kissed her before Rachel could even think of a reply. She felt his hand leave the wall, run down her back and prise her away from the safety of the edge of the room. He cupped her bottom, lifting her up in the air as if she weighed no more than a rag doll.

Rachel felt herself deposited unceremoniously on the stone table in the middle of the room. Malik's lips still didn't leave hers and she was drawn deeper into the kiss, forgetting her anger and indignation, consumed by the feel of Malik's mouth on her own.

'I can't have you, but I can't stop thinking about you,' he said, some of the rage leaving his voice. 'I thought if I stayed away from you I might be able to lessen *this*.'

Malik groaned as he ran his hands down Rachel's body, skimming her waist, feeling her curves underneath her dress. She felt her body responding instinctively, her hips tilting upwards towards Malik's hands, her shoulders rolling back and her legs relaxing. She wanted this, too. She'd wanted Malik for weeks, ever since their first kiss in the sunken garden. She'd revelled in his kisses and dreamed of so much more.

'And now you're here,' Malik said, pulling back a

little to look Rachel directly in the eyes. 'I'm going to give you ten seconds to get out of here. Leave now.'

Rachel didn't move, she couldn't move. She wanted to know what Malik had planned for her, wanted to give in to her deepest desires and give herself to the man she loved. Wasn't this what she'd secretly hoped for when she had realised what she was stepping into? She hadn't left when she'd seen Malik lying almost naked on the stone table and she wasn't going to leave now.

'Leave now or I won't be responsible for my actions,' Malik repeated.

Rachel stayed perfectly still, perched on the edge of the stone table, and Malik saw the defiant tilt of her chin and the rapid rise and fall of her chest, and he knew she wasn't going anywhere.

Wanting to shock her into movement, Malik took one of her hands and placed it on the bare skin of his chest. He felt her fingers tense and then move ever so slightly. Her eyes never leaving his, she began to trail her fingers over his muscles, tracing the contours and causing his skin to pucker despite the warmth of the room.

With an animalistic groan Malik kissed her roughly, wanting to possess her after all this time. He'd denied himself the pleasure of kissing her, touching her, for so long, now it was like a dam had burst. His hands flew over her body, caressing and stroking, and up above his lips devoured hers.

He needed to see her, to get her out of the prim dress that was buttoned up to the neck. None too gently he grasped the buttons at the top of the dress and he tore, working his way down the seam until he had reached her waist. Quickly, before Rachel had time to protest the destruction of her dress, Malik pushed the tattered material down over her hips and watched with satisfaction as it pooled about her feet.

Now she was clad only in a thin cotton shift, which was becoming damp from the humidity in the room and had started to cling to her body in places. Malik kissed Rachel quickly, then took the hem of her shift in both hands and lifted it over her head. Rachel gave a squeal of protest and raised her hands to cover herself.

Malik caught both her hands in his own and gently but firmly lowered them back to her side. Then he allowed himself to look at her, to take in every inch of her body, from her dainty feet, up over the creamy skin of her thighs, her taut abdomen, the mounds of her breasts and finishing at her soulful eyes.

A flicker of understanding passed between them and Malik knew Rachel wanted this as much as he did. Malik raised one hand and placed his fingers at the base of Rachel's throat, then slowly, savouring every moment, he began to explore her body. He ran his hand over her shoulders and down her arms, then gently cupped her breasts. He heard the soft moan escaping her lips as he grazed his thumb across one nipple and then the other, revelling in the instinctive way Rachel was responding to him.

Trailing his fingers further down Rachel's body, Malik paused before he reached her most private place. He raised his eyes up to meet hers as his fingers continued downwards, wanting to see her reaction to him. With the first stroke Rachel stiffened and tensed, but Malik pulled her towards him and murmured reassuringly in her ear. As he continued to tease and stroke her he felt her body beginning to relax. Slowly, Malik coaxed her legs open wide enough for him to dip a finger inside her. Rachel moaned, her head extending back, her breathing becoming shallower and more rapid.

Malik felt his own desire building. He wanted to be inside Rachel so much it was almost painful, but one thing Malik knew plenty about was self-control. He wanted to give Rachel everything first, to make her pant and scream with pleasure, and then he would give in to his own needs.

Slowly Malik began to build up speed, dipping his finger inside Rachel and then returning his attention to the spot that made her writhe with pleasure. He bent his neck, capturing one perfect breast in his free hand, and sucked her rosy nipple into his mouth. She tasted sweet, her skin warm under his lips, and Malik knew he could lose himself for hours just exploring every inch of her.

As he bit down gently Rachel raked her fingers down his back, pulling them closer together. Her breath was coming in short, sharp bursts now, and Malik knew she was close to climax. Taking a step back, Malik lifted Rachel up so she was fully sitting on the stone table, then gently pressed her back so she was lying, resting on her elbows. Before Rachel had time to realise what Malik was about to do he trailed a line of kisses from her breasts down to her thighs, then he began kissing her most private place. For a second Malik felt Rachel stiffen with surprise, but after a moment she gave in to Malik's assault on her senses and started to moan with pleasure. Malik kissed her and nipped her and dipped his tongue inside her, feeling his own desire almost at bursting point. Just as he thought he could not bear to wait any longer Rachel stiffened, her legs coming together, and she let out a long, high moan.

Before she had opened her eyes Malik stood, dropping the towel from his waist on to the floor, and straddled her. He waited for her breathing to slow and her eyes to flicker open before he began peppering kisses across her body again.

'Rachel, are you ready?'

He didn't know what he'd do if she said no.

Rachel moaned in response and pressed her hips up against his. Malik felt all his tightly wound self-control unravel and he knew he had to have her, right now, this instant.

He pressed himself gently against her, feeling her muscles tense as he slipped inside. He went slowly at first, not wanting to hurt Rachel, but as soon as he was fully inside her his primal instincts took over and his movements sped up. Underneath him Rachel's hips were rising and falling in rhythm with his own. Her eyes were shut and her mouth half-open. Every so often a soft moan would escape her lips and fire the already overheated desire deep inside him.

Malik knew he couldn't last much longer, the climax had been building for so long inside him he knew soon he would lose control. He felt Rachel's body tense, saw her eyes fly open and felt her muscles clench and spasm, then he was only aware of his own release.

Weeks of desire and passion flooded from him and Malik roared as he came inside her.

He collapsed down beside Rachel and scooped her into his arms, revelling at the sensation of lying next to a woman who didn't push him away. Rachel's soft breath tickled his neck and he could feel her heartbeat through her chest. Both their bodies were covered with a thin sheen of moisture and the *hammam* was certainly warmer than it had been before Rachel had arrived.

Rachel lay beside him in silence and Malik wondered whether she was already regretting her decision to stay with him in the *hammam*. Gently he traced a finger across her skin, waiting until she looked up at him. He wanted this moment to go on for ever, wanted them to spend eternity lying side by side in the *hammam*, with no questions about the future, no expectations or disappointments.

Rachel was unusually quiet, she hadn't really said a word since he'd given her the option to leave. She'd moaned and sighed with pleasure, Malik remembered with a smile, but she hadn't said anything.

Eventually Rachel shifted so she was propping herself up on an elbow. He loved that even now, even after the heat of the moment had subsided, she was confident enough about herself to not cover up. Most women would try and hide beneath the bedsheets, or hurry to redress, but it was as if Rachel had hardly noticed she was naked.

'I never imagined I could feel like that,' Rachel said, and all of a sudden Malik wanted her again. He knew soon she would come to her senses, realise the folly in what they were doing and he wanted to kiss her and touch her right up until that moment.

Quickly he stood and scooped Rachel up into his arms. He strode through the *hammam*, feeling the cool night air prickle against his skin as he emerged from the steam rooms. Malik kicked open the door to his bedchamber and lay Rachel down on the bed. Immediately he was on top of her, kissing her, running his hands over her body.

Rachel kissed him back feverishly, as if she, too, were worried about running out of time.

'Malik.' She sighed as he kissed her neck.

He loved that he could do this to her, that he could be the man to make her melt with pleasure. All through his marriage his couplings with Aliyyah had been cold and dutiful. Never once had she moaned his name or writhed beneath him. Rachel was giving him everything, she wasn't afraid to bare herself to him, to let him see her at her most vulnerable.

'I love you,' she whispered.

Malik froze. Rachel's eyes flickered open as if she was wondering why he had stopped.

He felt his whole world imploding. Carefully he pushed himself off Rachel and took a few steps away from the bed. He needed space, time to think. He glanced back at Rachel and saw the devastation on her face, and hurriedly looked away. He couldn't deal with her heartbreak on his conscience.

'Malik,' Rachel said, holding out her hand, 'come back to bed.'

He almost gave in, but he knew if he returned to her he would be guilty of a terrible deception. He couldn't give Rachel what she wanted, what she deserved. Rachel deserved love, all-encompassing love. She deserved to be worshipped and treasured and showered with affection. Malik wished he could be the one to do those things, but he knew it was impossible. He'd seen what love did to a person, Aliyyah had been destroyed by love and she'd nearly taken Malik with her. Malik didn't know how to love Rachel, he wouldn't give her what she needed. He knew in the long run she'd be better off without him.

'I can't love you, Rachel,' Malik said.

He saw her heart break and all he wanted to do was gather her in his arms and make the pain go away.

'I have to focus on Huria,' Malik said. 'I can't love you.'

These past two weeks had been hellish for him. He'd done everything in his power to try to focus his thoughts and energies on his kingdom, the kingdom Rachel made him want to abandon so he could spend long days in bed with her. He'd even pulled back from his children, telling himself the best way to serve the young Princes and Princess was to build a kingdom they could be proud to inherit one day. Malik had wanted to prove to himself that he would not be so shallow as to give up his birthright and duty for a woman, and in doing so he knew he had swung too far the other way. He had glimpsed Hakim's hopeful face every time he emerged from some meeting or mediation and he had told himself Huria must come first.

Looking at Rachel, he knew the truth; he shouldn't be given the responsibility for anyone's heart. He'd even failed his children when all he wanted was the best for them.

'Stop saying that.'

Malik shook his head, unable to tear his eyes away from her devastated expression.

'I can't love,' he said, finally acknowledging the truth. He couldn't love anyone, he just didn't know how.

Rachel sprung to her feet, wrapped herself in a sheet and fled from the room. Malik sunk down on to the bed, wondering how he could have got it all so wrong.

Chapter Nineteen

Rachel hugged her arms around her body and sniffed. The tears had dried up an hour ago, but she still felt delicate, as if they might begin to roll down her cheeks again at any moment. She was curled up on her bed with the door firmly locked, trying to hide from the entire world.

She couldn't believe how stupid she'd been. She had been furious with Malik, angry that he'd been neglecting his children and avoiding her. When she'd stormed into his private rooms she had been intent on making him see the error of his ways and instead she had made a fool of herself and got her heart broken.

For years she'd promised herself she wouldn't allow herself to get caught up in love and relationships. She'd vowed she would never let another person get close enough to hurt her like her parents had hurt each other and then she'd succumbed at the first opportunity. It had only taken a few words from Malik, a few smouldering looks and Rachel had offered herself up as though she were a cheap prostitute.

She gave an involuntary shiver as she remembered

the way her body had responded to his touch, the pleasure she had taken from him and the feeling of contentment, of finally belonging. As Malik's lips had met her
own she had just assumed he felt the same way about
her as she did about him. She'd assumed he loved her.

Rachel gave a choked sob and flopped back on to
the bed. If it wasn't so devastating it would be em-
barrassing, too. She'd read too much into their long
talks and the mutual desire. She'd thought it was love,
whereas for Malik his attraction to her must have been
purely physical.

Trying to calm her breathing and slow her racing
heart, Rachel wondered why anyone would want to fall
in love if it caused this much pain. She'd seen her parents have blazing rows, not speak to each other for days
on end. She'd seen her mother sobbing in her bedroom
and her father silent and grim-faced. It was no way to
live. That was why she'd promised herself to never
make the same mistake, but the first opportunity she'd
got she'd opened her heart. And she'd been rejected.

I can't love you, Rachel. He'd even repeated it, just
to make sure she'd got the point.

If she'd just remained professional, never allowed
herself to get close to Malik, then she wouldn't be
hurting this much now. She couldn't even find it in
herself to really blame Malik. He'd never promised
her love, never even mentioned it. In fact, he'd done
almost the opposite by telling her of his dedication
to his kingdom, how that always had to come first.
Still, Rachel had spun a fantasy in her head, a reality where she and Malik could live happily ever after,
surrounded by love.

Rachel closed her eyes and then swiftly opened

them again. Every time she let her eyelids shut she could see Malik's face as he broke her heart.

She stood and paced over to the window, looking out into the courtyard. She half expected to see Malik down there, waiting for her, but it was empty and Malik was nowhere to be seen. She wondered what he was thinking, whether he regretted their intimacy in the *hammam*. He was a noble man, a good man, and Rachel knew he had never set out to deceive or trick her. She could not find it in herself to blame him. He had never promised her love… It was her own naivety that was her downfall.

Now more than ever Rachel wished she had her friends to talk to. She knew Joanna would always listen with a sympathetic ear and Isabel would be indignant on her behalf, ready to storm into Malik's rooms and demand he marry Rachel. And perhaps Grace would understand the most, she knew about heartbreak, about giving up someone you loved. She wanted their comfort and their strength and the closeness they'd shared whilst at school. Instead she was here alone, with no one to talk to, no one to make her see that life would go on, that she would get over this.

Walking away from the window, Rachel wondered how she would get over this. She loved Malik, she knew that now. She loved his stern visage and the kind heart that beat underneath. She loved how hotly he defended his kingdom and how he was willing to learn from his mistakes with his children to make him a better father. And she loved how she felt whole when he kissed her, as though he was the piece of her that had been missing all along.

The idea of leaving the palace, leaving Huria, made

Rachel feel sick. She'd miss the children too much and she couldn't bear the thought of never seeing Malik again. However, the idea of staying was just as bad, fumbling through forced conversations with Malik, always being reminded of the intimacies they'd shared and the fact that he didn't love her in return. She didn't want to leave, but she couldn't stay.

The tears came flooding back to her eyes at the thought of leaving all she held dear in Huria behind. In two short months she had come to love this desert kingdom, with its entrenched traditions and arid climate. She'd come to love Aahil's seriousness, Ameera's quick wit and Hakim's cuteness. The notion of having to start again, just because she was foolish enough to think she could find happiness with love, made her despair. She wanted to stay here, to go back to sharing mutual respect with Malik, but nothing else.

No, Rachel told herself, that was a lie. What she really wanted was for Malik to love her.

Knowing she needed to get her thoughts straight, Rachel sat down at the small writing desk in her room and pulled out a sheet of paper. She found it soothing to write down her thoughts, and although this was one letter that would probably never get sent, it would be cathartic to write it anyway.

Rachel let all the emotions flow from her. She wrote of her mistakes and she wrote of her heartbreak. She detailed every feeling and every option open to her, but by the end of the letter she still wasn't sure what to do.

Rachel was thankful for the dawn light filtering in through her window. She hadn't slept at all and felt drained and empty, but at least with the start of the new day she could get up and try and occupy her mind with something else.

Whilst getting the children up and ready for the day and starting on their lessons, Rachel felt numb. At first she kept half-hoping Malik would appear, grasp her around the waist and tell her he had made a terrible mistake. By mid-morning it was clear that wasn't going to happen. Rachel really was going to have to decide whether to remain in Huria with the knowledge that Malik didn't love her, with a supreme awkwardness between them, or whether to leave the children and position she loved so much. She realised how much she had still been hoping Malik might have changed his mind, that he'd realised he did love her, but he just hadn't been able to admit it.

At lunchtime Rachel emerged from the classroom with the children in tow. Aahil and Ameera were ahead, arguing about something, but Hakim had hung back and was now holding her hand and chattering as they walked.

'Miss Talbot.' Malik's deep voice startled her and Rachel spun around to see where he was.

'Your Majesty.'

'Daddy.'

Hakim's hand slipped out of Rachel's and the small boy launched himself at his father. Malik scooped Hakim up into his arms and kissed the top of his head.

'I've missed you, Daddy.'

Rachel felt a lump form in her throat. Sometimes she wished life could be as straightforward as it was for a four-year-old.

'I've missed you, too, little one.'

'Are you coming to have lunch with us?'

Malik's eyes met Rachel's briefly over the top of Hakim's head and she saw the momentary panic there. It made her want to cry. Summoning up all her inner strength, she smiled and nodded.

'What a lovely idea,' Rachel said. 'Unfortunately I'm getting a headache so I think I'll have a lie down before this afternoon's lessons.'

She turned away before she could see the look of relief that would surely cross Malik's face. Before anyone could protest she hurried across the courtyard and went up to her room, firmly closing the door behind her and then sinking down to the floor with her back pressed against the wall. Rachel tried to ignore the image of Malik's face, the panic that had been too strong for him to hide, but it just kept popping up in her mind. They couldn't continue like this; she couldn't spend her life sneaking around, trying to avoid Malik.

If she stayed in Huria then she would be hurting the children. They needed a close, healthy relationship with their father more than they needed her. She was replaceable, Malik was not. If she stayed Malik would keep his distance, just like he had been the last couple of weeks. He would try to avoid her company and that would result in him not spending as much time with the children as he would do if she weren't around. Rachel could never do anything to hurt the children, and if she stayed they would miss out on building a good relationship with their father.

The enormity of the decision she had just made came crashing down and Rachel felt her entire body sag. She really was going to leave. She would leave behind the man she loved, the children she cared for and the kingdom that had started to feel like home.

A small voice in her head called her a coward, told her to stand and fight for what she wanted, but Rachel dismissed it quickly. She wasn't going to force Malik to love her, that wasn't her way, she would leave him to get on with his life with his children and somehow look to rebuild hers somewhere far, far away.

Malik knew he was neglecting his children, but his mind was so preoccupied with thoughts of Rachel he couldn't seem to focus on anything else. Aahil, Ameera and Hakim had all been delighted to see him, but they'd been content to start chattering amongst themselves when it became obvious he wasn't going to bring much conversation.

He'd planned to take Rachel aside, to calmly and detachedly discuss last night and try and bring some closure to the situation. Instead he'd frozen. He'd seen Rachel, looked into her eyes full of hurt and he'd lost every coherent thought. Malik hated that she'd fled rather than come to lunch with him, but part of him felt relieved as well. The problem was he didn't know what to say to her, because he didn't know what he wanted.

Once again Malik cursed himself for giving in to his desire in the *hammam*. If he'd just controlled himself they would not be in this intolerable situation. Silently he shook his head—deep down he knew he was fooling himself. There had been a tension building between him and Rachel for weeks. If they had resisted one another in the *hammam*, it would only have been a matter of time before they found themselves alone together again and their resolutions would have faltered.

He just wished they wanted the same thing, although he wasn't too clear what it was exactly he wanted. He didn't want Rachel as his mistress—the very idea made him feel ashamed. She was too good, and she meant too much to him for him to even contemplate asking her to dishonour herself like that. Malik had thought he never would want another wife, he still bore his emotional scars from his marriage to Aliyyah, but he had to acknowledge that the idea of Rachel as his wife was actually rather appealing. She was kind and caring and would make a good mother to his children. And the idea of taking Rachel to bed every evening was tempting all by itself. The problem lay with the issue of love. Rachel wanted love, she deserved to be loved, and Malik didn't think he'd ever loved anyone before and he didn't know how to start.

Malik knew Rachel wouldn't stay in Huria as his wife if he didn't love her, but the idea of losing her for good ripped through him like a sword slicing through flesh. He couldn't imagine his life without her. Some days he endured the long, tedious hours of disputes and negotiations, buoyed along by the knowledge he would see Rachel's smile at the end of the day. He didn't want her to be anywhere other than in his arms, but Malik knew he was likely to lose her completely, that she would leave Huria for good. The only thing that would make her stay, a declaration of love from him, he couldn't give.

He needed to do something. Malik wasn't sure what, but he needed to be proactive, to see if he could come up with a solution that suited everyone. Dropping a kiss on each of his children's heads, Malik left them to their lunch and strode purposefully towards Rachel's room. He didn't know what he was going to say, or how he was going to persuade Rachel to stay, he just knew he needed to try.

Once he was outside her door Malik hesitated, but the years of fearlessly leading Huria had taught him to approach conflict boldly, so he knocked firmly on the door. Without waiting for an answer, he turned the handle, pushed open the door and stepped inside.

Rachel's shocked face looked up at him from the bed.

'Don't leave,' Malik said.

Rachel shook her head. 'I have to.'

Malik felt the pain slicing through his heart.

'Stay.'

'We will both be happier if I go.'

'No, I won't be happier without you.'

Rachel sat up, her eyes filled with sadness, and Malik knew that he had lost even before he had started.

'What do you propose?' Rachel asked. 'That I remain here as the children's governess and we spend our lives trying to avoid one another?'

'It wouldn't be like that.'

'It would, Malik. I won't be the reason you see less of your children. I won't come between you.'

Despite his sadness Malik felt his heart swell at Rachel's desire to nurture his relationship with his children. As always she was still putting them first.

He sat down on the bed next to Rachel and reached out and took her hand.

'It's just not meant to be,' Rachel said sadly.

Malik sensed a resigned air about Rachel that he'd never known before. He realised what a monumental deal it was for her to have told him she loved him, to have risked her heart and then to be rejected. He wished he could reach out and make everything right, but there was something inside him, holding him back, telling him he could never give her what she needed, what she deserved. To convince her to stay would be selfish and Malik couldn't live with himself if he was the reason her beautiful soul shrivelled and shrank each passing year because he couldn't give her the love she needed.

'Where will you go?'

Rachel shrugged, but Malik could see the pain behind the nonchalant gesture. He remembered both her parents were dead, and he knew she had travelled to Huria straight after leaving school.

'I'll find another position,' Rachel said. 'Maybe something in England for now.'

The idea of her being so far away was painful in so many ways.

'The children will miss you...' Malik paused. 'I'll miss you.'

Rachel turned to him with tears in her eyes. 'You look after those children. Be a good father to them. Tell Aahil you're proud of him, tell Ameera she's beautiful and spend time nurturing Hakim. They need you,' she said fiercely.

Malik nodded. He wanted to scream that they needed her, that he needed her, but instead he allowed her to gently guide him out of her room and shut the door firmly behind him. Malik felt his heart squeeze in agony as he heard the stifled sobs that came through the closed door and for a moment he could barely breathe. As he heard the unmistakeable sound of Rachel's trunk being dragged across the floor

Malik slumped against the wall and wondered if he'd got everything terribly wrong.

Malik sat in the courtyard with Hakim in his lap and Aahil and Ameera playing nearby. He'd hardly said a word to his children all afternoon and they were all subdued as a result. They seemed to sense something important was about to happen and kept glancing at him from time to time, but none of them questioned him or questioned Rachel's absence.

Absentmindedly Malik began to stroke Hakim's hair. He held his youngest son tight to him, relishing the comfort he got from just being close. He wondered how he had managed to mess things up so completely. He'd gone from having a superb governess for his children and someone he enjoyed spending time with to nothing in the space of a day.

Of course they'd lost governesses and tutors before, but he had hardly known them—he couldn't even remember most of their faces now. Rachel he would never forget, her face was etched on his heart and would remain there for eternity. She was more than a governess, more than a friend.

Surely he shouldn't be feeling such pain at the idea of her departure. He was a grown man, used to making difficult decisions and dealing with the emotional fallout of those decisions. Why, then, did the idea of never seeing Rachel again hurt more than anything he'd ever known?

A fleeting thought crossed his mind, but quickly Malik dismissed it. Of course he didn't love Rachel, people knew if they were in love. He cared for her, deeply, but surely he wasn't in love with her.

The mutinous part of him asked how he knew he wasn't in love with her—it wasn't like he'd ever loved before. Of course he loved his children, but that was different. He'd never even really seen love between a man and a woman. Apart from the destructive obsession that Aliyyah had harboured.

'Aahil, Ameera, come here,' Malik said, hugging Hakim closer to him in his lap. 'I've got something very important to say to you.'

Three faces looked up at him with a mixture of worry and intrigue.

'I need to apologise to you. These last couple of weeks I've been distant and I've neglected you. I got caught up in my own worries and I let you suffer because of it. I'm very sorry.'

'What were you worrying about?' Ameera asked suspiciously.

Malik sighed, knowing it would be best to tell his children the truth even if they weren't really old enough to understand.

'I was worried that I wasn't a good enough ruler for Huria. I had some doubts about what I wanted from life and that made me question my ability to care for our wonderful kingdom.'

'But you love Huria, Daddy,' Hakim said.

Malik looked down into his youngest son's face and a devastating realisation dawned on him. Even at four years old Hakim knew that his father loved his country, but he wondered if the young boy knew that Malik loved him. Malik had never uttered the words, never actually come out and told his children that he loved them. It wasn't something anyone had ever told him as a child, but he was realising that it was all right to be more affectionate and involved than his own father had been with him.

'I love you all very much,' Malik said simply. 'I don't tell you enough, but you are the most important things in the world to me.'

For a second none of the children moved and Malik felt a stab of panic. Would they reject him and his love, tell him it was too late?

'I love you, Daddy,' Hakim said from his position on Malik's nap. Ameera flung herself at him and Malik opened his arms, gathering her in for a cuddle. Only Aahil remained standing a few feet away.

Malik looked at his son and wondered if the aloofness he had learnt from his own father had been passed on to Aahil. He wanted to see the carefree boy Rachel had coaxed to life over the past few months and, more than anything, he needed his eldest son to realise he was loved no matter what.

Ten seconds passed, then fifteen. Eventually, just as Malik was losing hope, Aahil stepped in closer and allowed Malik to squeeze him into a hug with Ameera and Hakim.

'I love you, too, Daddy,' Aahil said.

Malik felt the pure joy in his heart and the tears spring to his eyes. He didn't care that it wasn't right for a Sheikh to be seen crying, he didn't even try to blink the moisture away.

'I love you children so much, don't ever forget that. And I won't ever abandon you again.'

They stayed locked together for a few minutes until Malik felt Hakim squirming in the middle of the group. Reluctantly he released the children and watched as they returned to their games, knowing he now had the much harder job of trying to understand his feelings for Rachel. Maybe he was sad at the thought of losing her purely because he enjoyed her company.

Forcing himself to face the truth, Malik asked himself why his heart hurt so much if he thought of Rachel solely as a good friend, someone whose company he enjoyed. If Wahid declared he was leaving, Malik would feel sad, but it wouldn't cause him physical pain. He'd wish his friend well and get on with his life. The idea of never seeing Rachel again made his heart squeeze and his breathing difficult.

Out of the corner of his eye Malik saw the door to Rachel's room open and he felt like shouting. He needed more time, he needed to understand what he felt for her. A man couldn't be expected to work out what love actually was under such time pressures. He wanted to go over every thought and every feeling he'd ever had for Rachel, to analyse and dissect every conversation, every kiss.

Malik's thoughts froze as something occurred to him. Maybe that was the problem, maybe he'd been thinking about things too much and not allowing himself to *feel*. For so long he'd protected himself from a distant wife by becoming analytical, by distancing himself from any interaction, but maybe that was the problem. Maybe he needed to stop thinking and start feeling.

Looking up to where Rachel's familiar figure was dragging her trunk from her room, Malik asked himself what he felt for this woman and for the first time ever let his heart answer.

Chapter Twenty

Rachel allowed the servant to pick up her trunk as she darted back inside the room that had felt like home for the last two and a half months. She looked around, taking in the sumptuous furnishings and beautiful fabrics, and she knew she would miss her lifestyle here in Huria. She doubted she would ever live in such a luxurious home ever again, but rather than let the sadness overcome her Rachel lifted her chin and took a deep breath.

Now she'd decided to leave Huria Rachel was eager to depart the palace and start the long journey back to England. She knew every minute she stayed close to Malik and the children her resolve would waver and she would find herself turning into someone she didn't much like or respect. She would refocus on things in her life that couldn't hurt her, like finding a nice family to work for or seeing a bit of the world, and she would most certainly avoid any sort of relationship.

Rachel stepped out of the room and closed the door behind her. It felt as though she had swallowed a boulder and it was sitting heavily in her stomach, but she knew she had to face Malik and the children and say her farewells. She didn't want to see the tears in Hakim's eyes as he realised she wouldn't be coming back, or the disappointment on Aahil's and Ameera's faces as they worked out another governess was leaving them. She wished things could be different, but they couldn't.

She made herself look around as she walked, soaking in the exotic flowers that climbed up the struts of the balconies and the verdant plants that filled pots along the walkways. She inhaled the spicy aromas coming from the palace kitchens and felt the heat of the Hurian sun on her face. This would be the last time she set foot in the palace, and although she knew arranging a passage home might take a while, it wouldn't be long before she had exchanged the blue skies of Huria for the greyness of England.

She could see Malik and the children in the courtyard below and allowed herself a moment to compose her face into an expression of serenity before she descended.

'Miss Talbot.' Wahid's low voice stopped her in her tracks.

Rachel spun to see Malik's most trusted confidant standing behind her.

'Wahid, I was hoping I might trouble you for an escort to somewhere to stay whilst I arrange my passage home.'

Wahid shook his head sadly. 'Please reconsider, Miss Talbot, do not do something you will both live to regret.'

Rachel felt her face colour and wondered if Malik had confided in the older man, but she realised Wahid had eyes and ears everywhere, he wouldn't need Malik to tell him what was going on.

'His Highness needs you.'

Rachel shook her head. She wished Malik needed her, but he didn't. He was a capable man who had overcome so much to be who he was today and even his relationship with his children had blossomed in the last few weeks.

'He is pig-headed and stubborn,' Wahid said, seeming not to mind speaking of his Sheikh in such a blunt way. 'He is a great ruler, but he cannot admit when he is wrong.'

'They will be better off without me. No distractions.'

Wahid sighed and started to speak slowly as if Rachel were the one whose first language was not English. 'They need you, all of them. You make him a better father, a better man. And he deserves some happiness after all he's been through in his life.'

Rachel thought of the years of misery Malik must have endured during his marriage to a woman who had barely deigned to speak to him. She felt herself begin to hesitate, but then pulled herself together. It didn't matter, Rachel was not going to be in a one-sided relationship. She would have abandoned her vow never to let love take over her life if Malik had actually loved her back, but she would not spend her life growing miserable knowing the man she loved did not feel the same way.

'What about the children?' Wahid appealed.

'The children will be just fine with their father. He's brilliant with them.'

Rachel did feel guilty about leaving the children

so abruptly, but she knew in the long term it was the best solution. If she stayed for a few weeks it would be harder for all of them for her to leave, by going now it would hurt less overall.

'I've known His Majesty for many years,' Wahid said quietly. 'He has never cared for anyone the way he cares for you. Give him time, be patient with him, he will get there in the end.'

Rachel wondered if it was true, maybe she did just need to give him time. It wasn't like Malik had ever had any examples of a successful relationship in his life; his mother had died when he was young and his wife had resented him. She felt a surge of hope and struggled to suppress it. She would not waver. She would not spend her life adoring a man who did not love her back. Instead she would take some time to regroup and then devote her life to teaching and see-ing the world.

A small voice inside her head scoffed and Rachel knew it was right. She would never properly regroup, her feelings for Malik weren't likely to fade just be-cause she put a couple of continents between them. But maybe not seeing his face every day, not hearing his voice and imagining his lips on her skin, would help the pain to ease in the long run.

Rachel stepped forward and took Wahid's hand. 'Look after him,' she said softly.

Taking a deep breath, she descended the stairs and entered the courtyard. Her heart was hammering in her chest and already Rachel was beginning to doubt herself. Something inside her screamed at her to stay, to fight for what she wanted, and with every step it was getting louder.

Her eyes fixed to the floor, Rachel couldn't bear to look up and see Malik and the children gathered together. She didn't want to say goodbye. She didn't know if she would even be able to get the words out of her mouth. Surely if this was the right thing to do it wouldn't be so hard, so painful.

With a supreme effort Rachel looked up and immediately her eyes met Malik's. They looked at each other for ten long seconds, all that had happened between them pulsing backwards and forward in one glance. Rachel remembered the man she had first encountered on arrival at the palace, the cool, distant Sheikh who barely spoke to his children. She remembered their first arguments over her teaching methods and the first time Malik had admitted he was wrong. She remembered the first few disastrous trips out Malik had arranged, and how, slowly, he had begun to feel at ease around the children. In two and a half months Malik had gone from a stern, detached father to a man who could easily understand what his children wanted and what they needed.

'Aahil, Ameera, come here,' Malik said, beckoning his eldest two children over to where he sat with Hakim on his lap.

Rachel knew two and a half months ago Malik would have left it to someone else to tell his children their governess was leaving, but here he was ready to talk them through the change himself, to answer their questions no matter how difficult.

As Malik opened his mouth to speak Rachel wanted to shout out and stop him. She didn't want to leave. She wanted to be a part of the children's lives, part of his life. She wanted to spend her days helping the children to develop and her nights curled up by Malik's side. Rachel realised she'd never wanted anything so much in her life and she was about to lose it all.

She wondered if she could compromise, if she could live a half-existence. Maybe remaining in Huria and having Malik's companionship and friendship was better than running away.

Malik looked up at her again and, as their eyes met, Rachel felt her heart almost bursting inside her chest.

Malik felt like he'd been struck by a lightning bolt. Rachel's soft brown eyes met his and Malik wondered how he could have been so obtuse. He'd been so preoccupied with trying to work out how you knew you were in love, he hadn't listened to his heart. Suddenly all the moments of joy and pleasure made sense, as did the pain and suffering he'd experienced since driving Rachel away. Of course he loved her. He rather suspected he'd loved her from the moment they'd shared a kiss out under the stars in the desert, after she'd listened to him so carefully whilst he'd spoken of Aliyyah. Now he couldn't quite believe he'd been able to deceive himself into thinking he didn't love her. He'd been scared, worried history might repeat itself and he would end up living a re-run of the years of misery he had with his first wife, but looking up at Rachel, Malik knew she could never hurt him, at least not intentionally.

He wondered if he was too late, if he had driven her away for good by his blindness and stupidity. Malik wouldn't be able to bear it if she left, not now that he'd realised what love actually felt like. Love was looking at someone and knowing you cared more for them than life itself. It didn't have to be anything fancy, just straightforward, old-fashioned adoration.

'Children, I've got something very important to tell you,' Malik said, gathering his children closer.

He wondered how to phrase his next few sentences, knowing he needed to explain things carefully to his children.

Rachel had stopped a few feet away and was looking as if she might cry.

'I know you are all very fond of Miss Talbot. In the months that she has been here with us she has made a big impact on all our lives.'

Ameera turned to Rachel, her eyes narrowing. 'You're leaving, aren't you?'

Rachel opened her mouth, but no words came out.

'Miss Talbot will no longer be staying here as your governess,' Malik confirmed.

Malik watched as Hakim threw himself off his lap and ran over to cling on to Rachel's legs.

'Miss Talbot, Rachel, has come to mean so much more to all of us,' Malik said and he watched as the puzzlement and hope dawned on Rachel's face. 'And I very much hope she'll agree to stay here in the palace with us, as my wife.'

Four pairs of surprised eyes regarded him for a few seconds.

Malik realised he was holding his breath. She could still refuse him, she could still leave. He had rejected her in the cruellest way possible, Rachel might be too hurt to agree to stay.

'You'll be our new mummy?' Hakim asked.

He watched as Rachel crouched down in front of

Hakim and felt his heart swell as she took the little boy's hand in her own.

'I love you all very much,' she said. Malik felt a momentary stab of panic as he wondered if she was going to say she still couldn't stay.

'And I love you,' Malik blurted out. It hadn't been how he'd envisioned telling Rachel he loved her, but he would have time for the romance and the flowery words later. Right now he just needed her to agree to stay.

She looked at him and Malik felt as though her eyes were boring down to his very soul.

'You love me?' Rachel asked, her voice so quiet Malik hardly heard the words.

'I love you,' he said.

'I cannot think of a single thing that would make me happier than marrying your father and being there every minute of every day to watch the three of you grow up.'

Malik crossed the short distance between them in four long strides and swept Rachel up into his arms. He kissed her deeply on the lips, ignoring the 'Eww!' from Ameera and the gasp of surprise from Aahil. Malik wanted to communicate in that one kiss how much he loved Rachel, how much he would cherish her for the rest of their lives and how grateful he was that she was giving him a second chance.

'I do love you,' Malik said when he finally released her. Rachel's cheeks were delightfully pink and her eyes a little glazed.

'I thought…' Rachel started.

Malik shook his head vehemently. 'I was stupid and afraid and plain wrong. Forgive me?'

Rachel answered him with a kiss of her own, much to Malik's delight.

'You're truly going to marry Father?' Aahil asked, as if he couldn't quite believe the turn of events.

'Yes.'

Malik felt his heart soar again at her confirmation. He knew he'd nearly sabotaged his own chance of happiness by failing to realise he was in love, but he'd been given a second chance. He was not going to waste it.

'Right now we are going to celebrate,' Malik whispered to Rachel. 'Everyone will want to wish us well, add their congratulations, but I want you to myself for at least a little of today. Meet me on the rooftop after the children are in bed.'

It seemed fitting to take Rachel to the place they'd sat down together on her first evening at the palace all those weeks ago.

As she turned to him and smiled Malik felt like the luckiest man alive.

Once Malik had kissed his children goodnight he made his way to the rooftop to check everything was in order. It was set out just as it had been on their first night together, with a low table and scattered cushions. Malik had requested a meal they could serve themselves so they would have complete privacy once Rachel arrived.

She stepped on to the rooftop terrace a few minutes later, her eyes shining with excitement and just a hint of nervous energy radiating off her. Malik took her hand and led her to the parapet and for a moment they just stood side by side, looking out over the kingdom.

As Rachel turned to him Malik raised her hand to his lips and placed a kiss on her knuckles.

'Rachel, I was a blind, stupid fool, but I want to spend the rest of our lives showing you how much I love you...' He paused. Although technically he had already proposed, it hadn't been the romantic gesture Rachel might have dreamed of. This time he would do it right.

'I tried to tell myself that I couldn't love anyone, that I didn't know how, but it seems my heart had a different view. I think I've loved you for a long time, but I was just too blind to realise it.' Malik pulled Rachel closer to him. 'Will you do me the greatest honour and agree to be my wife, my companion, my Shaykhah?'

Rachel smiled, that warm, loving smile that made Malik's heart soar.

'Nothing would make me happier. Of course I will.'

Malik wrapped his arms round her waist and pulled her towards him, kissing her gently, languorously, as if they had all the time in the world. He knew he had a lifetime to enjoy kissing Rachel, to explore every inch of her mind and body until he knew it better than he knew his own. Running his hands down her back, he pulled away slightly and looked at the woman who was going to be his wife.

'I'm a very lucky man,' he said.

'I think I'm the lucky one,' Rachel said, raising a hand to stroke his cheek.

He led her to the scattered cushions, sat down and pulled her in close to him. He wanted to feel the warmth of her body against his, to hold her tight and never let her go. Malik selected a small delicacy and popped it into Rachel's mouth, watching as she closed her eyes to savour the flavour.

'You do realise what you've just agreed to?' Malik said as he licked the remnants off his fingers.

'I've agreed to be your wife,' Rachel said, laughing.

'Not just my wife.'

'Well, of course there's the children as well.'

'Of course, but there's more, too.'

Rachel looked puzzled and Malik took the opportunity to feed her another delicacy.

'When we are married you will be Shaykhah of Huria. Every woman in the kingdom will look up to you, will want to emulate you.'

Malik thought he saw some of the colour drain from Rachel's cheeks.

'I think you'll be fabulous,' he whispered in her ear.

Epilogue

Rachel stood in the middle of the room and allowed the women to fuss around her. Despite all the excited chattering and the noise her mind was elsewhere, it was with the man she was going to marry in fifteen minutes time.

She thought of Malik, dressed in his finery, and wondered how she had been so lucky. To find the man you could spend your life loving, and to have him love you back, was a blessing indeed. Now all she had to do was marry him.

There had been months of preparation for the wedding. Rachel had never imagined herself getting married, but if she had she wouldn't have spared a thought for all the preparation that went into a royal wedding. For the last five months, ever since Malik had proposed, Rachel had done something wedding related every single day. And now, after all that preparation, the time was finally here.

'Do you like my dress?' Ameera burst into the room, twirling as she went, making the skirt of her dress flare and ripple with movement. The young Princess was dressed in a deep purple gown made of silk, with purple flowers in her hair.

'You look stunning, Ameera.'

Ameera looked up at Rachel and bit her lip.

'I don't think I've ever seen anyone look as pretty as you, Rachel.'

Today Rachel felt pretty—in fact, she felt beautiful. Her skin was glowing from the time spent in the *hammam* and the milk-and-honey paste the attendant women had applied, and her hair was sleek and shiny from the lemon juice it had been washed in. One of the women had applied a small amount of kohl to Rachel's eyes, just enough to accentuate their shape and colour without being overwhelming.

The whole wedding was a fusion of their two cultures. Of course this was Huria and Malik was Sheikh, but Rachel had been keen to bring some touches from home. Her dress was a magnificent gold-and-ivory gown, with hundreds of tiny pearls sewn into the bodice. Rachel had opted to eschew the more conservative English style of dress and had requested her gown be off the shoulder, revealing much more flesh than an English bride normally would on her wedding day. However, she had asked for a veil, something no one in Huria had really understood until she'd sketched a detailed picture. It was this lace-trimmed veil the attendants were now pinning into her hair.

Adding splashes of colour to her gold-and-ivory dress were the small pink flowers that were scattered all over Huria. She had a few woven into her hair style and Ameera was to carry an elaborate bouquet as they walked down the aisle.

Finally the women were finished and they stood back, admiring Rachel in the mirror.

'You look like a queen, my lady,' one said.

Rachel smiled. She supposed soon she would be a queen. Not that she felt like anything other than normal, down-to-earth Rachel Talbot. Throughout all the meetings with the country's nobles and the foreign dignitaries, every time Malik had introduced her as his new Shaykhah-to-be, Rachel had felt like giggling. It seemed surreal. But if marrying Malik meant becoming Shaykhah then she would take on the role with pride.

Not everyone in Huria was pleased of Malik's choice of bride and they had spent considerable time over the last few months convincing some of the more old-fashioned nobles and village elders that Rachel would be an asset to the country. Many people still thought marriage should be arranged between the Sheikh and a woman from a wealthy and influential family, a union that strengthened the kingdom, but most backed down when they saw the resolute look in Malik's eyes. Rachel knew only too well he was a hard man to deny anything.

The whole thing was made slightly easier by the fact that the normal people of Huria loved the idea of their Sheikh marrying for love. The tale of Rachel and Malik's courtship had been retold and embellished thousands of times, and the romantics amongst the population had called it the romance of the century.

Ameera grasped her hand and together they walked from the room. In the past few months Malik had told her time and time again to move into the Queen's rooms, but Rachel had refused, staying in the chamber she had lived in since arriving at the palace all those months ago. After today she would take up residence in the sumptuous Queen's rooms, but before that it hadn't seemed right.

They walked through the palace and Rachel smiled and nodded at the hundreds of staff and traders who had worked tirelessly to make this day possible. The women gently jostled each other to get a good look at Rachel's dress and the men bowed deferentially as she walked past.

'Are you nervous?' Ameera asked.

Strangely she wasn't. She was about to get married in front of hundreds of people, but all she could think about was finally becoming Malik's wife.

She couldn't wait to wake up next to him every morning, to stand by his side as he conducted official business, and to curl up next to him every night. She fell in love with Malik more every day and after five months of waiting she was more than ready to become his wife.

'I'm excited,' Rachel said.

They paused by the steps that would take them into the sunken garden and Rachel had to stifle a gasp as she looked down. Malik had made her promise not to enter the garden in the last few weeks, so Rachel knew he had planned something, but looking down she couldn't quite believe what she saw. As well as all the plants and trees, the entire garden was overflowing with flowers. Vases and pots held the exotic foliage and every guest had a flower pinned to their outfit. It was a riot of colour and Rachel found herself laughing in delight at the beauty of the garden.

The guests themselves were all standing. The layout

of the garden meant there wasn't that much free space, but Malik had ordered some raised platforms, also decorated with flowers, to be place in the open sections of the garden to give the guests a better view. The overall effect meant that although hundreds of people were attending the wedding, when Rachel and Malik said their vows it would seem like an intimate ceremony.

In the background music was playing and Rachel realised it wasn't the exotic notes of Hurian music she had become so used to these past months but the soft plucking of a string quartet. Malik must have scoured the continent to find musicians who could play the western instruments and his thoughtfulness made her heart swell with love.

After a few moments spent listening to the music, Rachel let go of Ameera's hand and ushered the young girl forward. The guests turned and followed her progress down the stairs and into the garden. Rachel was only alone for thirty seconds before she felt a presence behind her.

'Are you ready, my love?' Malik asked as he slipped into place beside her.

Rachel slipped her hand into the crook of his elbow and straightened her dress. Beside her Malik was dressed in a traditional Hurian tunic, richly embroidered with gold thread. He looked every bit the royal leader that he was.

'You look beautiful,' Malik whispered, as they started to descend the stairs, 'but I can't wait until all these people have gone home and I can peel that dress off you.'

Rachel darted him a scandalised look. 'Behave.

There's three hundred nobles and foreign dignitaries in this garden.'

'I'm not proposing to strip you right here in front of them,' Malik said with a smile. 'That would be quite an introduction to their new Shaykhah.'

Rachel felt him pull her closer as they reached the bottom of the steps. He'd been amazing through all the planning of the wedding and the preparation for Rachel to take up her role as Shaykhah of Huria. Expertly he'd guided her through all of their customs and traditions, helping her learn the most important things first and set aside the more trivial for another day. As Rachel had thrown herself into the role she could see Malik's pleasure at having someone by his side who was interested and willing to serve Huria.

'This is your last chance to make a run for it,' Malik said as they walked through the verdant garden, past the hundreds of guests.

'I never want to be anywhere else but here with you.'

It was the truth. Since Malik had proposed Rachel had lost some of the wanderlust that had filled her since a young age. Before she had come to Huria the closest place she'd felt at home was at school with her friends, but now, here with Malik, she had a true home she never wanted to leave. Of course that didn't mean she would object to the odd trip into the desert with her new husband, or maybe she could persuade Malik one day to make the journey to England, so she could show him and the children where she grew up and take him to meet her friends.

Her friends not being at the wedding was her one regret. Of course she'd written and invited them, but Rachel had known logistically it was almost impossible for them to receive news of the wedding, organise travel and get here in the time between the engagement and the wedding. So Rachel would just have to plan a trip to see Joanna, Isabel and Grace back in England soon.

They drew to a stop in front of the official performing the ceremony and the man gave a deep bow first to Malik and then to Rachel. The ceremony was conducted in Hurian and Rachel had spent a long time going over the words with Malik, so that when she said her vows her voice was confident and clear. Beside them Aahil, Ameera and Hakim stood proudly in their new clothes and Rachel knew that, as well as gaining a husband, she was gaining a family. Already she felt like a mother to these children. She loved them as much as she would love any child of her own blood and today their bond was being made official.

The ceremony itself was short and within a few minutes the official was confirming they were man and wife. Rachel felt a flutter of excitement deep inside her as Malik looked at her for the first time as her husband.

'You're all mine now,' he said in a low whisper. 'For eternity.'

Rachel smiled and for a moment it felt as though it were just the two of them. She looked into his eyes as his hand came to cup her cheek and he bent his neck to kiss her gently on the lips. Despite the hundreds of people watching Malik kissed her passionately and Rachel felt her heart begin to thump inside her chest.

Too soon he had to pull away and after a moment he guided her round to face the guests.

'May I present Rachel bin Jalal al-Mahrouky, my wife and Shaykhah of Huria?'

As one the assembled guests bowed low to Rachel. She'd expected to feel out of place with all these people bowing to her, but standing by Malik's side Rachel felt like a queen.

Slowly Malik led her back through the sunken garden, past the guests who were now applauding and up the steps. Their day had only just begun, with appearances to be made to the hundreds of people waiting eagerly outside the palace for a glimpse of the newlyweds, the wedding breakfasts with speeches from all the important tribal leaders and many, many people to meet and smile at and talk to. Rachel relished all this; she loved being at Malik's side, putting people at ease as they spoke to their Sheikh, but today she was looking forward to the moment when it was just the two of them.

As if reading her mind Malik stopped at the top of the steps, turned abruptly and pulled Rachel into an alcove where they couldn't be seen.

'I know we have a long day of duty, but I just wanted one minute with my beautiful wife all to myself,' he said as Rachel started to protest.

She fell silent. Of course she wanted to be alone with Malik, she treasured moments like this.

Gently he cupped her face with his hands and bent to kiss her lips, kissing her languorously as if they had all the time in the world.

'I love you, Rachel bin Jalal al-Mahrouky.'

She couldn't help but smile as he said her new name.

'I love you, Malik.'

Again he brought his lips to meet hers, pulling her in close to his body so she could feel his heartbeat under his skin.

'Today is for Huria,' Malik said. 'But every second of every minute I will be wishing for tonight when I get you all to myself.'

* * * * *

*If you enjoyed Rachel's story, you won't
want to miss the other three stories in*
THE GOVERNESS TALES *series*

THE CINDERELLA GOVERNESS
by Georgie Lee
THE RUNAWAY GOVERNESS
by Liz Tyner
THE GOVERNESS'S SECRET BABY
by Janice Preston

COMING NEXT MONTH FROM

⬥HARLEQUIN®

ℌISTORICAL

Available October 18, 2016

ONCE UPON A REGENCY CHRISTMAS (Regency)
by Louise Allen, Sophia James and Annie Burrows
Uncover three Regency heroes in disguise with these three magical
Christmas novellas to warm your heart!

UNWRAPPING THE RANCHER'S SECRET (Western)
by Lauri Robinson
Sparks fly when Crofton Parks, the stepbrother who heiress Sara Johnson
believed was dead, returns to Colorado to claim his inheritance...

THE RUNAWAY GOVERNESS (Regency)
The Governess Tales • by Liz Tyner
When runaway governess Isabel Morton is rescued by handsome stranger
William Balfour, she decides to save William in return...by becoming his
bride!

THE QUEEN'S CHRISTMAS SUMMONS (Tudor)
by Amanda McCabe
Lady Alys Drury's gaze lands on a familiar face. Why is Juan, the Spanish
sailor she nursed back to health, at Queen Elizabeth's Christmas court?

Available via Reader Service and online:

THE WINTERLEY SCANDAL (Regency)
A Year of Scandal (spin-off) • by Elizabeth Beacon
As the daughter of wild Pamela Winterley, Eve lives in the shadow of
scandal. Meeting Colm Hancourt is sure to get society's tongues wagging.

THE DISCERNING GENTLEMAN'S GUIDE (Regency)
by Virginia Heath
Bennett Montague, sixteenth Duke of Aveley, is seeking the perfect bride.
He knows exactly what he wants, but will the arrival of Amelia Mansfield
unravel all his plans?

REQUEST YOUR FREE BOOKS!

HARLEQUIN®

HISTORICAL

Where love is timeless

2 FREE NOVELS PLUS 2 FREE GIFTS!

YES! Please send me 2 FREE Harlequin® Historical novels and my 2 FREE gifts (gifts are worth about $10). After receiving them, if I don't wish to receive any more books, I can return the shipping statement marked "cancel." If I don't cancel, I will receive 6 brand-new novels every month and be billed just $5.69 per book in the U.S. or $5.99 per book in Canada. That's a savings of at least 12% off the cover price! It's quite a bargain! Shipping and handling is just 50¢ per book in the U.S. and 75¢ per book in Canada.* I understand that accepting the 2 free books and gifts places me under no obligation to buy anything. I can always return a shipment and cancel at any time. Even if I never buy another book, the two free books and gifts are mine to keep forever.

246/349 HDN GH2Z

Name	(PLEASE PRINT)	
Address		Apt. #
City	State/Prov.	Zip/Postal Code

Signature (if under 18, a parent or guardian must sign)

Mail to the **Reader Service:**
IN U.S.A.: P.O. Box 1867, Buffalo, NY 14240-1867
IN CANADA: P.O. Box 609, Fort Erie, Ontario L2A 5X3

Want to try two free books from another line?
Call 1-800-873-8635 or visit www.ReaderService.com.

* Terms and prices subject to change without notice. Prices do not include applicable taxes. Sales tax applicable in N.Y. Canadian residents will be charged applicable taxes. Offer not valid in Quebec. This offer is limited to one order per household. Not valid for current subscribers to Harlequin Historical books. All orders subject to credit approval. Credit or debit balances in a customer's account(s) may be offset by any other outstanding balance owed by or to the customer. Please allow 4 to 6 weeks for delivery. Offer available while quantities last.

Your Privacy—The Reader Service is committed to protecting your privacy. Our Privacy Policy is available online at www.ReaderService.com or upon request from the Reader Service.

We make a portion of our mailing list available to reputable third parties that offer products we believe may interest you. If you prefer that we not exchange your name with third parties, or if you wish to clarify or modify your communication preferences, please visit us at www.ReaderService.com/consumerschoice or write to us at Reader Service Preference Service, P.O. Box 9062, Buffalo, NY 14240-9062. Include your complete name and address.

HHI5

She would become the best songstress in all of London.
She knew it. The future was hers. Now she just had to
find it. She was lost beyond hope in the biggest city of
the world.

Isabel tried to scrape the street refuse from her shoe
without anyone noticing what she was doing. She didn't
know how she was going to get the muck off her dress.
A stranger who wore a drooping cravat was eyeing her
bosom quite openly. Only the fact that she was certain
she could outrun him, even in her soiled slippers, kept her
from screaming.

He tipped his hat to her and ambled into a doorway
across the street.

Her dress, the only one with the entire bodice made
from silk, would have to be altered now. The rip in
the skirt—thank you, dog who didn't appreciate her

trespassing in his gardens—was not something she could mend.

How? How had she gotten herself into this?

She opened the satchel, pulled out the plume and examined it. She straightened the unfortunate new crimp in it as best she could and put the splash of blue into the little slot she'd added to her bonnet. She picked up her satchel, realizing she had got a bit of the street muck on it—and began again her new life.

Begin my new life, she repeated to herself, unmoving. She looked at the paint peeling from the exterior and watched as another man came from the doorway, waistcoat buttoned at an angle. Gripping the satchel with both hands, she locked her eyes on the wayward man.

Her stomach began a song of its own, and very off-key. She couldn't turn back. She had no funds to hire a carriage. She knew no one in London but Mr. Wren. And he had been so complimentary and kind to everyone at Madame Dubois's School for Young Ladies. Not just her. She could manage. She would have to. His compliments had not been idle, surely.

She held her head the way she planned to look over the audience when she first walked onstage and put one foot in front of the other, ignoring everything but the entrance in front of her.

Don't miss
THE RUNAWAY GOVERNESS by Liz Tyner,
available November 2016 wherever
Harlequin® Historical books and ebooks are sold.

www.Harlequin.com

Turn your love of reading into rewards you'll love with
Harlequin My Rewards

HARLEQUIN®

A *Romance* FOR EVERY MOOD™

Love the Harlequin book you just read?

Your opinion matters.

Review this book on your favorite
book site, review site, blog or your own
social media properties and share
your opinion with other readers!